WHEN HATTIE FINDS LOVE

AMY LILLARD

ZEBRA BOOKS
Kensington Publishing Corp.
www.kensingtonbooks.com

ZEBRA BOOKS are published by

Kensington Publishing Corp.
119 West 40th Street
New York, NY 10018

All Kensington titles, imprints, and distributed lines are available at special quantity discounts for bulk purchases for sales promotion, premiums, fund-raising, and educational or institutional use.

Special book excerpts or customized printings can also be created to fit specific needs. For details, write or phone the office of the Kensington Sales Manager: Kensington Publishing Corp., 119 West 40th Street, New York, NY 10018. Attn. Sales Department. Phone: 1-800-221-2647.

First Printing: December 2023
ISBN-13: 978-1-4201-5526-6
ISBN-13: 978-1-4201-5527-3 (eBook)

10 9 8 7 6 5 4 3 2 1

Printed in the United States of America

Prologue

Hattie Schrock loved weddings. All weddings. But there was something extra special about a spring wedding. Maybe because no one else was getting married in the spring since most everyone stuck with tradition and got married in the fall after planting season was over. But since this was a second wedding for both the bride and the groom, and they were building a family out of two that had been broken over the years, the bishop decided a spring wedding to be appropriate as well. So *jah*, weddings were always fantastic, but as far as Hattie was concerned, spring weddings were the best.

"So how long do you think we have to stay?" Elsie Miller, Hattie's cousin, sidled up next to her. The two of them owned Poppin' Paradise Popcorn Shop that was down on Main. Hattie loved her cousin, but there were times when Elsie was just a little bit of a grouch. Times like this when Hattie was enjoying eating and watching people and the general loving feeling that surrounded a wedding.

"I want to stay for a while longer."

Elsie rolled her eyes. "Of course you do."

Second weddings were always lower key than first ones.

But this was a little bigger than most second ones. Maybe because it was the spring, and everyone was in a fresh new mood. The daffodils were in bloom and the redbuds and dogwoods were as well. Everything made such a cheery addition to the happy day as everyone gathered in the bonus room on top of Joy's barn.

Hattie, like the rest of the widows' group, had heard the story of how Joy's and Uriah's kids had brought them together. They were both being too stubborn and too prideful to see their way back to each other. But now it was beautiful. And their love filled the entire room. A body was smacked with it the minute they clamped eyes on the newly wedded couple. It made Hattie simply jubilant.

"I wonder how the girls feel about moving over here?" Elsie said. She dragged a carrot through the puddle of ranch dip on her tiny party plate and popped it into her mouth, waiting to see if Hattie had any comment on the matter.

"They'll have plenty of space as soon as the new addition is built on." They had no sooner gotten Johnny B's Johnny *haus* (Wasn't that cute?) built before they turned around to build extra rooms on for the other girls. Just two more rooms would round it out nicely. The house was beginning to take on a random sort of shape. But she didn't think Joy or Uriah cared all that much. "Besides, Rebecca is probably going to get married in the next couple of years, don't you think?"

Elsie shrugged. She didn't keep up with such things, but Hattie did. Rebecca, Uriah's oldest, had put in to go to the baptism classes this year. That meant she would be joining the church in the fall. From there, it was a short distance to marrying her unofficial boyfriend, Adam Yoder. Or it could be, anyway. Hattie was happy for all of them. They seemed so thrilled.

Uriah had even installed a ramp in the barn so Johnny B could push his wheelchair up it by himself. After last fall's nearly disastrous church service when Thomas Kurtz and Uriah had to pull Johnny B's wheelchair up the stairs with a rope, it was good of him to fix it. The ramp was long and zigzagged twice but Uriah claimed it was the best way to get Johnny B to the top.

"I'm kind of tired," Elsie said. "And my feet hurt."

Hattie nibbled at a piece of cheese that was still on her plate. "Give it to God," she murmured. It was her typical response.

Elsie scoffed. "You can't give it all to God," she said.

"Not true." As far as Hattie was concerned, a person certainly could give it all to God. Everything from financial problems to not being able to open a new jar of pickles. Trust in the Lord for all things.

"You shouldn't bother God with the trivial stuff," Elsie said for what was perhaps the hundredth time this month. It was a regular argument between them.

"If you can't trust God with pickle jars, how can you trust Him with money?"

Elsie harrumphed.

"You know you could use a little positivity in your life," Hattie said.

"What's positivity got to do with me?"

But Hattie was already on a roll. "People get along without positivity day in and day out," she continued. "But are they successful? Are they happy?"

"I don't know about happy, but there's one who's successful." She nodded toward Christian Beachy.

"If I had to live with Malinda, I'd be grumpy too," Hattie admitted.

Elsie shook her head. "Some of us are happy just the way we are."

"Is that so?" Hattie asked.

"It is," her cousin countered.

Hattie frowned at her. "You might be, but you can't honestly believe that a man as grumpy as Christian Beachy is happy." That went against every part of Hattie's heart. A man that grumpy, he needed a lot of things, and happiness was assuredly at the top of that list.

"Want to bet?"

"I do believe gambling is a sin," Hattie shot back.

"Not for money," Elsie continued. "How about chores?"

"Chores? Like the dishes?"

"Work chores," Elsie supplied.

"Like?"

"Like if you can't change his attitude in the next sixty days, you'll scrub the copper vats at work. For a year. All by yourself."

"And if I can change it?"

Elsie looked unconvinced. "Then I'll scrub them."

Hattie looked over to the happy couple. She hadn't seen anyone that filled with bliss since Sylvie and Vern's wedding that previous fall. More of that should be spread around. If there was anyone who could use the dose of good ol' healthy happiness, that person was Christian Beachy.

"Sixty days you say?" Hattie asked.

"Sixty days."

Hattie turned to her cousin with a smile. She stuck out a hand to shake. "You're on."

Chapter 1

"Hard to believe that Joy and Uriah have already been married for two weeks."

"Uh-huh." Hattie Schrock didn't bother to look up from her plate of spaghetti in order to answer her cousin. If grunting could actually count as an answer. But she knew what Elsie was getting at, and it wasn't something she really wanted to think about.

"Fourteen whole days."

"Uh-huh," Hattie said again, eyes still downcast.

"It's amazing how time flies."

Now that was something Hattie could agree with. And running from the situation was not going to make it any better. *God give me strength.*

Hattie pulled in a fortifying breath of air the good Lord had provided, then propped her elbows on the table and met her cousin's mischievous gaze. No . . . mischievous wasn't quite the look. Elsie was a little too much of a worrywart to be mischievous, but she was definitely trying to get her digs in tonight. "Go ahead and say it," Hattie commanded.

"Say what?" Elsie had the nerve to look innocent. "I was

just talking how it's funny that it's already been fourteen days since Uriah and Joy got married."

Hattie rolled one hand in the air in front of her. "And?" She drew out the word until it had three complete syllables.

"Oh!" Elsie's eyes grew big in mock surprise. "You're talking about the bet."

Hattie shook her head, tossed her French bread back onto her plate. "Of course I'm talking about the bet. Aren't you talking about the bet?"

"I was talking about Uriah and Joy."

"And the bet we made at their wedding."

Elsie shrugged. "Why would I be talking about the bet? If I win, you clean the copper pots, so waste all the time you want."

"I–I . . . You," Hattie sputtered. "I'm not trying to waste time."

"You're doing a real fine job of it, for sure."

Hattie twisted her mouth into something between a grimace and a frown. "It's not that easy."

Elsie leaned back in her seat and crossed her arms over her middle. Unlike Hattie, Elsie hadn't been wool-gathering instead of eating and had finished her meal. "I thought everybody could benefit from a positive attitude. Isn't that what you said?"

Thankfully her cousin's words held no malice; they were merely a statement of fact. Something that Hattie had said so many times they might carve it on her headstone. Well, they might if Amish did such things, but since they didn't, she supposed she could just consider it her mantra. That was the saying that you repeated to yourself often to get through your day. She heard some *Englisch* women talking about it in line in front of her at the grocery store. A positive attitude always helped her get through her day. So she figured it counted.

"I do believe that." With all her heart she believed it.

"I know. But you gotta put your money where your mouth is."

Hattie frowned. "We didn't bet money."

"Your scrubbing skills then," Elsie said. "You've already wasted two weeks. That leaves you thirty-six days to improve that man's life."

"Forty-six," Hattie corrected. Math never was Elsie's strong suit.

Elsie shrugged her thin shoulders. Math was never her strong suit and it never seemed to bother her. "Fact remains that time is running out."

"I know, I know." She knew. She did not need her cousin reminding her. But she had pushed the idea of the bet from her mind because it was easier not to think about it than to try to figure out what to do. "It's not that easy."

"You could have fooled me," Elsie said. "You walk around here like it's the easiest thing in the world to do. Like it comes natural for you."

A positive attitude did come naturally to Hattie, just as natural as Elsie's worrywart attitude came to her. That wasn't the point.

Hattie shook her head. "That's not the point."

"Then what is?"

"How is a middle-aged Amish woman supposed to make a man change a lifelong attitude? It isn't like I can strike up a friendship with him just out of the blue. That won't look weird at all."

Elsie gave her an apologetic yet not so apologetic smile. "I guess you better start scrubbing those pots then. Might as well just get it over with."

She was not throwing in the towel. Not yet anyway. "We just don't run in the same circles," she tried to explain. "And since I live in town and he is out there on the farm, in the country, growing vegetables, the only time I get to see him is at church. And I really don't think that's appropriate for church."

"I feel like church is the most positive place we have."

"Not positive stuff. I'm talking about me going up and trying to be friends with him or something. I know I can change his attitude. It's just we're not friends. A middle-aged Amish woman can't be friends with a single Amish man. It's weird."

Elsie raised her eyebrows in that way she had that Hattie considered her facial shrug. "I think you're past middle-aged now."

Hattie closed her eyes for a moment, then opened them again when she felt a little more composed. "Not the point."

"The point is the bet. If you don't figure out a way to go talk to him, then how do you suppose you can bring positivity into his life?"

Hattie hadn't thought it all the way through. She figured that like everyone else, he would see her living positive and want some of the same. Lead by example, but if she wasn't around him, it wasn't like she could do that. Even when they were at church together, he hung out with the men and she stayed around the Whoopie Pie Widows' Club.

Okay, so that wasn't the official name of their widows' group, a group both she and Elsie were members of. But over the years they had become known for their whoopie pie benefits for people who had been injured or gotten sick in the community. Somehow the name had just stuck. There were a few members that didn't care for the moniker, but Hattie thought it had a certain ring to it. Whoopie Pie Widows' Club. *Jah*, she could live with that. But the fact still remained that she was hanging out with her friends after church and he was hanging out with his friends after church and never the twain should meet. Or something like that.

"Let me get this straight," Elsie said. That was another habit that she had, repeating things so she was sure she understood it. If Hattie was being honest, she would tell her cousin flat out that she was a worrywart. But sometimes honesty could hurt, so she wouldn't say that to her best friend for anything in the world. They owned a business together, they lived together, they went to church together, and they had known each other their entire lives. Hurtful or not, Elsie was a worrywart. Even worrying that she might misunderstand someone and cause some kind of fracas. "You're not wasting time because you don't think that you can change his life and make him more positive, you're wasting time because you don't know how to approach him. Is that correct?"

Hattie sighed in relief. Now her cousin was getting it. "That's right. I mean, I know these young people run all over and do all kinds of crazy things that don't follow the same rules that we did growing up, but I just can't imagine approaching him if I have no reason to." It would look forward, untoward, and a bunch of other *wards*, so she hadn't managed to find a way to do it yet because she couldn't find a way that it didn't look forward and untoward and the other *wards*.

"I don't know what to tell you, cousin." Elsie stood, grabbed her plate off their tiny, drop-leaf table, and took it to the sink. She turned the water on to rinse it.

Hattie stared at her half-eaten supper, now cold and more unappetizing than it had been when this conversation had started. "I don't know what to tell me either." She grabbed her fork and twirled up a bite of the pasta. She'd been taught to clean her plate as a child and clean her plate she would.

She slowly chewed the bite, not really tasting the food as she continued to mull over this problem. She knew she could change his mind and his attitude. She knew she could make Christian Beachy live a little happier with a more positive attitude and a sunnier outlook. But the way it was looking she would need more than a little divine intervention in order to pull this off.

"Somebody needs to do something." Sylvie King propped her hands on her hips, apparently waiting for someone to respond.

It was Tuesday and the weekly meeting of the Whoopie Pie Widows' Club, officially known as the Paradise Springs Widows' Group. The meeting had just begun and everyone had gotten a plate with their whoopie pies.

It started off as a lark and now had become a tradition to bring whoopie pies to the meeting. It was, after all, how they got their name. It also gave them time to practice for the upcoming festival next month.

Every year in May, Paradise Springs held the Whoopie Pie Festival with a whoopie pie baking competition at its core. People—Amish and *Englisch*—came from all over to buy whoopie pies, get recipes, play games, and find out who would be crowned top whoopie pie baker until the next festival.

This past year, Sylvie had gone through a rough patch after losing her crown as the number one whoopie pie baker in the Valley to newcomer Sadie Yoder. But the group had understood that she was unable to make whoopie pies for a while. She had come out of it now and had only this week baked a delicious pumpkin spice whoopie pie with honey buttercream filling. It was a recipe they were all familiar with as it was the winner four years ago. Or maybe it been five. Anyway, it was a trusted recipe and surely not the one Sylvie would enter in this year's festival. She was good at keeping her recipe a secret until the day of the event. At least from anyone else who might be vying for the title of number one whoopie pie baker.

"And by 'somebody' I suppose you mean us," Elsie said.

"Do something about what?" Callie Raber asked. "What happened?"

Callie was the newest member of the Whoopie Pie Widows' Club. Her husband, Samuel, had died last year during the festival. The group had waited a few months before inviting Callie to join their ranks, and she had readily agreed. Hattie supposed that's what happened when you were widowed at fifty with no children to ease the loss.

"You didn't hear?" Katie Hostetler broke in. "You work at the buffet. I figured you would've heard."

Callie was the hostess for the Amish buffet, not to be confused with the Chinese buffet, which was also delicious.

Callie shook her head. "I haven't. I didn't."

"In all fairness it just happened today," Lillian Lambert added. Beside her, Betsy Stoll nodded to back her up.

Lillian worked at the variety store her father-in-law owned while Betsy was a shop owner in her own right. She owned Paradise Apothecary and pretty much had her finger on all the news in the Valley all the time.

"Well," Sylvie said, gearing up for the speech she had obviously planned since hearing the news. "Barbie Troyer has had a heart attack."

A few murmurs and gasps broke out among the women—

murmurs from those who had already heard and gasps from those who hadn't.

"That's right. And according to what I'm hearing it must've been a bad one. She's in intensive care at the hospital."

She didn't need to tell them that the bills were stacking up. They had all been in a similar position at one point or another in their lives, but the thing about Amish communities was they pulled together for one another. They might not have insurance like the *Englischers*, but they took care of their own. Hattie supposed some might look at it as an insurance policy in itself if you were Amish, and maybe it was. At any rate, Sylvie was right. Somebody had to do something.

"Is she going to be all right?" Callie asked.

Being childless, Callie didn't have as intimate a relationship with Barbie as the rest of the women in the group. All of them had had babies delivered by the midwife. All except for Millie King's baby who had been delivered by Barbie's apprentice, Annabelle Glick.

Well, that wasn't exactly true either. Annabelle had been called due to Barbie already being engaged with another birth. The apprentice had promptly sent Millie to the hospital. Or at least that was the way Sylvie told it.

"It was a bad one," Sylvie said. "But everything I'm hearing seems to say that she will pull through eventually."

"She needs to retire," Elsie muttered from beside Hattie.

Hattie loved her cousin. She did. But sometimes Elsie's doom and gloom attitude about everything was hard to stomach.

"She has a skill this community needs and the experience to back it up." Hattie kept her voice low where only Elsie could hear.

"She's older than dirt," Elsie shot back, not quite as quietly as Hattie. "And if her eyesight is anything like yours . . ."

Hattie pushed her glasses back a little on her nose. "And that's why the good Lord gave us the smarts to create a way to see better."

"She should still retire," Elsie said. "Annabelle can take over for her. She's good. Or so I've heard. And she's young."

"With age comes experience," Hattie reminded her. "And with experience comes age."

Elsie just shook her head.

Hattie supposed her positive attitude rubbed against Elsie about the same as her cousin's rainy-day attitude did to Hattie herself.

"What do you suppose we should do?" Hattie asked. "Besides pray, I mean. That goes without saying."

"We're known for our whoopie pie benefits," Sylvie answered. "And since everyone's gearing up for the festival, I figure there's a lot of whoopie pies floating around. We could sell those instead of letting them go to waste."

"I have never in my life heard of the whoopie pie going to waste," Elsie muttered from beside Hattie.

Hattie had to agree. The women always found a good home for their whoopie pie experiments. Even if it meant freezing them for a rainy day. Or a day you didn't feel like baking.

"That's a great idea," Callie said. She had never been on this side of the fence for a benefit event. Boy, was she in for a treat.

The chatter around them increased as Hattie half-heartedly nibbled on the banana whoopie pie she had chosen. She had a feeling it was a failed attempt by Lillian who had brought them. They were much too plain to win the title. But it was good. Good enough, anyway.

Elsie seemed more interested in her plate than determining when and where they should hold this benefit for Barbie.

"It's already Tuesday," Lillian reminded them all. "It might be better to have it next Saturday, instead of this upcoming one."

Sylvie nodded importantly. "Noted. Does anybody have an objection to holding it Saturday next?"

They all shook their heads, murmured no, and looked around to see if everyone else was in agreement.

Sylvie waited a heartbeat more to make sure everyone's vote was accounted for. Then she clapped her hands together and rubbed them as if gearing up for physical labor. "Now—"

Elsie raised her head excitedly, pinning Sylvie with an eager stare. "I've got an idea."

Everyone waited and held their breath for her to continue.

"Let's make it a Sadie Hawkins event."

"What in the world are you talking about?" Sylvie asked. Though Hattie could see she was intrigued.

Hattie herself was a little bit interested. Who was Sadie Hawkins and what did she have to do with their whoopie pie benefit? The only Sadie she knew was Sadie Yoder.

"A Sadie Hawkins event," Elsie said slower this time, as if that helped explain it, "is where the girls ask the boys. So it's opposite." She seemed so pleased with herself, and yet Hattie knew she was going to get shot down. Why would you want to invite a date to a benefit?

"Why would you want to invite a date to a benefit?" Katie protested, ever the voice of reason, Hattie supposed.

"It's a bake sale. Nobody brings a date to a bake sale. And then who's going to come? The *youngins*?"

"Well, *jah*," Elsie said. "And married couples, but they would have to pay an extra dozen whoopie pies to get in."

"So everybody's going to bring whoopie pies?" Sylvie asked.

Elsie shrugged. "If they want to. I mean, why not? And we can have games and little booths like a kissing booth."

A chorus of "no kissing booth," rose up in the crowd.

"Okay," Elsie backpedaled. "No kissing booth. But we do have those go-fish games and maybe we could add a beanbag toss. Anything like that and a cakewalk."

Katie sat back in her seat, shaking her head. "That sounds awful convoluted."

"Maybe it is," Elsie said.

Hattie could hear the hurt tone creeping into her voice. She never asked for anything. Never gave anybody a moment's trouble and was always willing to help. Surely they could give her this one thing.

"I think it's a very . . . unique idea. And it's something we've never done before." Hattie was pleased with herself for coming up with such a brilliant word to describe this fiasco Elsie was currently concocting.

"It's unique, all right," Sylvie muttered. "I've run quite a few of the benefits," she continued. "But if we were to do this it's your baby."

Elsie sniffed and sat up a little straighter in her chair. "Okay then. I'll handle it all."

Hattie turned toward her cousin. "All of it?"

Elsie nodded with great conviction. "All of it." Her tone was emphatic, and Hattie thought she might have been surer about this project than anything they had done, aside from opening the popcorn shop together.

Yet for all of Elsie's confidence, Hattie could look

around the room and see the doubts shining on everyone's faces. She wasn't sure if they were trying to hide them or not, but there they were all the same.

"Okay then," Sylvie said, repeating Elsie's own words. "If you want to take care of it all, then I suppose we have ourselves a Sadie Hawkins Whoopie Pie Cakewalk Benefit."

"Are you sure you know what you're getting into with this?" Hattie couldn't help but ask Elsie as they walked back to the popcorn shop.

It was well past dark even though the time change had already come to Paradise Valley. As the summer continued, the days would get longer and longer and the sun would be out until almost nine-thirty at night. She loved those beautiful long summer days. They reminded her of her youth when she still believed that not much wrong could happen in the world. Yet those bad things had happened and she had met them all with a smile and a prayer. Always hoping for the best. It was the only thing that got her through.

"I did this for you," Elsie said, her tone almost accusatory.

Hattie froze in place, in the middle of the sidewalk, halfway between the Paradise B&B and the Poppin' Paradise Popcorn Shop. "For me?"

Elsie stopped as well, propped her hands on her hips, and turned back to face Hattie. "For you," she said. "This whole Sadie Hawkins thing is so you'll have a way to ask Christian to go someplace, then you can work your charms on him and help him have a more positive outlook on life."

Well, it certainly did give her a reason to ask him out and, Hattie supposed, to even have a pass to ask him out as well. Since it was a Sadie Hawkins thing and girls would be going around willy-nilly asking boys, then she supposed no one would blink an eye if she asked Christian Beachy to go. Not that she wanted to. There had to be another way.

"It's the perfect idea," Elsie said.

Hattie shook her head. "I don't think so."

"I believe the words are *thank you*."

"Why should I say thank you—"

"You're welcome," Elsie said, and turned on her heel, marching toward the popcorn shop.

Hattie stared after her, mouth agape. She almost had to physically push her chin back into its proper place before following behind her meddling cousin.

"I didn't want to ask the man on a date," she said as she made her way up the side stairs to their apartment door.

There was another entrance that led from the back room of the shop to their kitchen, but in times like this when the shop was closed for the evening, they always went in by the side stairs.

"Did you have another plan?" Elsie unlocked the door and stepped inside their apartment without waiting for her answer.

"Well, no." Hattie started up the stairs not sure whether her cousin heard her or not. Like it mattered. Elsie seemed to have her mind already made up. "But how am I supposed to go out there and ask him to go with me to a whoopie pie cakewalk benefit?"

"The horse and buggy? That's how most Amish get around." She set her purse on the side table by the door. "I mean, you could hire a driver, but it's really not that far."

"Ha. Ha. Very funny." Hattie closed the door behind her and turned the lock. Elsie had already switched on the propane lamp they used in the living room.

"You just go out there and ask him," Elsie said calmly.

Hattie didn't have a rebuttal for that. It was too true and sent chills down her arms. Which was ridiculous. *Just go out there and ask him.* "How about we just forget the whole thing?"

"Not a chance." Elsie shook her head with a smile. Her cousin hated cleaning the large copper vats they used daily for their popcorn, and if she won, Hattie would have to clean them herself for a whole year. What was she thinking when she agreed to this nonsense?

She had been thinking that a positive attitude had served her well her entire life and everyone could benefit from one. She hadn't been thinking about the *how*. Like *how* was she going to get Christian Beachy's attention in order to show him the way? And *how* was she going to approach him with her ideas and plans for his improved life? She wasn't friends with the man. She barely spoke to him when he brought by their vegetables in the summer. Or when he stopped to get a bag of popcorn.

She did know that caramel-cheddar was his favorite and he always picked up a packet of siracha salt to sprinkle over the top. So he liked sweet, cheesy, and a little heat. It wasn't much, but it was a start, she supposed.

"You shouldn't drag your feet on this," Elsie quietly warned. "I mean it's okay with me if you don't want to prove your point. I love being right." She beamed at her then, and Hattie felt that hot burst of familial rivalry flash through her.

"I'm not dragging my feet," Hattie muttered, doing her best to control her competitive nature. It had always been this way between she and Elsie. They were as close as sisters, had been their entire lives. Now they lived together, worked together, went to church together, naturally. And

Elsie knew just which buttons to push in order to set Hattie into motion.

The problem was . . . even though Hattie knew all this, she still managed to let her cousin get her goat.

"I'm just saying . . . I wouldn't wait too long. There aren't that many eligible bachelors our age here in the Springs. Someone's bound to snatch Christian up. Even if he's the grumpiest man in Paradise Valley."

She wouldn't say that he was the grumpiest man in Paradise Valley. Paradise Springs maybe, but she didn't know all the men in Paradise Hill, and there could be a few others over there who could give Christian a run for his money. She wasn't sure. She didn't know. But she figured anyhow.

Hattie sucked in a deep breath to try to calm her spinning thoughts, but the palms of her hands were slick against the leather reins. Her heart was pounding in her throat, and her thoughts were completely out of control.

She could do this. She could walk up to his house, knock on his door, and ask him to go to the Sadie Hawkins benefit with her. She would tell him that it would help Barbie Troyer. Hattie supposed that most, if not all, of Christian's children had been delivered by the midwife, just as Hattie's own had been. Barbie might have even delivered him as well. *Jah*, Barbie had been helping babies come into the world for that long.

Hattie shouldn't have to explain to him that it was for a good cause, but she might ought to tell him that she only wanted to attend as friends. Though she would buy the entry ticket for the both of them—even though it wasn't a date. And she didn't want it to be a date, just two friends out to help a mutual member of their community. Or something like that.

She pulled in another deep breath. The closer she got to his farm, the more she wanted to slow her buggy. She didn't have her words nailed down. She didn't know exactly what to say to him. Even though she had barely thought of anything else since she had hitched up her horse at the stables and pulled her buggy out of the long storage shed there, built for the sole purpose of keeping the buggies close.

It wasn't that she was trying to delay the encounter, she just wanted a little more time to practice, but all too soon she was pulling into the drive at the Beachy farm.

It was a beautiful property with green grass and a white fence and a row of greenhouses tucked behind the main house. It had been Christian's parents' house before it had been his, and somehow in the transaction from father to son, Christian inherited the care of his unmarried adult sister as well. Hattie considered it a miracle that they had managed, even after Christian had married Elizabeth Miller, one of Hattie and Elsie's many cousins. Despite the relation, Hattie hadn't been that close with Elizabeth and didn't have any privy information on how the five— Christian, his wife, his sister, and his aging parents— managed to get along. Probably better when said parents moved in with Christian and Malinda's brother David who lived over in Paradise Hill, having married a Hill girl a few years before.

But as she said, the property itself was beautiful, worthy of the calendar that the co-op printed every year and gave away around Christmastime. So worthy, that the farm had been pictured not once or twice, but three times.

Coming out here, smelling the freshly cut grass and the recently turned earth made her miss her days living on a farm. But a few years after she and Elsie had opened the popcorn shop, it became harder and harder to make that drive into town every day. It was hard on the horse, hard on the buggy, and hard on Hattie. The only solution was to move into the apartment above the popcorn shop and allow the farm to go to one of her children. They could plant and harvest the land, live in the house, and care for it. Not only would she be closer to work, but she also wouldn't have those responsibilities to worry about. Since then her life had grown increasingly easier. But she did miss the mornings in the country and the sunsets and the fresh air.

She pulled her buggy to a stop, nearly losing the reins, her palms were so damp. She had to get ahold of herself. This was absurd, outrageous. This wasn't a date. It was a bet. And something that Christian would benefit from. What she was doing, teaching him how to be more positive, would improve his life exponentially.

Exponentially. It was in the crossword puzzle this morning though she had to look it up in order to get it right. Then she had vowed to use it in a sentence today. Look at her go! It was barely nine o'clock, and she had already completed that goal. Now all she had to do was get out of the buggy, go up to Christian's door, and knock.

She forced herself to get down and slowly walk over to the porch steps. She took them one at a time, for safety's sake, she convinced herself. She wasn't a spring chicken any longer. Though at fifty-nine she thought she got around better than most. And for that she was grateful.

That was important to always be grateful. Just one of the things she planned on teaching Christian about the power of positivity.

She raised her hand to knock.

So when he opened the door . . . she brought herself

back on track . . . when he opened the door she was going
to say—

"You need something, Hattie?"

No, that's not what she wanted to say at all. Her thoughts
screeched to a halt as she blinked at him. Christian Beachy
was standing there, watching her as if he had never seen
her before. His mouth was turned down into a heavy
frown, but his eyes remained their normal clear blue,
maybe filled with questions, but clear all the same.

"Hi, Christian."

He waited for her to continue.

She cleared her throat.

He waited.

"See, there's a benefit for Barbie Troyer and I came out
here to invite you to go with me it's a Sadie Hawkins cakewalk but with whoopie pies and all the money goes to
Barbie she had a heart attack you know so we got the
benefit together and the women are asking the men and I
am asking you to go with me not as a date or anything but
as friends helping friends." She sucked in a breath, realizing she hadn't paused once while speaking.

He blinked, and she wondered if he was still taking in
all of her words and trying to decipher them. It was quite
a tirade.

Then as firmly and as succinctly as if he was speaking
to a child he responded. "No."

Chapter 2

As he stood there in the doorway of his house and watched Hattie Schrock stare back at him, Christian began to wonder if she had heard him. "Is that all you need?" he asked, hoping to prompt her to action. He had things to do. It was the middle of planting season. Plus he had all the plants and herbs in the greenhouses to attend to. He couldn't stand on the porch and just stare at Hattie Schrock all day.

She blinked at him and opened her mouth as if she was about to say something. She closed it. Opened it once more. Closed it. Blinked. Opened it. Then shook her head and made her way back to her buggy.

Christian shut the door.

"What was that all about?" His sister, Malinda, came up behind him.

He shrugged. "Hattie Schrock and something about Barbie Troyer. I guess there's a benefit. Whoopie pies and a cakewalk and something else. I don't know."

Malinda nodded. "I've heard about that. Barbie Troyer had a heart attack and is in the hospital."

Christian frowned at her. "I know that."

"So the Whoopie Pie Widows' Club is hosting a benefit

in a couple of weeks to help pay her bills. It's supposed to be a lot of fun and should bring in quite a bit of money."

"If she's in the hospital, she's going to need it."

"Did she . . . invite you to the benefit?"

"I haven't talked to Barbie Troyer in such a long time. Maybe not since Lizzie was born." That had been twenty-one . . . No, twenty-two years ago.

Malinda pursed her lips and waved his words away with one flick of her hand. "You've talked to her since then," she said. "Not that it matters. I was talking about Hattie. Did *Hattie* invite you to the benefit? It's a reverse thing where the women ask the men."

Christian eyed her dubiously. "That's the craziest thing I've ever heard."

"Is that a yes or no?" Malinda asked, following behind him as he made his way back through the house. He really had a lot of work to do.

"Yes or no about what?"

"About the benefit." Really, when Malinda got her teeth into something she wouldn't let go, like one of those dogs that could lock their jaws and would hang on the end of rope for hours until somebody made them get down.

"I guess it's a little of both."

"Christian, for pity's sake would you stop for a second and turn around and talk to me?"

"I have a lot of work to do, you know." He said the words but stopped, turned, and faced his sister. He had almost made it to the back door.

"You can give me five seconds of your busy day," she told him. "Now what does yes and no mean?"

Christian bit back a sigh. "It means yes, she asked me to the benefit. Or at least I think she did. And no was my answer to her and I'm sure of that." It was about the only thing he was sure of this afternoon except for the fact that he was going to be behind come tomorrow morning having to listen to Hattie Schrock prattle on about benefits and his sister having to know every minute detail of every minute of his day.

"Why did you tell her no?"

He frowned. "I don't want to go to some whoopie pie thing the crazy widows have come up with. I just don't have time for such nonsense."

Malinda pressed her lips together before replying. "You should have told her yes."

Scratch that. He was going to be *way* behind come tomorrow morning. "I'm sure you're going to explain that."

"I think it would be good for business."

"So you think she's going to quit using our services because I won't go to this whoopie pie nonsense thing with her?"

"That's not what I'm saying at all. It would just be good for business that you were out among the people."

"And how am I supposed to grow vegetables if I'm out among the people? The vegetables are here."

"I swear, Christian. Sometimes there's just no getting through to you."

"You shouldn't swear."

Malinda growled under her breath. It was a noise he was very familiar with. In fact she'd been making it their entire lives.

He started toward the back door once again.

"You shouldn't have shut the door in her face."

He stopped once more. He was going to be way *way* behind come tomorrow morning. "I didn't shut the door in her face. I told her no, she said okay, and she left. I had to close the door sometime."

"Unapproachable," she said in a singsong voice that

held the superior tone that set his teeth on edge. He really hated that voice, and she knew it.

He waited for her to continue.

"For the business," she said again. "You need to be more approachable for the business. You know, you never smile."

"I grow vegetables. What does smiling have to do with growing vegetables?"

"It's not the growing; it's the selling. When you're out, you need to be more approachable so people want to buy their vegetables from you. Smile. I can't remember the last time you smiled. Smile right now," she demanded. "Come on. Give me a smile."

Christian curled his lips into what he thought was a smile. It sort of felt like a smile, but he wasn't sure what it felt like to smile as he had never consciously tried to smile and think about the fact that he was smiling.

Dear Lord, he was starting to sound like the both of them—Malinda and Hattie.

He waited for his sister to approve the look so he could actually get back to work. But instead she shuddered. "You look like one of those horror film bad guys on the movie posters at Paradise Theater. You are not approachable. In fact, that's downright scary."

"I'm not approachable?" he asked incredulously. "What are you talking about?"

"If you can't smile, at least don't wear a frown all the time. A girl hears things, you know."

Christian didn't remind his sister that she was no longer a girl and was quite unapproachable herself. Mainly because everyone was scared to talk to her since whatever they said would surely be spread all over the community by the afternoon. *Nee*, he decided to keep that to himself. Rumors and gossip were just part of Malinda's personality.

He couldn't remember her any other way. But back when they were running around, going to singings and such, she was so involved in who was dating whom that she never had time for a beau of her own. By the time she got around to it, the opportunity had passed her by. Now he was stuck with her.

"Is that all?" Christian asked.

Malinda just shook her head as if he were a lost cause. Whatever.

"Fine," Malinda said.

Christian started for the door, then stopped. "You're sure? That's it?"

Malinda closed her eyes as if she just couldn't stand it any longer. "That's it. You won't hear any more from me."

"Have you ever thought about growing hemp?" Betsy Stoll asked the next afternoon as Christian was bringing in her weekly order of herbs. He had devoted an entire greenhouse to growing herbs—lavender, lemongrass, even things like catnip, chives, and rosemary. He loved rosemary.

"I hear it's hardy," he replied. "You got a use for it?"

"Many," she replied. "Hemp seed milk, lotions, rope for tags and bows for gift wrapping here."

"I don't mind giving it a try," he told her. "I never much got into it and now that marijuana is legal . . ."

"You thinking about getting into the marijuana business?" she teased.

He shook his head. "Nope." Though he had no aversion to it. He wouldn't use it himself, but he had heard a great many people talking about its benefits to terminal patients and those with chronic pain. "It just seems a little too controversial." Whereas hemp seemed more accepted, and a great of amount of CBD could be gleaned from hemp, that much he had learned.

"If you grow it, I'll take it," she told him.

"We're still talking about hemp, *jah*?" He laughed.

"*Jah*." She chuckled in return.

"It's going to be so fun," he heard someone behind him say, and he was fairly certain they were talking to someone else. Still he turned to make sure.

Frannie Lambright, the deacon's wife, bounced a toddler on her hip as she waited behind him. She was talking to Geraldine Lapp who owned Paradise Lawn and Garden with her husband, Joel. Christian didn't keep up with all the comings and goings in Paradise Valley but he did know that the baby Frannie held belonged to Benjamin Lambright, Frannie's brother-in-law. According to Malinda, Frannie shouldn't be taking care of such a small child this late in her life, at least not one that didn't belong to her. But when her sister-in-law Diana died last year giving birth to the baby, someone had to step in. The other four children went to live with Benjamin's mother-in-law who lived on the other side of Paradise Hill. Benjamin got to see the older kids once or twice a month, but that didn't seem like enough. Malinda had told him that as well.

Christian didn't know how they managed. He'd been lucky enough to raise his children with his wife before she had died.

"It will be like a mini-festival," Geraldine agreed.

"And it will be for a good cause."

The ladies continued to talk, and Christian could only assume that they were talking about the upcoming benefit for Barbie Troyer, that whoopie pie thing that Hattie Schrock had invited him to. It was a good cause, he supposed; he just didn't quite understand the concept. Of course, it didn't help that Hattie spoke fast and seemed a bit nervous when she was talking to him. He didn't know why she was nervous. As far as that went, he didn't know why she had asked him in the first place.

He finished his business with Betsy, nodded to Geraldine and Frannie, then headed back out into the beautiful April sunshine. Next stop was the Amish buffet. He had some hothouse tomatoes to show to Aaron Lapp, the owner. He just about got his hybrid down so that his hothouse tomatoes were just as good as the ones grown out in the sun. Almost.

It was just after lunch and the parking lot was mostly cleared out as he tied his horse's reins to the hitching post and made his way inside the restaurant.

Callie Raber was standing at her usual spot at the hostess station.

"Hey, Christian." She greeted him with a smile though her eyes still seemed so sad. Her husband had died just about a year ago. To hear Malinda tell it, it was a shock to everyone in the community. Samuel Raber had been fine one moment and dead the next. Dead from a massive heart attack.

She looked at the basket in his hand. "You don't have tomatoes already?" Callie asked, questions in her voice.

"I grew them in the hothouse." Christian nodded. "I figure they'll be better than those ones y'all get from Mexico."

"I'll get Aaron." Callie came around the hostess stand and started toward the kitchen.

Christian reached out a hand to stop her. "Say, Callie," he began, "you wouldn't happen to know anything about this whoopie pie thing they got going on for Barbie Troyer, do you?"

She nodded. "It's just a benefit," she said. "But there's going to be games and things like that. A cakewalk, and they are selling tickets."

That much he knew already. "I heard something about a woman's name, but it wasn't Barbie's."

"That's right." She smiled in remembrance. "It's a Sadie Hawkins event."

"Who in the Sam Hill is Sadie Hawkins?" He only knew one Sadie and that was Sadie Yoder. And he didn't know her all that well. She'd been in Paradise Valley for nigh a year, but he hadn't said two words to her.

Callie laughed, but again her eyes remained sad. "It's just a fun way of saying the girls get to ask the boys to the event. I think they're trying to get young people to participate."

"I see," Christian said. Though he really didn't. What difference did it make anyway? All he knew was that Hattie Schrock had asked him to go, and that he had said no. But it did seem like a worthwhile endeavor. Now it did anyway. It was just yesterday he had gotten confused with everything else she had said.

Callie went to the back and got Aaron.

Christian sold his tomatoes, got back into his buggy, and headed for home.

On the drive out to the farm, he thought about what he did know about this Sadie Hawkins whatever. One, he didn't know who Sadie Hawkins was. Two, he needed whoopie pies to attend. And three, he wasn't very good at making whoopie pies.

"Malinda," he called as he walked into the house a short time later. His horse had been brushed down and had been put away. The buggy was stored. Now Christian had to figure out this whoopie pie mess. "Malinda!"

She came out of the kitchen wiping her hands. "Have

mercy, Christian," she admonished. "What's all this racket about?"

"Who is Sadie Hawkins?"

"That's the big deal? You want to know who Sadie Hawkins is? I don't know." His sister propped her hands on her hips. "You called me out here for that?"

"It's an honest question."

She gave a small shrug. "I suppose it is. But I don't think anybody knows who Sadie Hawkins *is*. Just that a Sadie Hawkins dance or a Sadie Hawkins party means that the girls can invite the boys. Or the women can invite the men."

That's exactly what Callie had told him. And that was why Hattie had come over. "And this is for the bake sale?" It wasn't exactly a question or a statement. Just somewhere in between. "How can you have a date for a bake sale?"

Malinda was shaking her head before he even got finished. "It's not a bake sale exactly. It's sort of a mini-fair. At least, that's my understanding; for they're selling tickets and there will be dates."

"And whoopie pies," Christian finished for her.

"That's right." His sister seemed relieved that he was finally understanding.

"So we need to make some whoopie pies."

Malinda gave a shrug. "Or some kind of dessert. I would think that there's going to be more than whoopie pies available. Perhaps there even *needs* to be more than whoopie pies, but from what I hear, Elsie Miller came up with the idea and Sylvie King is pulling the strings."

Which explained why it was all about whoopie pies. Sylvie, who was not the current reigning champion of the Whoopie Pie Festival they held every May there in Paradise Springs, had held the title for seven years previous.

"I suppose we're going to go."

"You need a date," his sister said.

"You're my date."

Malinda shook her head. "The girls ask the boys."

He propped his hands on his hips and nodded in her direction. "So ask me then."

"I will not." She perched her hands on her hips and mimicked his pose. "I don't want to go with my brother." Which was strange as they usually went to things like this together. Of course things like this didn't normally have a person requiring a date.

"This is dumb."

"Perhaps you shouldn't have turned Hattie Schrock away when she asked you." With that Malinda spun around and marched back into the kitchen, leaving Christian to wonder whether she had already asked someone to go herself. It was possible, he supposed. It just seemed unlikely. This was Malinda he was talking about. She was more interested in the community as a whole than she was in one person.

"Fine," he called after her. "I'll go by myself then. You'll bake the whoopie pies though, right?"

She stuck her head back out of the kitchen entryway, a patient yet strained smile on her face. "If you want whoopie pies, you are going to have to bake them yourself."

"Just go over to his house again," Elsie said for what had to be the umpteenth time since they had started the afternoon, after-church meal. But the thing was Hattie was not going to just go over there again. He had turned her down. So she was going to have to think of some other way to show him how a positive attitude was exactly what he needed.

"No" was all she said. She had explained it so many times to Elsie that she wasn't about to do it again. Plus there were too many people around who could possibly overhear.

"I'm not letting you out of the bet," Elsie said.

"Shhhh . . ." Hattie shushed her cousin. "Someone could hear."

Elsie lowered her voice. "I'm not letting you out of the *b-e-t*."

Hattie rolled her eyes. "I'm pretty sure everyone around us can spell." But it didn't seem as if anyone was paying them any mind. Which was good.

"I don't want out of our . . . agreement," Hattie said. "I just don't want to go talk to him. He's already said no. If I ask him again, it will look too forward. I'm not trying to date the man; I'm just trying to bring some positivity into his life."

"Might I remind you that you only have sixty days and you've already blown twenty-one of them."

As a matter of fact, she didn't need reminding. As another matter of fact her cousin saying the words out loud made her stomach clench. She should just give up now. It wasn't that Christian Beachy couldn't use some positivity in his life and it wasn't that she didn't think everyone could benefit from a more positive attitude, it was the dynamics of it all. It wasn't like she and Christian were friends. Obviously. They wouldn't be in this situation if they were friends, because she would be able to lead by example, and Christian would already have a more positive attitude because Hattie's positive attitude would have worn off on him already.

Hattie closed her eyes against her whirling thoughts.

"Twenty-one of what?" Sylvie King demanded.

"Nothing," Hattie said, while her cousin replied, "Days."

Sylvie looked from one of them to the other. "Which one is it?"

"Nothing," Hattie said, while glaring at her cousin.

"Nothing," Elsie reluctantly agreed.

"It's a sin to lie on a church Sunday," Sylvie said, looking at each of them pointedly.

"It's a sin to lie on any Sunday," Lillian Lambert added.

Hattie glanced over Lillian's shoulder to see half of the Whoopie Pie Widows' Club standing behind her.

It might be a sin to lie on any Sunday, or any day for that matter, but here she was jumping in feetfirst. "It's twenty-one days until we release our new flavor of popcorn."

"What?" The ladies all gasped at once, but no screech was louder than Elsie's. There was no new popcorn flavor. And now Hattie had twenty-one days to come up with one. Plus figure out a way to get Christian Beachy to see that a positive attitude was all he needed in life and bake whoopie pies for the whoopie pie benefit. No pressure.

"He's got quite a tan," Aaron Lapp said, then took a drink of his water.

Christian sipped his own and looked across the yard to where Titus Troyer was chatting with a man Christian had never met before. Must be a visitor from another district, he thought. He knew everyone in the Valley, both sides. Hill and Springs.

He had to admit Titus Troyer did look tan. But it wasn't the tan that drew his attention. It was more the rested look he had. See, Titus had just returned from a ten-day trip to Pinecraft in Florida. Titus was a goat farmer. Or rather, he had been. He had recently turned his farm over to his new son-in-law. His last daughter had gotten married to a hardworking young man named Jacob Detweiler who eagerly took over the farm from Titus. That's when Titus headed to the Sunshine State.

Goat farming never ended. A person just couldn't leave goats unattended for ten days, but since Titus now had a built-in goat sitter . . .

Aaron continued talking about Titus and his tan, but all Christian could think about were the other things that he'd heard Titus say since he'd been back. He had come home talking of shuffleboard and fresh fish and beaches. Why, a person would think that he was living the high life. The Amish high life anyway. Still, Christian couldn't help but wonder how Titus, at forty-five, liked living in his own *dawdihaus*. But to look at the man he would say he didn't mind at all. And for the first time in his life Christian felt like he missed something along the way. He never thought about it much. He had simply gone about things. He fixed things when they broke, he planted things when it was time to plant, and he read the Bible every night. Now all of a sudden he was old. He supposed it didn't make much difference, but he hadn't done anything extra in his life. Yet this was something that Christian had never thought about before, wouldn't be thinking about now if Aaron had not been lamenting it in relation to his own life. And Titus Troyer.

Christian nodded at whatever Aaron was saying and hoped it was the proper response. He hadn't been paying attention to the man. He felt bad about it, but he didn't think he should ask him to repeat it. He didn't want to tell

Aaron that he had been thinking about life and death. About what a person could manage to accomplish in the world and all the other parts of everyday Amish life.

He had been taught since he was a boy to accept life as it came, trusting God's will and living a righteous life. But now he wasn't sure that was enough. The thought was more than unsettling. It was practically earth-shattering.

Chapter 3

"Hattie?"

He must've scared her for she startled and whirled around to face him.

It was getting close to three o'clock in the afternoon. Almost everyone else had left the preacher's house where they had held their service today. Only a few stragglers remained and Christian figured now was his moment. He just didn't mean to frighten her.

"*Jah*?" Her voice trembled.

Should he apologize? He already felt strange enough coming over here getting ready to ask her what he thought he was going to ask her. That was if he could find the words. He tried to decide what to say on the way over, but everything he started with sounded desperate. And that wasn't how he felt. He wasn't desperate. He just made a mistake, that was all. He'd been a little hasty in turning down her invitation and now he wanted to go back on it. There was nothing desperate about that.

"Did you need something?" Hattie asked, a small frown of concern wrinkling her forehead. "A drink of water to take with you on the way home?"

Christian shook his head. "No. I'm fine. Really."

The frown disappeared completely, but the wrinkles only half so. He supposed that was another mark of getting old. Not that he would say Hattie was old. She was a couple of years younger than he was and he didn't consider himself old, even though he felt old now. All thanks to Titus Troyer.

"Okay then." Her voice had a lilting quality like she wasn't sure if she should make that a question or not.

"It's just that . . ." Christian stopped, trailed off trying to find the right words to tell her that he would like to go to the Sadie pie whoopie Hawkins thing. Maybe those were the words. But couldn't seem to get his mouth to say them. He frowned.

She took a step back.

"The cakewalk thing," he managed. "The one for Barbie Troyer. The whoopie pie whatever. I would like to go with you after all."

Her chin dropped down, mouth open in fly-catching position as she stared at him.

"Did you hear what I said?" He asked the question and pressed his lips together. It'd taken him so much to come over here and talk to her, and now she was just staring at him as if he was a piece of gum stuck to the bottom of her best shoes. "Hattie?"

Hattie jumped forward as Elsie came behind her. Christian had a feeling that Elsie poked her cousin though he couldn't figure out why.

"*J-jah,*" Hattie stuttered, then seemed to gather herself. "The invitation to the whoopie pie whatever, er the Sadie Hawkins Whoopie Pie Cakewalk Benefit still stands. I would love for you to go with me. That will be . . . fun." She said the words but her tone implied otherwise.

But if she didn't think she would have fun with him at

the benefit, why was she willing to go? The thought made his frown deepen.

Hattie took another step back and continued to stare at him.

Not sure of what to do next, Christian gave a stern nod. "How about I meet you Saturday morning at the entrance to the benefit?"

She nodded.

"Okay then. Thanks," he said. "I'll see you there."

She nodded once more without saying a word.

He turned on his heel and headed for his buggy.

Hattie pushed down the smug feeling that rose inside her as she turned toward Elsie. "How about that?" she said.

"That is all well and good," Elsie replied. "But the bet isn't over. You still have to get him to be positive."

That was going to be the hard part. How in the world was she supposed to get a man who frowned that much to see that a positive attitude would benefit his life? She knew it would, but she had to convince him. All he did the whole time was frown at her. It almost made her wish to say that she didn't want to go with him, though in truth she did. Not because she was interested in Christian in any romantic manner, but she wanted to bring some joy into his life.

She had been watching him lately and had noticed more and more that the man never smiled. Never. He didn't smile when he was greeting people. He didn't smile when he was walking away from people. He didn't smile when he got a plate of the after-church meal. Hattie couldn't fathom what would make a man never smile. Everyone needed to smile. Everyone. So she had to do it. She had to go with him. She had to present him with a positive alternative, and she had to get the man to smile. Right then and there she decided she was going to use whoopie pies to do it. Everyone loved whoopie pies and she was certain Christian Beachy did too.

What was he thinking?

He didn't know. He'd gotten so caught up in Aaron Lapp's lamenting and Titus Troyer's suntan that he lost himself for a minute. He had lost himself to the tune of agreeing to go with Hattie Schrock—ever-smiling, ever-positive, sometimes a little nauseating Hattie Schrock—to the whoopie pie benefit thingy. He wasn't sure she even wanted to go with him when he got right down to it. She had stared at him the whole time, like he'd crawled out from under a rock or something.

Then to take that much time off from work on a Saturday was just ridiculous. He would be so far behind schedule. A lot of his customers would be home on Saturday where he could run by and talk to them about their orders in the upcoming growing season. About the new hothouse tomatoes and additions he'd made in his greenhouses. He could also talk to them about hemp and whether anyone else had the need for it besides Betsy Stoll. He had a lot to do. The people of the community depended on him to give them their food. At least part of it.

He had already said yes. And he supposed there was no going back on it. He would just have to make up the time some other way. But he needed to make a mental note to himself not to get sucked into the whatever this was ever again.

* * *

As if Christian wasn't regretting agreeing to go with Hattie to the benefit Hawkins thing enough, he had to endure endless ribbing at the men's meeting. So many times he never made it to the meeting because he was busy. But today he remembered and now he wished he hadn't.

Vern King came up and elbowed him in the ribs. "I hear you're going to the benefit with Hattie Schrock."

Christian sighed. "I believe everyone knows this by now." The whole entire community knew it. He supposed that's what he got for going home and telling his sister that he had invited Hattie, or rather had rescinded his original answer to her invitation to the whoopie pie benefit.

"Well, Hattie is a handsome woman." Vern nodded at his own words.

"I hadn't really thought about it," Christian said. And that was the truth. He hadn't thought about it; he just thought about life passing by. That maybe he should get out more and that happened to be the last invitation he had from someone. Plus, he wanted to support Barbie Troyer. That was all.

"Trust me. We grow them good here in the Valley." Vern gave a knowing nod as he moved away.

Christian supposed that was the truth as well. There were a lot of handsome women in Paradise Valley on both sides of the line. But he had never noticed much. He had been widowed for fifteen years or better and never once had he thought about remarrying. Possibly because there were days when he still missed Elizabeth. She'd been the first girl he'd ever taken home from a singing and the last girl as well.

Or possibly because Malinda had never moved out. Christian had taken over their childhood home from their parents. Both Wilma and David Beachy were gone now, but Malinda still remained. So Christian had her there to help. He didn't need to worry about washing clothes or cooking dinner. Or raising kids. Though there were times when he could use the companionship of someone special. He never thought about it until now. What had shifted in the world that had caused him to start thinking about it all of a sudden? What made him feel lonely now after all this time? What made him envious of Titus Troyer's tan?

That wasn't true; he wasn't envious of Titus's tan per se, he was envious of something new. Lizzie had been married for two years; that was probably the last thing that happened in his life. His youngest daughter got married. And since then, in those two years, in those entire twenty-four months, nothing new had happened. Unless you counted hothouse tomatoes. And truthfully he didn't.

"Don't pay him any mind." Henry King came up behind Christian, gently nudging him out of the way to get to the spinach dip.

It was his contribution to the evening refreshments. Just another of Malinda's efforts in Christian's life. She made sure he had dinner on the table every night, breakfast every morning, and something to eat midday. She took care of the food for the church services and the benefits and anything else that arose. So why wouldn't she make him some whoopie pies? That one he couldn't figure out.

"I don't mind," Christian said, but he kind of did. Widowed fifteen years and he asked one person out on a date that was not really a date. Though he really didn't ask her, she had asked him. He had simply agreed to go after saying no first. But why should he take a ribbing for all that? Fifteen years and he had never gone out. He just couldn't understand it.

Henry made a face. "It looks like you do," he said.

"It does?" Christian crossed his arms. "How's that?"

Henry nodded in Christian's general direction. "You're frowning."

"I am?"

Henry nodded, then got another scoop of spinach dip and a couple more crackers. Then he headed toward the circle of chairs set up in the practice room in the town's community theater. They used to move the men's meetings around from house to house, but when Sammie Franklin, the mayor of Paradise Springs, offered them the theater, they had jumped at the chance. It was more central and kept the single men from having to clean up and host the others.

"Frowning? I am?" He said the words softly to himself. He hadn't even realized it.

He got himself a plate and started filling it with the goodies everybody had brought. Of course Sylvie had made some whoopie pies, Christian's favorite plain chocolate with delicious vanilla filling. Nothing beat the original. Then he made his way over to the circle of chairs.

He sat down next to Jason Stoll, owner of Paradise Stables.

Jason leaned a little closer to him. "I hear you're going to the whoopie pie benefit with Hattie Schrock. Good on you."

"We're just friends," Christian said. It was a knee-jerk reaction. Because they were just friends. Weren't they? *Jah.* They were just friends.

"Just sayin'," Jason said with a small shrug.

Really. This was getting out of hand. So out of hand that he almost wanted to get up from the men's meeting, march down to the Poppin' Paradise, and tell Hattie Schrock that he had changed his mind back to his original answer. But he had already said yes. And he had the strangest feeling that his answer was important to Hattie. Which was more than strange, truthfully. They had lived in the same community for . . . well, forever, and never had they exchanged more than two or three words at a time.

Cheddar Candy Mix today, Christian?

Jah. Danki, *Hattie.*

Yet it seemed to please her that he changed his mind and agreed to go to the silly whoopie pie whatever thing with her. Weird.

"So how are married people supposed to come to the benefit?" Lillian asked Tuesday at the Whoopie Pie Widows' Club meeting.

The ladies were hammering out the last details of the rules. Though Hattie wasn't sure a benefit truly needed rules. Yet this one had more than plenty.

"I've got it right here." Elsie held up a stack of papers stapled together. It had been something to get a staple through all those pages.

Hattie and Elsie had gone down to the library the day before. Elsie had typed up all the rules on how everybody would qualify to get into the benefit. She was such a worrywart about the whole thing that she provided for every little detail. Like how married men were allowed in without their wives in the event that the wife had to work during the event. And that was to bring another dozen whoopie pies.

Basically that was every contingency. Single woman with no date—a ticket and a dozen whoopie pies. Single man with no date—a ticket and a dozen whoopie pies. Married man with no wife in attendance—a ticket and a dozen whoopie pies. Under sixteen and no date—well, you know.

"What if someone brings a cake?" Lillian asked.

All heads swung to Elsie and her incredibly thick packet of papers full of rules.

It might've been perhaps the one thing Elsie hadn't counted on. She delicately set the rulebook—how Hattie had started to refer to the thick stack of papers—in her lap and closed her eyes ever so gently, like they were fluttering down for her to go into a peaceful sleep. Hattie knew the truth: It stressed her out to the max.

"If someone brings a cake," Elsie started before her eyes flickered back open, "they will be allowed in. We're not about to discriminate against other desserts."

Hattie bit back a laugh. Elsie was taking this way too seriously. But that was Elsie. Somewhat over the top, always concerned, never taking life as it came.

"Don't you think we should write that down?" Betsy asked.

Hattie resisted the urge to kick her to keep her mouth quiet and instead shot her a *be quiet* look. The last thing they needed was for Elsie to start adding more rules and regulations to her already over-ruled and over-regulated event.

"What about Paradise Hill?" Lillian asked. "Surely people from Paradise Hill are going to want to come."

Elsie nodded, and Hattie could tell that she'd gotten her feet back on solid ground. "Of course they're going to want to come. Barbie serves both sides of the line. And they will be as welcome as anyone else. This is a benefit to help Barbie, not try to keep up with a county feud."

"Maybe not," Katie said. "But how are we going to know if women invited the men?"

Hattie scoffed; she couldn't help herself. "That's not the point of the whole thing. It doesn't matter who invites whom as long as people show up with whoopie pies and money for tickets so that we can help Barbie." This whole thing was starting to make her a little irritable. Maybe because they just kept talking about it and talking about it and talking about it.

"Well, I only mentioned it because you are the one that came up with that idea, Hattie," Katie said.

Lillian shook her head. "No, she didn't. It was Elsie."

"Well, everyone in town knows that Hattie has invited Christian Beachy to go." Sylvie nodded emphatically.

"Everyone in town?" Hattie squawked. "Why would everybody in town know?"

"Because Christian lives with Malinda," Sylvie replied.

Everyone nodded slowly. *Jah*, that was the exact reason.

"Wait a second." Betsy turned in her seat to look at Hattie. "You two hatched this whole idea so that you could invite Christian Beachy to the event." She crossed her arms and sat back, satisfied with her deduction.

Hattie shook her head, fully prepared to fib her way through. "No," she said as Elsie threw up both hands into a surrender pose and said, "You got us."

Sylvie looked from one to the other. "So which is it?"

"Obviously Elsie hatched this plan so that Hattie could invite Christian Beachy to the event. Am I right?" Katie asked.

"It's not like that," Hattie said. "It's just that—that—that—"

"That—that—that what?" Sylvie asked.

"He never smiles," Hattie said trying to land on the one thing they could all agree on. And they could all agree that he never smiled. "Has anyone in here ever seen him smile?"

The women looked around at each other, and Hattie waited patiently for them to come to a collective determination. Finally Millie spoke. "I know I haven't lived here very long, but I've never seen him smile."

"I've lived here nigh on seventy years," Katie said. "And I've never seen him smile."

"See?" Hattie sat back, hoping they would accept her explanation, such as it was.

"See what?" Sylvie asked. "What does never smiling have to do with you inviting him to go to a whoopie pie cakewalk for Barbie Troyer?"

"It's like this—" Elsie said, jumping ahead of Hattie, who was almost a little thankful that her cousin stepped in. She didn't have a good explanation for the whole thing without telling the absolute truth. That she and Elsie had hatched this whole thing as a bet, trying to bring more joy into Christian's life.

To hear it in her head it sounded terrible. She was sure that if she said the words out loud, it would just be horrifying. She couldn't.

"It's like this," Elsie repeated. "Hattie and I were talking over supper about how Christian seems so utterly unhappy. And we wanted to bring some joy into his life. So we did rock, paper, scissors, and Hattie got to be the one to try and make his life more positive."

"I see," Sylvie said. But Hattie had the impression that Sylvie only believed about half of what she had just heard. Though she supposed that was about standard for Sylvie. The woman was very skeptical. But all in all Elsie did a great job of avoiding the real issue and bringing forth the one that was the most important—trying to bring positivity and sunshine into Christian Beachy's life. After all, everyone could use positivity and sunshine.

"Never seen him smile, that I can remember, but that doesn't mean he hasn't smiled before," Katie said, back-pedaling over her earlier words. "Surely he smiled when he was married to Elizabeth. Or when his children were born."

The low murmur spread around and nods went up among the widows and previous widows. It was true. None of them could remember seeing Christian Beachy smile, but that didn't mean he hadn't smiled when they weren't around. Or that they simply hadn't noted his smile. Either way they could agree that he seemed to frown an awful lot. That's what everyone remembered.

"Why do you suppose he frowns so much?" Lillian asked.

"I don't know," Elsie said. "But it is sort of worrisome."

"His wife died," Sylvie said.

"Your husband died, and you don't go around frowning all the time," Millie pointed out.

Another low murmur and round of nods went up among the widows.

"Well, his children are all grown, and I'm sure his grandchildren bring some happiness," Sylvie added.

"It is hard on some people when their children move out. Or so I've heard," Lillian said.

Everyone knew she was counting the days until Esther married Mark Esh and moved on with her married life. No one knew exactly what Lillian was to do when that happened, but it seemed to bring her great joy to just think about the time to herself.

"It's not like he lives by himself," Katie said. "He does have Malinda there with him."

It was almost as if the air had been sucked out of the room. Everyone paused, stopped, looked at each other then gave a collective nod. "*Jah*," they said, and everyone knew what the others were thinking. They would be frowning too if they had to live with Malinda.

"*Danki* for letting us come down and bake whoopie pies," Hattie said after Sylvie had opened the back door to the kitchen of the B&B and waved them inside.

"Don't thank me," Sylvie said, chuckling. "You're still cleaning up the mess."

The four women laughed. Millie was already seated around the large kitchen worktable with little Linda Beth asleep in a nearby portacrib. She really was a precious little thing.

It had been too long since they had had *boppli* in the family. But now that Hattie's youngest, Mary, had gotten married and was pregnant, there would be another one in the family soon. That would get her up to eight grandchildren though she had a feeling that the twins would never bless her in that way.

All in all Hattie had six kids, all girls. All were married except for the twins who had taken over the family home when Hattie and Elsie moved into the apartment upstairs from the popcorn shop. The twins, Iris and Ada, lived there still, and there were days when Hattie figured they probably always would. At twenty-five neither one showed the faintest interest in getting married.

"Come," Sylvie said, gesturing toward the table. "Let's sit down and have a snack before we get started."

They settled around the table as Sylvie poured everyone a cup of steaming coffee.

A beautiful coffee cake with brown sugar crumble sat in the middle of the table, just waiting to be eaten.

"That looks good," Elsie said, with a small nod toward the delicious-looking dessert.

Sylvie looked at it as if it had crawled out from under a rock and landed in the middle of her table by some random, horrific, act of nature. "Not that." She waved her hand in its general direction as if it were unworthy. "That's for the guests. I have something special for us to try."

Her eyes sparkled as she turned away to retrieve a large plastic container from next to the stove. She shot them all a secretive smile as she opened the container. "What you think about these?"

It was hard to tell anything by just looking at them, but Hattie's mouth started to water as a wonderful spicy banana aroma rose from the container.

"What are they?" Elsie asked.

Sylvie quirked one brow. "Whoopie pies."

"Really," Hattie drawled. "I had no idea."

"Right," Elsie said. "Flavor?"

Sylvie pressed her lips together in another secretive smile. She really was proud of herself for this one. "They're hummingbird cake whoopie pies."

"It sounds delicious."

"Try one." Sylvie held the container out to them. First Hattie, then Elsie. Millie shook her head as Sylvie offered her one. "I've had one too many already." She smiled as she patted her midriff. "Any more and I might go into a whoopie pie coma."

Though they all knew she preferred plain vanilla whoopie pies, they still all laughed. Then the laughter was short-lived as Hattie bit down into the moist delicious cake. It was perfection. Hummingbird cake in itself was amazing and delicious, but to have it in a whoopie pie with just the right amount of cream cheese frosting in the center did something special to her heart. Not only were they delicious, they were whimsical, even reminiscent. It brought back all those memories of when she was young.

"You like?" Sylvie asked.

"They're delicious," Elsie said as she reached for another.

Sylvie held one out to Hattie. But she shook her head. "If I eat too many, I won't be able to get in my dress come church Sunday."

"That's why we pin our dresses," Sylvie told her with a knowing chuckle.

Hattie smiled but continued to shake her head. Even her pins were starting to get tight. It was time to watch what she ate before she had to make all new dresses.

It was true that Hattie had been a little on the chubby side her entire life, then after six kids, especially twins, it seemed her midsection liked to grow a little every year. If she wasn't careful, she would completely surpass kind of chubby and end up right smack-dab in the middle of fat. Her mother had been big and had trouble getting around her whole life. As she aged, her knees and her hips hurt and her feet swelled. It seemed that she always had one ailment or another. That was something Hattie didn't want for herself. She was enjoying her life. She might be a little overweight, but she could still be active. She could still work a full shift on her feet at the popcorn shop and have energy left over for later. She could still get down on the floor and play with her grandchildren. And that was just the way she liked it.

"If I eat one, I'll have to eat two. And then if I eat two, I'll have to eat three, so I'm stopping right now."

Sylvie smiled and closed the container, but not before Elsie grabbed one more of the delicious pies from inside.

"So you like?" Sylvie asked, obviously needing their approval. Losing last year's whoopie pie competition to Sadie Yoder had done a number on Sylvie's confidence. But if her entry this year was anything like what she had just given to them, she was certain to be a finalist, if not top dog, once more.

Hattie nodded as Elsie managed to speak around a bite of whoopie pie. "Love them."

"Are you going to bring these to the benefit?" Hattie asked. If so, she just might try to win them so she could take them out to the twins. They liked to bake, but Ada did pies and Iris baked cookies. Whoopie pies would be a nice change for them.

Sylvie shook her head and pointed to the pastry boxes sitting on the buffet table by the door. "I went traditional for the benefit. Vanilla and strawberry."

Elsie nodded. "That sounds yummy. Like strawberry cream?"

"No," Sylvie said. "Like strawberry and vanilla. Two different types not together."

She certainly did go traditional. Sylvie was very creative when it came to coming up with unique ideas for her whoopie pies. Last year's entry would have won hands down had Sadie Yoder not been so incredibly creative and used brownie instead of cake for her halves.

But something like these hummingbird cake whoopie pies? Delicious. Of course she said she made vanilla and strawberry like they were plain, but Hattie had a feeling they were superior in every way. Somehow Sylvie just had a knack for making whoopie pies.

"What kind are you going to make?" Sylvie asked. "Anything really special?"

"I'm making chocolate with chocolate filling," Elsie

said. "Hattie says she is making cherry, but I keep telling her since she's going with Christian Beachy, she ought to make lemon." She pursed her lips like she tasted something sour.

Hattie took a sip of her coffee and rolled her eyes at her cousin. "That's so funny."

Elsie laughed. "Just a joke, cousin."

"Seriously, though," Millie said, looking at all of them in turn. "Is he really grumpy all the time?"

Sylvie slipped into the chair opposite Millie and propped her elbow on the table, her chin in her palm. "I wouldn't say grumpy. When you talk to him, he seems nice enough. He just frowns all the time."

"He seems blessed," Millie said.

Sometimes Hattie forgot that Millie had only moved to the community the year before. She fit in so well with everyone in Paradise Springs, it was like she'd been born there. But after her husband had fallen from the roof and died, she had been pregnant and alone and needed to get away from all the memories her home community offered. That was when she moved to Paradise Springs to live with her aunt. And that's where she met Henry King who was now her husband and father to Linda Beth.

"*Jah*," Elsie said. "I would say he's blessed."

"It makes me sad," Hattie said. "I would just like to see him smile."

"I'd pay to see that," Sylvie said.

"Oh, there's no money involved," Elsie replied. And before Hattie could stop her, she finished up with, "It's the cleaning of the copper pots."

Sylvie set up a little straighter, her interest piqued. "What do you mean, no money but copper pots?"

Hattie coughed, hoping to divert everyone's attention. "Elsie is just joking."

"It's the truth," Elsie said, a little hurt it seemed that Hattie was talking over her. Or maybe it was the swift kick that Hattie had given Elsie's shin.

"Ouch." Elsie turned to Hattie. "What is wrong with you? I didn't tell them about the bet we made over Christian Beachy."

Chapter 4

You could have heard a pin drop as Millie and Sylvie both turned to Hattie.

"What sort of bet?" Sylvie demanded.

Hattie gave a nervous laugh, then cleared her throat and finally pressed her lips together as she tried to come up with a logical explanation that wasn't quite a lie. But there was none. "We were just worried about him. That's how it all started," Hattie admitted. "We were watching him at the wedding. Joy and Uriah's. And then I said that everybody can use some positivity in their life and somehow Christian got brought up and we decided to make a bet. It was done. And we shouldn't have. And I have tried to get out of it, but Elsie won't let me."

"Me? If I let you out of this bet, you'll be crying for years that you didn't have an opportunity to show that your theory is correct."

"And what theory is that?" Sylvie asked.

"That anybody can be happy if they want to," Hattie said. And she stood by it. Stood by it enough that she would have embroidered it on a pillow. Everyone could be happy if they wanted to be. No matter what you went through in your life or how bad things could get, there were times when everybody got sad and depressed. Times when everybody cried a little, everybody stomped their feet. But then you had to pull yourself up by your bootstraps— or your prayer *kapp* strings, whatever you wanted to pull yourself up by—and live life. Hattie for one didn't want to live life unhappy.

"So you came up with a plan to try to make him happy?" Sylvie frowned as she said the words.

Hattie shook her head. "It's not that I think he's unhappy," she said. "I just think he needs to realize that he's happier than he lets on."

"How do you know he's not happy?" Millie asked.

"He frowns all the time."

"Why does that mean that he's unhappy. Does it? Maybe he just doesn't smile," Millie said, but her voice sounded unsure. How was a person supposed to know if another person was happy if they didn't smile. Which would mean that if you didn't smile you had to be un-happy, right? At least that's how Hattie viewed it.

"Maybe going out with our Hattie here will make him smile and then he'll realize he's happy." Sylvie smiled that smile of women in love with their men.

Hattie shook her head. "It's not like that," she hastily corrected. "We're not going as a date or anything. I mean, I invited him and Elsie made it a Sadie Hawkins thing so I could invite him, but only so that I could talk to him and help him be more positive. But it's not a date."

Sylvie was still grinning. It was as if she hadn't heard one word that Hattie had said. Great. If Sylvie thought that Christian and Hattie were going on a date, it wouldn't be long before the whole town thought the same. Malinda included.

* * *

Christian looked around him in stunned awe. It was perhaps the biggest mess he had ever seen. Even that time when the kids decided to give him breakfast in bed on his birthday and they had pretty much used up every dish trying to make pancakes, eggs, and sausage. The difference was that Deborah, his oldest, had been six at the time and the youngest, Lizzie, hadn't been born yet.

See, unlike a lot of men, he knew his way around the kitchen. He could fry up some eggs for breakfast and put together a sandwich for lunch. He could even make a half-decent casserole for supper. But never in his life had he ever tried to make a cake.

Come to think of it, if they were called whoopie *pies,* why would they be made out of cake? He had never understood that. And now he had a big mess on his hands. There was flour everywhere and he used up almost all the eggs to get the recipe right. He still had three deliveries he had to go make and there were no whoopie pies in sight. He didn't know how the women did it, stayed in the kitchen and whipped up these things like it was nothing. A biscuit now and then was something he could get behind. Maybe add some blueberries from the freezer and a little honey butter filling, but these were whoopie pies. And they were made of cake. Not biscuit dough.

He was still trying to decide where exactly to start tackling the mess and clean up when Malinda breezed into the kitchen. She stopped; the song she had been humming stuck in her throat as she eyed the mayhem. "I just came to get a drink of water."

"It's safe," Christian said. "Come on in."

Malinda moved slowly, as if facing off against a large jungle cat, as she made her way to the kitchen sink. She grabbed a glass from the drainer and got herself a drink from the tap.

"What are you doing?" The words were reluctant, as if she wasn't sure she even wanted to know.

"I was making whoopie pies."

She braced her back against the sink and stared at the mess in front of her as she sipped her water. "I see. And why are you making whoopie pies?"

"Because Hattie and I are going to the whoopie pie thingamabob for Barbie Troyer and we're all supposed to bring whoopie pies."

And he figured since the women were asking the men that the man ought to be making whoopie pies. It made about as much sense as the woman asking a man on a date as far as he was concerned. But the whole whoopie pie baking just wasn't coming out like he had planned in his head.

"You can always tell her you don't want to go."

He turned to face his sister. Her eyes were innocent and she sipped her water. She looked harmless, as she if she hadn't just told him to break a date with someone that he wasn't going on a date with but who was a nice person and whom Christian didn't want to hurt.

Hattie might be intolerably positive. But she didn't deserve to be just cut down. He had already done that once, and he wasn't about to do it again. "I'm not going to do that," he told Malinda.

She shrugged as if it were no big deal and turned back to rinse her glass. She set it back in the dish strainer. "Suit yourself. But you've got to get the mess in here cleaned up before supper." She looked at the battery-operated clock that hung on the wall next to the refrigerator. "You only got four hours. You better get started."

Christian frowned at her. "Ha ha," he said. "Very funny." Though it was a big mess in the kitchen. He still wasn't going to need four hours to clean it. He couldn't take that long. He already had to make at least a dozen whoopie pies and that would take some time. And time was running out. The event was tomorrow. He had hoped to have them made by this afternoon, put in a container, and waiting for the morning.

"I just don't think you should go out on a date with her. You don't have any intention of being with her." She stopped but continued to stare at him. "You don't, do you?"

Christian closed his eyes and tried to get everything back in line. Aside from the kitchen, it seemed this deal with Hattie was turning out to be a big mess as well. "She asked me."

"Only because of Sadie Hawkins."

There was that name again. He still hadn't found out who Sadie Hawkins was. But she seemed to be wreaking havoc on his life, even more than Hattie Schrock. "Just because I'm going out with Hattie doesn't mean that the date will lead to anything. Because it's not really a date. We're going as friends to support Barbie Troyer. Surely you can understand that."

"I understand it, but you don't have to go with her in order to support Barbie. All you have to do is make another dozen whoopie pies and you could get in. At least I think that's what Elsie said."

"I'm going with Hattie because she asked."

"But didn't you tell her no to begin with?" Malinda countered.

It wasn't one of Christian's prouder moments. "I did. But that was before I understood what she was really asking me. We are going to support Barbie. You remember Barbie Troyer, the midwife who has delivered just about every baby in this community in the last sixty-something years, including you and all my children and all my grandchildren."

"I remember Barbie. I just don't understand why you changed your mind and told Hattie that you would go with her."

"I just did. And I just am." He hoped his words held enough conviction that she would let the subject drop. He couldn't say exactly why he backed up and decided to go to the benefit with Hattie. Well, he could say. But he wasn't going to say it out loud. Especially not to his sister. He wasn't about to tell her that somehow his life had turned a little flat and that he had turned old. That he felt like there was a little bit more of something out there for him and that he hadn't realized it until now. Lord only knew what she would do with that sort of information.

"Suit yourself," she said with a sniff. She spun on her heel and started for the door.

Christian turned away from her, back to the mess before him. "I don't know how women do it," he said, still trying to determine the best place to start. Sweeping the floor would help but so would emptying the trash. And then there was the flour that coated everything.

Malinda turned, critically examining the mess as well. "I always use the cake mix from the store."

One good thing about this whoopie pie benefit that the widows had going was that it was being held in the empty field next to Paradise Stables. Since Christian was coming in from the country with his horse and buggy, it was no big deal to drop it off with Jason and have him store the buggy and the horse until the benefit was over.

The bad thing was Christian was nervous. His heart had steadily pounded faster and faster, in rhythm with the clop of his horse's hooves and the whir of his buggy wheels as he'd made his way to town. Now that he had turned his horse over to Jason and his buggy was safely parked in the opposite field across the street from the stables, it was time to go meet Hattie.

And yet he lingered.

"So you're not going to go at all?" Christian shifted the box of whoopie pies he held as he directed the question to Jason Stoll who owned the stables.

Christian just hoped that whoever ended up with his whoopie pie efforts didn't judge them too harshly. He'd done as Malinda had suggested and gone to the store for a cake mix. He still had to add water, oil, and eggs, mix it all, and bake them in the oven. So really the effort and time was about the same as those who started from scratch. At least, that was what he was telling himself.

"Nah," Jason said with a sheepish smile.

Jason was a good man, a little younger than Christian himself though a widower as well. He had shaggy brown hair that stuck out from underneath his straw hat and big brown eyes that somehow seemed to offset his beefy countenance. He made Christian think of the blacksmiths of olden times who beat iron into submission. It was a fanciful thought, but that's what Jason brought to mind whenever he saw him. Or maybe it was just the fact that he worked in the barn and worked with horses that made all that blacksmith stuff come to light. There was a blacksmith in Paradise Springs, but he was on the other end of town closer to the line where you crossed over into Paradise Hill.

"Not even for a little while?" Christian pressed.

"I've got enough here to keep me busy."

He supposed he did. Christian looked around. There was some sort of horseback riding lesson going on in one pasture. The Amish horses whose owners had gone to the benefit were in another. A great many people milled around, those who came to look at the horses and those who actually worked at the stables. *Jah*, he had enough to keep him busy. But it looked like he also had enough staff on hand that he could get away for a little while if he really wanted to. Which meant he didn't want to. And Christian wondered if like him, Jason was a little reluctant to head over. Except Jason hadn't promised Hattie Schrock that he would go with her.

"Okay then. But if you want to walk down with me . . ." He trailed off. Shameful, that's what it was. Puredee shameful that he was trying to get a buffer. Even though he knew that he and Hattie Schrock were not going on a date. They had never talked about it being a date anyway.

"*Danki.*" Jason had the grace to color a bit. "Have a good time."

Christian paused one more heartbeat. "It's for a good cause," he said, trying to tempt the man. Definitely shameful.

Jason's color deepened one more shade. "I donated," he said, then he turned away, leaving Christian no choice but to head down to the benefit alone.

It was a short walk. Just down the sidewalk. In fact, the sidewalk ended right where the entrance to the benefit was. Normally that field was empty, fenced in with simple wire and baled for hay come the end of May and sometime again in August. But today it was teeming with people. Folks of all kinds had turned out for Barbie Troyer. Even *Englisch* folks.

The gate had been propped open and some sort of plastic bunting had been draped about to add a festive nature to the place.

Just outside the fence, Lillian Lambert sat behind the table with Katie Lapp next to her.

"Hey, Christian," Lillian greeted.

Katie gave him a small nod.

"Hi, ladies." He paced to the other side of the entrance, shuffling the box in his now-sweaty hands. "I'm just waiting for someone."

Lillian gave him a secretive smile and a small nod.

This was where he said he would meet Hattie. Right? He doubted his own memory. *Jah*, this was where he said they would meet. That they would meet at the entrance to the benefit. He paced back to the other side.

She should be here soon. He hoped anyway. He wasn't sure exactly what time it was, but it was perhaps a few minutes after time for them to meet. Which meant she wasn't there yet. And suddenly he had the heavy feeling that she might not come at all.

The thought shouldn't have bothered him, but it did. What if she stood him up? What if she didn't come at all? What if she forgot that she had asked him to begin with?

The thoughts made his heart pound in his chest. As if he wasn't nervous enough. And he didn't even know why he was nervous to begin with. This wasn't a date. So if it wasn't a date, she couldn't stand him up, right?

No, it wasn't a date. They had said just friends.

Hadn't they?

Even if they had, you know women. They say one thing and mean another. He stopped midpace. Was it a date? Maybe he should ask her. No, he decided quickly before he could think twice about it. He didn't need to ask her anything. And she wasn't going to stand him up. Because—

There she was.

Hattie rushed toward him, a little out of breath as she ran-walked hurriedly down the sidewalk. The strings of her prayer *kapp* trailed out behind her.

"I'm so sorry. We got caught up with an order at the shop and . . ." She allowed her words to trail off. She stopped dead in front of him. "I hope you haven't been waiting long."

Only long enough to get himself all worked up that she wasn't coming. Not long at all. "No," he said. "Not at all." Then he looked down into her empty hands. "No whoopie pies?"

She smiled. She had a nice smile, and he had never thought about it because it was always hanging around. But today he noticed. And it really was a nice smile. "I brought mine over earlier." She dropped her voice to a whisper so Lillian and Katie couldn't hear. "Mine are the red velvet."

He thought she was telling him that because she wanted him to win them. Maybe. Maybe not. He had no idea. "I'm not a big red velvet person," he admitted.

"Really?" There was that smile again. It seemed to light up her entire face. It made her eyes twinkle and her dimples show. He'd never thought much about dimples, but right then and there he decided that he liked them.

"Isn't it just food coloring and cream cheese frosting?"

For the first time ever—at least the first time he noticed it, anyway—Hattie frowned. "Heavens no. Red velvet is something else entirely."

"Malinda—" he started, then cut off his own words. "I didn't know that. Maybe I can win yours today and give it a try."

Her smile returned. "I tell you what. If you don't get them today, I'll make you a batch this week. Deal?"

"I'd like that." He nodded toward the entrance. "Shall we go in?"

It was the nicest way he could think of to see if she had bought tickets for the event. That was the whole point, wasn't it? There was no sense in him buying tickets if she had already bought some. But since this wasn't a date, had she bought some?

This whole event was making his head ache.

"*Jah*," she said with a smile. She unsnapped the flat little purse she had dangling from her wrist and pulled out two slips of bright blue paper. Tickets for the event. She handed them to Lillian.

The woman smiled knowingly as Katie stamped the back of their hands with a red smiley face. "That's in case you leave and need to get back in."

Christian frowned. "Aren't you going to be here?"

Lillian shrugged. "Theoretically I suppose one of us would be here, but just in case somebody else takes over. Now they know you paid to get in."

They nodded their thanks and headed into the benefit.

Someone—the widows he supposed—had decorated the field and set up booths. Some of those he remembered from the Whoopie Pie Festival, such as the beanbag toss and the horseshoe stakes. Poppin' Paradise had a booth and was selling popcorn with Rachel Lehman, Uriah Lehman's daughter, at the helm.

The games and the booths were all on the outside edge of the field and in the center of all that, the grass had been mowed down low. Squares for a cakewalk had been spray-painted onto the space. Buckets had been scattered around with Barbie's name on them, the lids all boasting slits so people could easily slide their donation inside.

And the whoopie pies. A table had been set up near the entrance where people could deposit their contribution to the cakewalk. Well, it was actually three of those long rectangular tables lined end to end to make a highway of whoopie pies. Boxes of all kinds were stacked, some labeled with the flavor, others not.

Christian placed his box on the table, a little anxious and awkward, trying to figure out what to do with his hands. He rubbed them on his pants and looked around.

"Want to play a round of horseshoes?" she asked.

He shook his head. He was quaking so bad inside that he was pretty sure he would be a danger to anyone standing close. "I haven't pitched in years."

"Come on," Hattie cajoled. "You're not afraid I'll beat you, are you?"

He scoffed at the idea, then found himself moving toward the game. "I'll take red." He picked up the two crudely painted horseshoes in his chosen color and went to stand at one end of the playing area. He waited patiently for her to do the same. "You can pitch first," he told her as she went to stand on the opposite side.

Horseshoes was a relatively simple game. Two stakes were planted forty feet apart and the object was a ringer. That's when the mouth of the horseshoe was actually around the stake. Points were given for having the horseshoe touch the stake and points were also given for the closest pitch in that round. That's where that old saying came from, that close only counted in horseshoes and hand grenades. He could definitely attest to horseshoes, though he didn't know much about hand grenades.

Hattie scored two on the first round and smiled encouragingly when his tosses both went a little too wide. He hadn't been joking when he told her that it had been a while since he had pitched horseshoes. It had been a while since he played any game it all, come to think of it. There was something nice about standing there in the sunshine, a cool breeze blowing, and the sound of other people's laughter filling the air. Suddenly he felt all the tension leave his shoulders. And for the first time since he got up that morning, he wasn't nervous at all.

After the next three rounds and so many ringers, Christian had a substantial lead.

"I thought you said you hadn't pitched in a long time." Hattie looked at him skeptically. Her normally sweet smile had taken on a forced edge and he had a feeling that she had a competitive streak. It wasn't something he would've thought about her. She was just so . . . sweet all the time. So nice and pleasant and helpful and just so . . . Hattie, that he had never dreamed she would have a drive to win.

"I haven't," he said with a small shrug. It was the truth.

Her expression turned serious, and after a few more pitches the score evened up a bit. But she still hadn't had any ringers. She gained several points from having the horseshoe touch the stake, where he had blown his streak of ringers three in a row.

Two more rounds and the score was fifteen to nineteen with him in the lead. He just had to score two close, and he would win. If Hattie wanted to take the victory, she would need two back-to-back ringers, something she hadn't managed in any of the pitches so far.

Maybe he was concentrating too hard. Or maybe there was something in him that didn't want the game to be over just yet. Whatever it was, both his pitches were a little bit wide; that only left him with one point for the round. He needed twenty-one for the win. "Your turn," he called.

"Come on, Hattie Mae," he thought he heard her mutter as she drew back for her first toss.

If it had been a basketball shot through a net, it would have never touched the rim at all. If it had been a baseball, it would've been hit over the fence straight down the middle. The horseshoe wrapped around the stake without even touching it. It fell to the earth with a solid thud.

Christian stared at it for a moment then looked back up to Hattie. "It's a ringer." His voice held a note of awe and disbelief.

Her mouth fell open. "It is?"

"You want to come look at it?"

"You're really telling me the truth?"

He frowned at her. "Why would I lie about horseshoes?"

"You wouldn't," she said. But apparently she had deceived herself as she walked slowly over to where he stood. She looked down at the horseshoe then back up to him. Her eyes were twinkling and her dimples starting to show. "That's pretty nifty."

He shook his head at her. "Pretty nifty," he said. "You do it again."

The mask of determination descended on her features so quickly it was as if it had been there all along. "We shall see," she said, then spun around and marched back to her spot at the end of the pitch.

Apparently her competitive streak was about a mile wide. Just watching her gear up for this possible final toss of the game, was akin to the *Englisch* athletes he caught glimpses of on the TVs at Walmart and other places. Where they warmed up, danced in a circle, stretched their legs and arms in a variety of motions, as if all that would be the determining factor in their performance. Hattie didn't dance around or stretch her arms and legs, but she was breathing deep and steady. He could almost see her try to pull in a calm breath as if that would allow her to ring the next one. She got into position, both arms bent at the elbow, horseshoe open side lined up in front of her eyes as she leveled her gaze on the stake. She stooped a little at the waist as if to get a better line on the stake. Then she took in another deep breath.

"You going to throw that today?"

She straightened with a frown. "Christian, I was just about ready."

He eyed her skeptically. "If you say so."

"I say so." She started to get back into position. "Now be quiet so I can concentrate."

He almost chuckled out loud at her antics. It was a game of horseshoes, but she was acting like it was for some big title.

Down in position again, Hattie closed her eyes, blew out a deep breath, opened them again, and tossed the horseshoe.

Clang! The horseshoe hit the top of the stake and spun around all the way to the ground where it rang against the other.

Hattie stood on the opposite end of the game field as still as a statue. Two full heartbeats passed before she got herself into motion again. A wide smile took over her face. She raised her arms in the air and jumped up and down, whooping and hollering. "I won! I won! I won!"

She was so happy that a part of him wished he had thrown the game a few rounds ago. But he didn't think Hattie would've appreciated that. She wasn't the kind that wanted to win because someone had let her. But he did like to see her happy. Well, she was always happy. This was a different kind of joy. This was the excitement of life and the victories that came with it. Celebration.

"You want to go again?" she asked.

He could tell she wanted to see if she could beat him again. And perhaps they would play once more. "Later?"

She nodded, eyes twinkling and dimples still flashing. "Definitely."

Hattie couldn't believe the day she was having. When she got up that morning, she'd been so nervous, terrified that Christian wasn't going to show up. It wasn't a real date so it shouldn't have mattered. But since everybody at the Whoopie Pie Widows' Club knew that she had invited him, if he decided to stand her up, she would look ridiculous. And then the fact that she had made the bet with Elsie . . . It would just be so embarrassing if she got to the benefit and he wasn't there.

Worry had made her stomach hurt and her fingers clumsy. She barely ate any breakfast and then she seemed to drop anything she touched. Then everything seemed to take twice as long as it should and their deliveryman took the wrong order over to the bowling alley. Once that got straightened out, she realized that she was late to meet him. So she rushed out the door barely remembering to grab her wristlet purse before she left.

But now . . . now everything seemed just fine. She'd been worried about nothing.

"And you made the whoopie pies yourself?" she asked as they took their sandwiches to the tables under the blue-and-white striped tent that had been set up.

She was oh so aware of all the strange looks that they were getting. And those looks were coming from all sorts of directions. Members of the Whoopie Pie Widows' Club smiled and nodded as if it were a normal occurrence to see the two of them together walking side by side. Sylvie and Millie both gave them knowing looks along with their smiles of greeting. And Hattie had to say a small prayer that Christian didn't notice. Everyone else watched them as if a budding romance was starting right beneath their noses. If Christian noticed, he didn't say a word.

They found two chairs together and sat down across the table from each other, unwrapping their bag lunch. Aaron Lapp had promised all proceeds to go to Barbie Troyer from the sale of his sandwiches. And though he was known for his fried chicken and mashed potatoes and other yummy buffet food, the man could make a good sandwich. Aaron was offering chicken salad, roast beef, or ham and cheese. Each sandwich came in a brown paper sack along with a bag of chips, a pickle, a tangerine, and a piece of honey candy made by Katie Hostetler. Katie was Rufus Metzger's sister and Rufus the community's local beekeeper.

"This is good," Christian said, taking a large bite of his roast beef.

Hattie had chosen the chicken salad. It was, hands down, her favorite. "You've had Aaron's sandwiches before though, *jah*?"

Christian took another big bite and shook his head. He chewed and swallowed before answering. "No. It's delicious."

She shot him a small, perplexed frown. "Not even at one of these benefits? He always makes sandwiches for the benefits."

Christian shook his head. "Most times I go home for lunch."

But that would mean . . . "You don't stay for the whole thing?" Benefits and helping the community and fellowship, Hattie lived for this sort of thing.

"I usually have to get home to check on everything. Those vegetables don't grow themselves, you know."

If she wasn't mistaken, she thought she heard a teasing note in his voice. But when she examined his expression, there was no trace of it. "Of course they don't. And the popcorn doesn't make itself either. But you have to take time for your community."

"I take time. I just don't take all the time."

Hattie mulled that over. "Work's important," she said. "But so are friends."

"Is that why you invited me here today?"

Her mouth went instantly dry and the chicken salad turned to ash. How in the world was she supposed to answer that one? "*Jah*," she finally managed. "I guess you could say that. And it's for a good cause." She gave a small shrug hoping that the action hid her sudden nervous nature. "I guess I thought you might like to come here."

Shut up now, Hattie. Before you embarrass yourself further.

She pressed her lips together somehow taking her own advice as she waited for him to say something in return.

But this was Christian Beachy she was talking about. He only nodded, his eyebrows pulled into a small frown as he took another bite of his sandwich. He grabbed a couple of chips and chewed everything together before swallowing and then finally answering. "It's been fun so far."

"You think it'll be fun when I beat you at horseshoes again?"

"Who said you were going to beat me again?"

"That sounds like a challenge."

"You just let me finish my lunch, and you're on."

Hattie smiled at him, noting that he didn't smile in return. She was going to get a smile out of him one way or another. "You got yourself a deal."

They pitched horseshoes until Christian's arm was so sore he didn't think he'd be able to lift it the next day.

Finally he begged off with Hattie beating him by one match. It was surprising that she was so competitive, but he found that he liked that about her. Or maybe it was because they were just there as friends that she could be open with him. It made him think about back when he was dating Elizabeth. He never asked her, though there were incidents when he felt like she did her best to make him feel big and strong and in charge. This was a lot like that. Because he and Hattie were just friends. It would be like him playing horseshoes with Titus Troyer.

Speaking of which . . . Titus was over there laughing at something Irene Lapp was saying. Irene had to be the oldest person in Paradise Springs, and if Christian didn't know better, he'd think that Titus—who was at least half her age—was flirting with her. But that couldn't be right. It was just that Titus seemed so happy these days. Though no one knew why. At least no one who was talking. Surely if there was something new going on in Titus's life Malinda would have shared it over supper. Surely.

Now truthfully most times Christian tuned his sister out, but he was fairly certain he would remember if she had said something about Titus.

But seeing the man laugh and joke with Irene made Christian feel like he was missing out again. The feeling had left him that day as he ate whoopie pies, pitched horseshoes, and talked with Hattie.

"What sort of whoopie pies are yours again?" Hattie said, nodding toward the foil pan she held. Been something of a joke between them, but she had bought his whoopie pies and he had bought hers.

"Sprinkle Delight." He said it where he hoped no one else around could hear.

"What?" She leaned in a little toward him.

"Sprinkle Delight," he said a little louder.

She stopped and he kept walking. So he had to go back to where she was. "You mean like the kind at the grocery store?"

He felt himself grow warm. He couldn't remember the last time he had blushed, and yet here he was turning all sorts of colors over whoopie pies. And in front of Hattie Schrock, no less. "*Jah*, like in the grocery store."

"I thought you said you made these."

She tilted her head toward him as if encouraging him to respond. It was perhaps the last thing he wanted to do. "I didn't buy them," he said pulling her to one side. The benefit was over and everyone was starting to move out of the field. People were heading for their houses, their cars, and other people like them were headed up toward Jason Stoll's stables. Hattie had to walk that direction anyway so she was going to walk him as far as the stables and then head on to the popcorn shop. But with so many people around, he grabbed her elbow and pulled her to one side. He really didn't want anybody hearing all of this. It was his dirty little secret.

"Malinda wouldn't make me the whoopie pies to bring," he said. "So I tried making them from scratch."

She nodded once again, encouraging him to continue.

"That didn't work out. So I went to the grocery store."

"And you thought you would bring store-bought whoopie pies to the benefit?"

He shook his head. "Nothing like that. It's a cake mix."

"Don't let Sylvie King hear you say that. That's downright blasphemous."

"I was going to make chocolate," he continued. "But then I saw all those sprinkles. They looked like so much fun. So I bought the cake mix and the icing to match."

She shook her head. "There's still a kid in there somewhere, isn't there?"

He shrugged. "I guess." Maybe there was. And maybe it was coming out today. Which might be why he had that weird feeling that something was missing. That he hadn't done everything that he wanted to, everything that he needed to.

It was a strange to think about that. Had he done the things he wanted to do? He had married a beautiful woman. He had brought up a wonderful family; he raised delicious, nutritious crops for his community. He had extrafine grandkids. There wasn't anything missing. But yet that emptiness in his stomach seemed to remain.

"You're going to eat the red velvet, aren't you?" she asked.

"Of course," he replied. "I wouldn't have bought them otherwise."

"Not even if it was just for a good cause." She started back in the direction of the stables.

In two steps he caught up with her. "I told you I would try your red velvet. Though I still don't see what all the big fuss is about."

"That's because you've never had real-deal red velvet."

And that might be true considering that the red velvet he had was chocolate cake mix with food coloring in it.

"It's my grandmother's recipe."

"If it's so good, why don't you enter it into the Whoopie Pie Festival each year?"

She gave a tiny shrug. "It means so much to Sylvie and she does such interesting flavors." She trailed off, then picked back up again with "Then we have the popcorn booth and it just seems like such a busy time. Plus it's my grandmother's recipe."

He nodded. "You've already said that."

"Well, she's Elsie's grandmother too."

"So it wouldn't be fair of you to enter your grandmother's recipe when she wouldn't be able to enter the same thing."

"Just between you and me, I'm a better baker than Elsie and if I were to win with the same recipe . . ." She closed her eyes and shook her head, then opened them once more. "That would make for bad times in paradise."

He chuckled, and the sound was rusty, as if it was water forced through creaky pipes. Had it been that long since he had laughed at something? He couldn't remember. He cleared his throat. "That wouldn't be good."

Her expression turned more serious than he had ever seen Hattie look before. She shook her head. "No, it wouldn't be. Plus I think you have to be really creative in order to win. And my grandmother's red velvet is awesomely delicious, but it's not unique in any way."

"So if you enter, it would be to win?" he asked.

She turned toward him. "Why would a person who didn't want to win enter in the first place?"

He had no answer for that.

They stopped at the entrance to the stables. It was basically a big barn that sat off the road just a tad to allow people places to pull in their buggies or cars and get situated before going inside the barn. Then there was a series of barns behind where Jason kept horses for people, boarded other large animals, and otherwise conducted whatever businesses a stable conducted.

She turned to him, the aluminum foil pan she held crinkling a bit. "*Danki* for going with me today." She smiled, and he thought he saw her lips tremble just a bit. But that didn't seem right at all, not for Hattie.

"It was my pleasure," he said. And that was the truth. It truly had been a pleasure to hang out with her today and just get away from the farm. He would have more work to do tomorrow, which he wasn't supposed to be doing because it was Sunday, but some things just had to be taken care of. And this was a good cause, *jah*?

"Well," she said backing away a couple of steps, "enjoy the red velvet."

"Enjoy the Sprinkle Delight."

She smiled even wider. "I will. Oh!" She had backed into someone trying to go around her. "I'm sorry."

The man nodded and continued on his way. Hattie turned the brightest shade of pink Christian had ever seen.

"Well, thanks again," she said. Then without waiting for him to respond, she turned on her heel and hastily walked away.

Chapter 5

"Malinda," Christian started, halfway through dinner the following evening.

It was Sunday, a nonchurch Sunday for the two of them, and Christian had spent most of the day pretending to tend to his greenhouse and daydreaming about Hattie.

He'd really had a good time with her the day before, a better time than he had expected to have. That made him wonder why he didn't get out of the house more. It wasn't like he consciously stayed at home. It just sort of fell that way, and now it seemed like things were whizzing past him and he wasn't able to keep up. It wasn't a very good feeling.

"What is it?" his sister asked.

They were eating leftovers from the day before, along with cheese, meat, and pickles. It was an eclectic mix of food, just pretty much what they could find to put on their plates. It wasn't really a dinner at all.

"Is something missing?" She glanced around the kitchen as if to discern the problem before he could say the words.

He put down his fork and sighed. "I don't know. Just here lately I've been feeling . . ." Old. But he didn't want to say that word out loud. It sounded so *Englisch*. Like he was worried about getting old. He didn't know anyone who worried about getting old. No one. It was just part of life, something that people accepted and moved on from. But it seemed like the time passed faster and faster and the days became weeks and the weeks turned to months and nothing changed.

Did he want something to change?

He didn't know. Yet that was why he felt like he was missing something. But he couldn't verbalize that to Malinda. He didn't think his sister would understand.

"What?" Malinda prompted. "Lately you've been feeling so what?"

"I don't know, like maybe we should do more things. Go to meetings, clubs, benefits. Something."

Pitching horseshoes with Hattie yesterday had been such a satisfying activity. He didn't know why. His life should be satisfying. God helped him grow the best vegetables in the Valley. He took seeds and God's beautiful earth and created something with His help. It was a miracle in itself. He read his Bible, he went to church, and knew in his heart all that should be enough. Yet somehow it didn't seem to be. That was something he didn't understand.

"And what meetings am I going to go to?" She sat back with a small snort.

He probably shouldn't've brought that up. It had been a sore spot with Malinda for many years now that she hadn't been invited to join the Whoopie Pie Widows' Club. The problem was she had never been married, and she certainly wasn't a widow. So she didn't fit their criteria. But she felt she was a decent enough baker they should make some sort of exception for her. Though no one had. And it wasn't as if she had asked. If she asked, maybe they would allow it. But she didn't ask and they didn't invite her and Malinda was very tender about it.

"There's more than just the Paradise Springs Widows' Group," he said, calling the club by its proper name.

"There's not a lot of groups for me out there," Malinda said. "Most women my age are already married or have been married. And the younger girls that are single . . . I don't quite fit in with them."

Then there was the fact that if Malinda was around and found out news, the whole town would know it by the end of the day. But that was just how things worked in Paradise Springs.

"You've got your friends though?"

She had friends, didn't she? Of course she did.

Malinda gave a small shrug. "I guess so. But I know what you mean. Sometimes there just seems to be a hole there somewhere. Like maybe if I'd gotten married things would be different."

Married. There were just a handful of people in Paradise Springs who knew the truth about Malinda's single status. That she had been in love once but the man had been *Englisch*. Their parents hadn't approved and Malinda was planning to secretly run away with him. Then he had gone to a family reunion at Lake of the Ozarks and drowned. Heartbroken, Malinda never married. She threw herself wholeheartedly into the church. And everyone associated with it.

"I was thinking about inviting Hattie to go do something," Christian said.

"Do something?" Malinda asked, her eyes so big that her eyebrows nearly collided with her hairline. "Hattie Schrock?"

It was Christian's turn to shrug. "Why not? She invited me to that thing yesterday, and we had a good time. She's not married. I'm not married. We can hang out together. Be friends."

Malinda shook her head. "A man and a woman cannot just be friends."

"I was friends with Elizabeth."

Malinda shook her head and made a face. "That was completely different. You were married. So you had to be friends."

"Well, we're in a new century now," Christian pointed out. "And—and the Amish are evolving. We're not the same as we used to be a hundred years ago. Just think. The elders decided to let us have bicycles now."

Like a lot of the more conservative communities, Paradise Springs had not been allowed to use bicycles. Nothing with rubber tires. Not like some of the communities down south who weren't allowed to use bicycles but drove around on tractors. He'd even heard of bicycles being used in northern Indiana. But not in Paradise Springs. Not until now.

"That still doesn't change the nature of a man and a woman. A man and a woman cannot be *just friends*. It would never work. What if she's friends with you and then decides to get married again? Do you think her husband is going to let her hang out with you? No. See? It would never work to be just friends."

Sometimes Malinda could just be so negative. He had a feeling if he had mentioned that to Hattie, she would be smiling and laughing and clapping her hands, maybe jumping up and down with her arms in the air like she had when she had won that first match of horseshoes.

Speaking of which . . . he rolled his right shoulder. His arm was so sore today. But he supposed it was a good workout. Next time maybe they should switch off and play one game right-handed and the next game left-handed so one arm didn't get quite so sore. He thought Hattie would think that was funny.

"Just because Zebadiah Miller decided to cave and allow everyone to go around willy-nilly on bicycles doesn't mean you should."

"It might be fun though." Something else he'd like to talk to Hattie about. He wondered what she thought about bicycles. He wondered what she thought about the bishop allowing them to have them now in their district.

Malinda shook her head. "You may feel like something is missing in your life," she said. "But I can promise you this: It's not a bicycle."

"I hope you bought yourself some new rubber gloves," Elsie said, pinning Hattie with a serious look.

Hattie turned from stacking their dirty dishes in the sink to look back at her cousin. "I don't normally wear rubber gloves when I do the dishes."

It was Hattie's turn to wash up. They had a system. One week one would cook and the other would clean, then the next week they would switch positions. This was Elsie's turn to cook and Hattie's turn to clean. It was a system that had worked well for them. But in all the years that Hattie had been washing the dishes, she never wore rubber gloves. It seemed unnecessary when she was just dealing with regular detergent. Now cleaning up downstairs was a whole 'nother ball game.

"For the copper pots." Elsie shot her a smug look. "I saw you two on Saturday."

"We had a good time," Hattie protested. "At least, I mean . . . I had a good time. And I brought a lot of positivity into Christian's life." She had. Pitching horseshoes was positive. Walking around the benefit was positive. Eating sandwiches from the Amish buffet booth was positive. Even discussing whoopie pies was positive. She had practically flooded the man with positivity.

"But I didn't see him smile one time."

Hattie frowned. Come to think of it, she hadn't seen him smile either. So all the while she was having such a good time, he was just . . . enduring?

When they got to the stable, he laughed. She remembered him laughing. 'Course it almost sounded like he had choked, and at the time she had resisted the urge to pound him on the back. But she was pretty sure it was a laugh.

"These things take time," she told her cousin.

Elsie just shrugged. "Maybe you should have given yourself more than sixty days, then. Or maybe Christian Beachy is just a hard nut to crack."

That couldn't be it. He didn't seem unhappy. He hadn't said anything to make her think he was unhappy. So why didn't he smile?

She had a feeling he had a nice smile. He had a good chin and a strong jaw, and he was really quite handsome. Well, she thought his jaw was strong underneath his short beard. He was one of the men in the area who trimmed his up so it didn't hang down to his chest. It was dark like his hair and shot full of gray, but that was to be expected. He was in his sixties, after all. And she liked what the *Englisch* said about men with gray hair, that it was distinguished. Right there was a sign of years past and service to the Lord, as far as Hattie was concerned. But there were times she wished her hair wasn't quite so gray. But that was life.

"You're definitely running out of time," Elsie prodded. That was the one thing about her cousin that was sort of annoying to Hattie. She tended to poke the bear whenever she could. Not that Hattie was feeling too bearish. Most of her life was a complete joy.

They had just come up with a fantastic new popcorn combo that was selling out daily. Her whoopie pies—though not as good as Sylvie's—still seemed to be a hit. And God was good all the time. The problem was she didn't have another reason to ask Christian to go anywhere with her. And because of that she was about to have to forfeit the bet.

The Whoopie Pie Festival was coming up in four weeks and there wouldn't be enough time to get him to smile and take a more positive outlook on his life if she waited until then. There was nothing else in between. She certainly couldn't call him up and invite him to dinner or bowling or coffee. It just wasn't done.

A knock sounded on the door, the one that led down into the shop. Had to be a problem with something there.

Hattie waited as Elsie turned to open it.

"I'm sorry to bother you." It was Rachel Lehman, Uriah's daughter, who had taken up the position as night manager in the popcorn shop. "Christian Beachy is downstairs."

Hattie almost got excited, but then told herself to calm down. He wasn't here for anything other than their order. They hadn't talked to him yet about what they wanted this season.

"It's okay, Rachel," Hattie said. "Tell him we want our same order as last year. Except if he can add another watermelon to it, that would be fantastic. Every week, that is."

Rachel nodded. "Same order as last year. Add another watermelon every week. Got it." She turned and headed back down the stairs.

Elsie shut the door behind her.

There were a few people who lived in town who still managed to have gardens to grow food for their table. One of them being Millie at the B&B. Jason Stoll of Paradise Stables also had the land. The rest of the town's Amish had to rely on the grocery store and Christian's home-grown vegetables.

They paid a fee and got so much of the crops every year. It kept fresh food on the table. Truth be known, Elsie and Hattie didn't even have room for a houseplant much less a garden.

"I'm just saying," Elsie said, poking the bear once more, going back to what they had been talking about before Rachel interrupted: Hattie running out of time to help Christian change his ways.

By now Hattie *was* beginning to feel a little bearish. "Well, you said," she replied, then turned back to the sink.

She just had to finish up the dishes, then she could go in her room and stare at the ceiling and try to figure out some way to get Christian Beachy to smile. Some way to show him that life was positive.

Her determination didn't have anything to do with cleaning the copper pots. Hattie simply hated to lose. It had always been part of her nature. It had gotten her into trouble when she was younger. But now she managed to contain it for the most part.

But this. She had to win this. Positivity was her *thing*.

She was just putting the last plate in the drainer when a knock sounded again.

Elsie came out of the living room as Hattie dried her hands to open the door.

"I'm sorry again," Rachel said. "I hate to bother you. But that's not what he wants. But he did tell me to tell you thank you for the order, and he will make sure that an extra watermelon comes every week."

Hattie nodded. "What does he want?" she asked, wondering why he hadn't just knocked on their outside door.

They had two entrances into their apartment. One was on the outside and opened into their living room while this one started in the back room of the popcorn shop and put a body smack in their kitchen.

"Will you just come down and talk to him?" Rachel shifted uncomfortably from one foot to the other. "I think he just wants to see you."

"Okay," Hattie said. She smoothed her hands down her apron, then over the part of her hair that showed under her prayer *kapp*. Then she cleared her throat and followed Rachel down the stairs.

She was oh so aware of Elsie following her. But as Rachel moved behind the counter and Hattie waved to Christian, Elsie lingered in the back room.

"Hey," Christian said quietly as she approached. He had his hat off and was twirling it in his hand. He looked nervous, which was strange. But she supposed it was a little out of the ordinary for him to be there. Yet it was nothing to make a man nervous.

"Everything okay?" Hattie asked.

Christian nodded. "I was just at the men's meeting down at the community theater," he said. "Then I decided I would stop by. Just to see how you are doing."

That was sweet, she thought. But a little bit strange. She was certain he'd come to men's meetings before but had never stopped in to see how she was doing then.

See? Her positivity was rubbing off if he was just stopping by for a visit. That meant he enjoyed her company, which in turn meant he enjoyed her positivity. It was obvious.

"I'm glad you did," she returned.

He nodded, twirled his hat some more, then finally got down to business. "Would you go have coffee with me tomorrow?"

It might've been the last thing that she would've expected him to ask her to do. "Coffee?"

"At Perks of Paradise," he said, talking about the coffee shop that was on the other side of Main. "I want to talk to you about something." He looked around. "You know."

She really didn't, but she nodded politely wondering where this was all going. "I'll go have coffee with you." It might not have been what she had expected, but it was an opportunity to spend more time with Christian and show him what a more positive attitude could get a person in life. Then Elsie would have to clean the copper pots and would have to change her attitude about a lot of things. That was what Hattie was really after. Well, that and the win.

"Okay then. It's a date," he said. Then he shook his head. "Just as friends, right?"

Hattie nodded, grateful that he got it. At least she hoped he did. "Perfect," she replied. "Just as friends."

She waited until he had left the popcorn shop before heading back to the stairs.

"So you're going to take off in the middle of the day to go have coffee with Christian Beachy?" Elsie was obviously annoyed with the whole ordeal.

"You can't tell me that I can't do this," Hattie said. "You have to give me an opportunity to do my thing."

"I suppose," Elsie grumbled.

"You have to be fair."

"Do we have enough people here tomorrow?" Elsie asked, still in a bit of a huff.

"There will be plenty of people here. I will not be gone that long. And you have to let me have a chance to make him more positive."

"I suppose," Elsie said. And though she wasn't the one with the competitive nature, Hattie knew her cousin hated to wash the copper pots.

Chapter 6

It should have been an easy thing, Christian thought the following day as he lingered near the tables outside at Perks of Paradise. And yet it had nearly been a disaster. So much so that when he had asked Hattie to go to coffee, he fully expected her to turn him down.

His plan had been easy enough. If you wanted to call it that, a plan. He had been at the community theater enjoying the men's meeting and thought how easy it would be to walk down to the popcorn shop. He would go in, ever so casually, and there Hattie would be, behind the counter. He would order some popcorn to take home to Malinda, and he would ask Hattie if she'd like to go have a cup of coffee the next day. Today. Whatever.

The problem was none of that worked out the way he thought. Well, the part about walking down to the popcorn shop did, he supposed. It was after that when everything went sideways.

First of all, Hattie wasn't behind the counter when he'd come in. So he looked around and waited for a turn to get popcorn. But then when he got to the counter, it was as if his brain and his mouth stopped working together. He couldn't seem to find the words to ask where Hattie was and if he might talk to her for a moment. When he did find the words, they sounded ominous, even to him. He could tell that Rachel Lehman felt the same about them. Her eyes grew kind of wide, and she seemed to be a little nervous as she told him that she would go upstairs and check and see if Hattie was available.

While she had done that, he had walked around, looked at the popcorn flavors, shook his head over some of them, and hoped that Hattie would indeed agree to see him tonight. Otherwise, he would feel so very foolish. Then he saw dill pickle and candy mixed popcorn. Who ate this stuff?

He didn't have a chance to ask as Rachel came back through the door that led to the back and over to where he loitered about. She had told him that Hattie and Elsie wanted the same order as last year plus an extra watermelon.

Sending her back upstairs to tell Hattie that he wanted to actually speak to her was perhaps the hardest thing he had done in a long time. With the exception being telling her that he would like to go with her to the whoopie pie benefit after all.

No, if he was comparing them, this was harder.

Rachel looked almost as if she was going to tell him no, that he could go to the outside staircase and knock on the door himself, but she gave a small nod and headed once again for the back room of the popcorn shop.

What seemed like an eternity later, Hattie was finally standing in front of him, green eyes sparkling and inquisitive smile simmering just around her mouth. Somehow he managed to get it out that he wanted to go have coffee with her and somehow he managed to actually decide on a time they would meet. Then somehow his legs managed to take him from the popcorn shop.

Now as he waited for Hattie, he seemed to be having similar troubles. This was necessary. According to Malinda it was necessary for his business. He didn't want to put people off. But he just didn't know how Hattie Schrock went around smiling all the time. Not that there wasn't a lot to smile about. He just didn't do it. So how did a person get from where he was to even close to where Hattie was? He didn't know. That's why he was there.

He saw her rushing up the sidewalk and he noted that she always seemed to be rushing somewhere. Like she was running late all the time. It also seemed kind of odd to him that Hattie was always bustling around and was sort of round through the middle, while Elsie, her cousin, seemed to be almost methodical everywhere she went, yet she was thin as a rail. But that wasn't what he was here to figure out.

He raised his hand and waved at Hattie.

She waved in return, her steps increasing their speed. "Sorry," she panted, out of breath as she finally made it to stand just in front of him. "We had a small rush right when I was supposed to come over here."

"Everything okay?" Christian asked, thankful that his words seemed to be back. For the time at least.

"*Jah*," she said. "But I don't think I can stay for long."

"Busy day?" he asked, gesturing toward the tables. "Would you like to sit outside or inside?"

"No more than usual," she said. "And inside."

That's when he realized that he had asked her two questions without allowing her to answer first. His words were back, but falling from his lips with a vengeance.

"Let's go inside then." Christian opened the door and allowed her to step inside in front of him. He'd been able to smell the coffee all the way outside the building, but now that he was inside, it was almost overwhelming. But in a delicious sort of way. "You want a pastry or something?" He checked the menu behind the counter.

How could there be that many coffee drinks? It was coffee. As far as he was concerned, there were three options for coffee. Black, with milk, or with sugar. Okay, four, if a person liked milk and sugar.

Perhaps he should have just invited Hattie to the diner. He understood their menu and a cup of coffee there was a cup of coffee.

"I would like a double vanilla latte with a shot of espresso and just a squirt of hazelnut syrup."

The words were English but he felt as though she was speaking another language.

"A double vanilla latte," he repeated.

She nodded as he spoke.

"With a shot of espresso and what else?"

"An extra squirt of hazelnut syrup. But not too much."

He nodded. "Got it."

She reached for her little wristlet purse, but he shook his head.

"I've got this."

His legs felt awkward as he walked toward the counter. A young blond-haired girl in a black T-shirt and matching hat waited expectantly to take his order. Somehow he managed to get Hattie's order right. And he ordered himself a cup of coffee. Black. His favorite way. He also ordered a slice of lemon pound cake because he knew it came from Joy's bakery. Malinda was always telling him that he ate too many sweets. Maybe he did. But if he could get Hattie to share it with him . . .

He paid for the coffee and they were sharing the cake. Did that make this a date? No, they had said they were just friends and just friends was all they were going to be.

The young blond-haired girl grabbed all of their items,

placed them on a tray, and gave him a smile as she told him the total.

He almost choked. "For two coffees and a piece of cake?"

Her smile never wavered, and he had a feeling he wasn't the only person to balk at the price of things in this little shop. Truth was he had never been in here before. He wasn't one of those coffee people. Though it appeared that Hattie was.

"A coffee, a vanilla latte with an extra shot, and a piece of cake," the young girl corrected.

"Got it," Christian said. What was the *Englisch* saying? *My bad*.

He pulled his money from his wallet, paid the woman, and took the tray over to where Hattie waited.

She shifted expectantly in her seat as he set down the tray. "You got a piece of cake?"

"And two forks." He held up the plastic utensils.

He saw a small flash of concern in her eyes. *Jah*, sharing a piece of cake definitely made it feel a little more like a date.

"Just friends," he told her.

She managed to smile and give a small nod.

"How's your coffee?" he asked after he had sat down and she had taken a sip of that special brew.

"Very good," she said. "It's my favorite."

He tilted his head to one side and studied the coffee with this big glob of whipped cream on top. It wasn't even served in a regular coffee cup. This one could hold soup. "And it's really that good?" Like seven dollars' worth of good? He could remember when coffee cost sixty-five cents a cup.

"You want to try a sip?" She pushed the large saucer with the extra-large coffee cup on it toward him a bit.

He picked up the cup and took a tentative sip. She was right. It was good. It was more than good; it was like dessert in a cup. Why hadn't he been drinking these all along? He took another sip, then resisted the third. He could drink that whole cup in nothing flat, even as big as it was.

"You like?" Hattie asked.

"I do."

She nodded toward the counter and the young girl who was now making another coffee drink for someone else. "Why don't you get yourself one?"

"*Jah*," he said, pushing back from the table and grabbing up his plain coffee. He hadn't even taken the first sip, and he already didn't want it. Maybe the girl could turn it into something like what Hattie had.

The girl finished making the drink for the other customer and moved off to the side. Christian stepped forward, coffee cup in hand.

"Is something wrong with your coffee, sir?"

He shook his head. "I, uh—" He wasn't really sure what to say about it. *It's too plain? I made a mistake?*

The girl could only have been a teenager, yet she gave him an understanding, knowing smile. "First time in?"

He almost sighed in relief. "*Jah*," he said. "Yes, I mean."

"Would you like for me to doctor this up a bit so it's a little more like your friend's?"

"That would be good. I'll pay extra," he continued.

Her smile deepened. "This one's on the house."

He waited as she went about adding this and that from bottles he didn't recognize, then she stirred it with an extralong, twisted spoon and handed it back to him. Now it was in a bigger cup, more like the one Hattie had. He supposed with everything that she added there needed to be more room for the coffee. Understandable.

"*Danki*," he said.

"Anytime," the girl said. "Enjoy."

Christian made his way back to the table and sat down across from Hattie once more.

"What did she do to it?" Hattie asked.

"I don't really know," Christian said taking a small experimental sip. It was beyond delicious. Definitely dessert in a cup. Coffee flavored with all sorts of creamy textures and warm sweet layers. It even had a dollop of whipped cream on the top.

It was the closest thing to heaven on earth he'd ever had.

He set down his cup to keep himself from guzzling it down like a child.

Hattie chuckled a bit, then stirred in her seat. "You have a little"—she gestured toward his face and pushed a napkin across the table to him—"whipped cream," she finally said.

He picked up the napkin and wiped at his face. He turned to her for inspection. "Better?"

She smiled and nodded. "Better. I suppose you should watch the whipped cream with your beard," she suggested.

Christian nodded. "*Jah*."

"This cake is delicious," Hattie said.

"I hear that they get all their pastries from Joy's bakery."

Joy Lehman had opened a bakery in her basement after her husband had died. That had been a few years back, and it was still going strong. Though now she was remarried. She was still Joy Lehman as she had married Uriah Lehman, her husband's brother. If anyone in the community thought it strange, he hadn't heard a word. Not that he listened to idle gossip, but he was Malinda's brother.

The fact was that it was only natural for Joy to help Uriah take care of his family after his wife died, and for Uriah to help Joy take care of her family after her husband died. It just took them seven years to get there. Seven years and her son Johnny B falling out of the hayloft breaking his back. But that was another story.

"Why do you suppose Joy never enters the Whoopie Pie Festival baking competition?" Hattie mused.

It was like something Malinda would've asked him. He had absolutely no idea. But when Hattie asked him, it didn't annoy him like it did when Malinda posed such questions. "I wouldn't begin to know." He took a bite of the cake. It really was good, though a little sour after drinking such sweet coffee. He had a feeling that the young girl kept the cake in mind when she was mixing up his drink. The flavors seemed to go together very well.

"I suppose after you bake all day it wouldn't be as much fun to enter a competition," she mused.

That seemed logical enough. "I suppose."

"I mean Sylvie King bakes a lot, but not as much as Joy."

Christian took another bite and shook his head. Maybe he should have gotten two pieces of cake.

"I mean, I wouldn't want to enter a popcorn-making competition."

"Speaking of which," he said taking one more sip of coffee to wash down the last bite of cake. "Dill pickle and candy?"

"That was Rachel's idea."

"It sounds disgusting," Christian said.

"We can't keep it on the shelves."

Christian shook his head. "I guess there's no account for some people."

She chuckled. "I suppose not." She glanced up to some point behind him and her eyes grew wide. "Oh no, I gotta go."

She gulped down the rest of her coffee, then picked up her wrist purse from the tabletop.

They had been sitting there talking so long about coffee and popcorn, about cakes and the baking competition that he had not had a chance to ask her how she managed to keep a smile on her face all the time. Or what he could do to have the same.

He stood as she did.

"*Danki* for the coffee," she said.

Christian didn't know what else to do, so he nodded. He couldn't just let her leave. He had things to ask her. The only solution would be to ask her on another date . . . uh, meeting. And maybe then he could go over everything he wanted to know.

"Hattie," he started, unsure of what he was about to say. "There's a new pickleball court on the other side of the park."

She stopped her fidgeting and bustling around and stared at him, mouth slightly open. "What in the world is pickleball?"

He wasn't quite sure himself, but he had been hearing Titus Troyer talk about it. It was something that they had all over the place in Florida. Christian wasn't sure how it made its way from there up to here, but someone had certainly imported the game.

"I don't know myself, but I'm certain we can find the rules. We can learn enough to play. It might be fun. Give me a chance to even the score after your crushing victory at horseshoes."

"Crushing victory, huh?" The beginnings of a smile twitched at the corners of her mouth.

"You got something else to call it?"

Again she suppressed that smile. "You're on," she said.

"I'll call about getting us a court and let you know when we can play." Maybe by then he could get up enough of whatever it was he needed to ask her, questions he really wanted to ask her. Nerve? Gumption?

"It's a date," she said. Then she stopped.

"A meeting," he corrected. It was much better than a date. That word had all sorts of weight on it that had nothing to do with the word itself.

"A meeting, then," she said. And with a small wave she bustled out the door.

"It's very good news," Callie said that Tuesday night at the widows' club meeting.

Lillian Lambert had just told everyone that Barbie Troyer was coming out of her coma or whatever it was that they had put her in so she could heal after her heart attack. It seemed she was on the mend. Though she was far from healthy.

"She really should retire," Katie said. "She's older than dirt. She was old when I was coming up. In fact she delivered Imogene and I thought she was ancient then."

Katie's daughter, Imogene, had once attended the widows' meetings. But she had recently fallen in love with a man from Paradise Hill and moved over across the line. They seem to be very happy even though it wasn't her intended match. See, Imogene had gone to Paradise Hill to hire a matchmaker, who turned out to just be a romance author. But the author, Astrid Kauffman, wanted to set Imogene up with the hardware store owner, Ira Oberholtzer.

Instead, Imogene fell in love with Astrid's brother, Jesse. It was kind of confusing, but it sure made for good talk at the Widows' Club. Of course, Imogene didn't come to the meetings anymore, and they sorely missed her. But at least they had Katie.

"How do you suppose she is?" Millie asked.

"She seemed to be in good spirits the last time I was in there," Katie said with a firm nod. "Good spirits for Barbie anyway. She can't talk yet since she had all those tubes down her throat. But her color looks good and the doctor seemed to think she's on a more stable ground now. I don't think she's out of the woods completely yet and will have to rest a lot before she can even think about going back to work."

The ladies all nodded in commiseration. They had all gathered round for the meeting, each one checking out the whoopie pies that the others had baked. It wasn't long before the competition and everyone was starting to narrow down their possibilities for entries.

So far on the table were lemon sour cream, chocolate chocolate chip, some kind of zucchini bread concoction, strawberry, and of course, vanilla. Because that was Millie's favorite.

Sylvie always managed to have vanilla available for their meeting. Millie was really thin after having Linda Beth and she seemed to be getting thinner still, instead of the other way around. Hattie supposed it was because she had taken up a more vigorous position at the B&B since Linda Beth had been born. Hattie hoped that's all it was, and that it wasn't something more serious.

"Annabelle came and helped with Linda Beth. Well, she sent us to the hospital," Millie reminded them. Hattie supposed that was help in its own way too.

Millie had had a difficult birth with Linda Beth, and

both were lucky to have survived it all. Just another thing to thank the good Lord for.

"She's a wonderful midwife," Katie continued. "Don't get me wrong. But I think it's time she stepped aside. I'm not the only one in town that thinks that too. Poor Annabelle's always been her shadow."

Sylvie settled herself down in the chair, her full plate perched delicately on her lap. "I think Barbie deserves a break, for sure. She's worked so hard all these years, delivered all these babies. It's time to enjoy her golden years."

Katie scoffed. "I'm in my golden years," she said. If Hattie was remembering correctly, Katie was somewhere in her seventies. "And she's way past me." She looked around at all the other widows. "Way *way* past me."

Sylvie shook her head. "At any rate, she should be enjoying these last times of her life instead of running around delivering babies, especially when Annabelle can step in."

They continued to discuss Barbie Troyer, her age, whether or not she should retire, and her chances of having another heart attack considering all the bacon the woman ate.

"I want to know about Hattie and Christian at the whoopie pie benefit." Sylvie turned all of her attention to Hattie.

She felt the heat rise into her cheeks and knew that she had to be as bright pink as the strawberry whoopie pies Callie Raber had brought. It was embarrassing really to sit there and blush like a schoolgirl when those years were way *way* past her. But there she sat, pink as all get-out, trying to find some explanation for the time she spent with Christian Beachy at the whoopie pie benefit. If she said they were just friends no one would believe her, and it would probably make it even worse. So she decided to just meet it head-on, pretend like everything was normal. Like she always asked Christian to go places with her.

"I had a great time." She smiled to back up her words. "I beat him at horseshoes." But mentioning that didn't make her overcompetitive. At least not as competitive as Elsie claimed she was.

"It looked like you were having a good time, but I didn't see Christian smile even once." Katie looked around to see if anyone else agreed with her.

"How would you know that?" Hattie demanded. She had been with Christian the whole time and no, she hadn't seen him smile either, but to have Katie say that . . . "You were taking tickets for the longest time."

"I said that I didn't see him any of the times I looked at him. And I looked at him plenty enough times to think that man didn't smile at all."

Elsie leaned a little closer to Hattie and whispered, "You can go ahead and just buy a year's supply of rubber gloves and then you wouldn't have to keep going back to the store."

"Hush," Hattie said. And she might have popped her cousin on the leg if she hadn't been holding her plate with both hands. For the most part, the Amish were nonviolent people, but sometimes a cousin could just use a smack on the leg when they got a little too impertinent. Right now Elsie was a little too impertinent. Just because no one else saw Christian Beachy smile, didn't mean he didn't smile. Hattie was the only one who knew. And she knew that he hadn't smiled. But that wasn't something she wanted to discuss with everyone. She was working on it.

The thing about it was he didn't seem wholly unhappy. Every time she talked to him or met with him, he seemed perfectly fine. Perfectly happy. He just didn't seem to express it in the same way that others did. And truly there wasn't anything wrong with that. Though she would lose the bet if she didn't get him to smile and appear more positive on the outside. She still hadn't worked out how she was going to accomplish that.

"You suppose he's still grieving over Elizabeth?" Millie asked. She hadn't lived in the Valley when Christian was married to Elizabeth, but Hattie had. But she had been married to her own husband. She had been busy raising kids and hadn't noticed if he was any different now than he was then. She remembered him slightly from school. From what she could recall, he was as serious then as he was now. Or maybe that was just her memory playing tricks on her.

"And then they went to the coffee shop together," Elsie confided.

Really. If she hadn't been holding her plate to keep it from dumping over, she would've right then smacked her cousin on the leg. Nonviolent types or not. Elsie didn't need to be going on and telling everybody that.

"Wow," Sylvie said. "You went to have coffee together? That's like a date date. Who invited whom?"

"He invited her." Oh that Elsie.

"It was not a date date. It was a meeting meeting. Well, it was a meeting. It had nothing to do with dating," Hattie explained. Though she had enjoyed watching him enjoy his coffee. But even that hadn't brought a smile to his face.

"Meeting?" Elsie made a face. "You're at a meeting now."

"If it wasn't a date, girl, why did he invite you?" Katie asked.

Hattie pressed her lips together, unable to find a suitable quick answer. Finally she said, "I think he wanted to talk to me." Though the words came out sounding a little like a question.

"About what?" Lillian asked.

"I don't know," Hattie replied. "We didn't get around to talking about it and then I had to go."

"You had to talk about something," Elsie said. "You were gone for almost an hour."

Callie's eyes grew wide. "Do tell," she said.

"There's nothing to tell. We talked about coffee and the lemon cake they serve at Perks of Paradise." She thought about it another moment. "And we talked about the dill pickle and candy popcorn—"

"Gross," Katie said.

"You're not our target audience," Elsie said. "And we sold out of it every day this week."

Katie shuddered.

Everyone laughed.

"And we talked about whoopie pies and pickleball." Hattie sat back in her seat, a self-satisfied smile on her face. None of that was date talk at all.

"Dill pickle popcorn and pickleball in the same conversation?" Sylvie asked.

Hattie shrugged. "That was it."

"What in the world is pickleball?" Katie asked. She shook her head. "You young people."

"I'm not sure myself," Hattie said. "But we are going to play sometime this week. Apparently there's a court on the other side of the park. I never knew it was there."

"Oh, they've been building on that for a while," Callie said. "It's supposed to be a lot of fun."

"Are there pickles involved?" Sylvie asked.

Callie laughed. "No, no, just a ball and a racket and a net and a court."

Elsie frowned. "That sounds a lot like tennis."

"I've never played," Callie admitted. "But I've heard others talking when they come into the restaurant."

Hattie guessed you heard a lot when you were the hostess at the most popular eating establishment in Paradise Springs. Next to the Chinese buffet, anyway.

"I guess it's a lot like tennis and somewhat like badminton, and then I even heard it has elements of ping-pong," Callie said.

As far as Hattie was concerned, Callie knew quite a lot about the game.

"The ball is plastic and the paddle doesn't have holes in it like a tennis racket or badminton racket. Then you hit the ball across the net. I think they're just revamping the old tennis courts so that they're marked for both games."

That seemed efficient, Hattie thought. She hardly ever saw anyone playing on the tennis courts in the park. The kids who played used the courts over at the high school. But there had been a time in her life when she liked to play tennis. However, that had been during her *rumspringa* when she was fifty pounds lighter and able to wear pants and sometimes shorts, if no one was watching. So she could actually run and play without her skirt tripping her up. But a person couldn't stay in *rumspringa* forever, which meant she couldn't play tennis forever unless she played in a dress. Then life happened—marriage and kids—but what she wouldn't give to play now. . . .

"Hattie." Callie turned her attention to her. "You'll have to tell us when you go play with Christian."

Beside her, Elsie snorted. Once again Hattie had the urge to pop her on the leg. Sometimes a cousin just couldn't do a body right.

"I'll be sure to." Though the more they talked about it, the less she wanted to play. And not because she didn't want to play pickleball, or she didn't want to play with Christian, she just didn't want everybody in the room to think it was a date. Playing pickleball was not a date. It just couldn't be. A date meant maybe holding hands, eating, talking, not sweating on a court hitting a ball back and forth, trying to score points. To think that was ridiculous.

Which made her think, if Christian really had something important to talk to her about, how was he going to ask her that if they were running on opposite sides of the court chasing a ball?

Just add that to all the questions that she had concerning Christian Beachy that didn't have answers.

Chapter 7

"Poppin' Paradise, how may I help you?"

"Hattie?"

"*Jah*?" Her insides shouldn't have felt so warm at just the sound of his voice. But they did. Perhaps that was why she didn't act like she knew who he was straightaway.

"It's Christian Beachy."

She hid her smile as Elsie shot her a look to see who was on the phone. Not that it was unusual for the phone to ring during their workday. That happened all the time. But something in her voice must've tipped off Elsie as it being an important call.

"Christian, how nice to talk to you."

Elsie raised her eyebrows.

Hattie shot her a frown. Then turned away. "Is everything okay?"

"*Jah*," he said. "I was just calling to let you know there's been a cancellation and we have the pickleball court for Thursday. Well, one of them. There's four altogether, but we're just playing on one."

He sounded about as nervous as she felt at that moment. Of course this probably wouldn't be happening if everybody wasn't making such a big deal out of all of this. Their friendship.

"A cancellation?"

"Apparently it is a very popular game."

"Then I definitely feel lucky and blessed," Hattie told him.

"*Jah*," he said. His voice sounded a little strange, like maybe he was about to choke on something. Or maybe she was just a little too over-the-top sometimes. Especially when she got nervous. "So meet you there on Thursday at four?"

"Sure," she replied.

"See you then."

"Wait, Christian?" She had almost let him get off the phone without asking the most important question. "What about equipment? Don't we need a ball and such?"

"I got all that covered as well." The choked sound had left his voice and he sounded almost happy.

"*Danki*," she said. "I'll see you then."

They hung up the phone, and Hattie continued to stare at the receiver in her hand. He did sound happy. Maybe nothing was missing from his life. Maybe he just needed to get a few more life experiences under his belt, so to speak. Like pickleball. Who couldn't have a good time playing something called pickleball?

Pickleball turned out to be a lot harder than she had thought it was going to be.

Hattie fanned herself as she stopped to catch her breath. "I still don't see how that didn't score a point."

Christian held up the well-worn copies of printer paper that he had brought with him today. He told Hattie that he had gone down to the apothecary and Betsy Stoll had printed out the rules for pickleball. Betsy was good with stuff like that. She was always printing out information about her herbs and stuff for her customers. So it was no wonder he turned to her. And apparently he found the used equipment at old Honest John Beery's. How he found anything in that maze of junk was a miracle. Hattie figured he'd most likely asked Honest John himself.

"I told you, you can't score if you're not serving in pickleball."

Hattie shook her head. "That's dumb. If you score, you should get the point."

"But you didn't score. Because you weren't serving."

Hattie shot him a look. "Are you sure you're not making this up as you go along?"

He held up the papers once again. "You want to look at this?"

"No," she grumbled. "Just serve it."

There were so many parts of pickleball that were just like tennis. And it was so easy to swing the racket. Having to serve underhand wasn't always the easiest to remember, but it helped that the court was smaller and the net a little bit lower. It would have helped too if she had been fifty pounds lighter and wearing something other than a dress, but that was beside the point. She would've been having a lot more fun if she could score when she was supposed to score and not have that weird rule that a player couldn't score if they weren't serving. She didn't understand that one at all. But okay, she was having a good time. Even if she was losing.

"Oops," Christian said, pointing to the timer in the corner of the court. "Our hour is up."

Thank the Lord, she thought. She was hot and sweaty and a little bit grumpy. She couldn't let him know that. "But we didn't play to eleven or whatever it was."

He gave a sheepish shrug. "I guess next time. Someone else gets the court now."

She shook it off as if it were no big deal. But in truth she was grateful.

"I'm so hot," he said, looking at his shirt. "How about a water and an ice cream? That should cool us off."

"Are you sure?" She hadn't meant to ask that question. It just sort of popped out of her mouth when she wasn't paying attention.

"Why do you ask that?"

Great. Now she had to answer that. "Well, it's just that you haven't smiled all evening." She waited a heartbeat to see how he would respond.

He frowned. "That's a weird thing to say," he replied. "What does my smiling have to do with anything?"

It had a lot to do with everything, including the bet she had with Elsie. More than anything she wanted to see Christian happy. She hadn't really known him before and the more she got to know about him, the more she really wanted him to be a happy person. Yet the only way she knew how to tell if a person was happy was to see if they were smiling. Christian never smiled.

"Okay," she said. "I'll explain, but you are going to have to buy me an ice cream. Explanation à la mode."

He gave her a strange look and nodded. "Okay."

They walked from the park over to Paradise Cones. It was a small truck that served ice cream out of the back. Though it was on wheels, it never moved. But it was central enough that no one complained. The ice cream was made in small batches and then mixed with fruits and nuts to give it added flavors and textures.

"What flavor do you want?" Christian asked.

"Pistachio with almonds and cherries."

Christian gave her a dubious look. "If you say so."

"I say so."

Hattie found a seat at one of the picnic tables and used the printed instructions for pickleball to fan herself. She was going to have to take these home with her and study them in case she decided to play with him again. Not that she thought he would cheat, but she wanted to be sure of the rules when she played a game. But it wasn't like she was competitive or anything.

Christian made his way back over a few minutes later with two cups of ice cream, hers green with bits of bright red throughout. His was creamy white, very plain, with only a few pieces of strawberry here and there.

He set hers down in front of her, then hustled back over to get their waters. "Please tell me you didn't get vanilla," Hattie said with a pointed nod at his ice cream.

"So what if I did?"

"It would just be a shame," she said, taking the first delicious bite. There was nothing like the pistachio ice cream at Paradise Cones.

"Why would that be a shame?" he asked.

"Because you have all those great flavors and to just get vanilla . . . Well, that would be a shame."

He held his hand out across the table toward her. "Give me your spoon."

"What?"

He flicked his hand in her direction. "Your spoon."

She eyed him dubiously but gave him the utensil. He scooped up a bite of his pristine white ice cream with one little bite of strawberry inside, then he handed the spoon back to her.

She took it but stared at it as if it contained something not as tasty as ice cream.

"Try it," he said.

The thought crossed her mind that maybe he wanted

her to see what flavor ice cream he really got, or maybe he was trying to make a point about the vanilla ice cream at Paradise Cones. Anyway there was only one way to know what he wanted. She took the bite. Not vanilla.

The ice cream had just the right amount of creaminess and the strawberry just the right amount of tartness. "Cheesecake. Strawberries and cheesecake."

He nodded, though for a moment she almost thought she saw him smile. Then he took another bite of his ice cream and his mouth was too busy eating to do anything else.

"Things aren't always what they seem on the surface."

He was right about that. Just like him. There were layers to him that people around him didn't see. So what if he didn't smile? Yet it bothered her nonetheless to think of him going around all the time without smiling at all.

"Paradise Cones is good," he said, Then he leaned forward a little and lowered his voice. "But I know a better place to get ice cream."

Hattie glanced around as if the place would be close by, then she returned her gaze to his face. "You do?"

He nodded, pressed his lips together as if it was a serious matter, then said, "It's all the way over in Paradise Hill though."

"Maybe next time you can take me there," she told him, realizing that she was flirting and wondering just what had gotten into her. Next time? Was there even going to be a next time? They talked about maybe playing pickleball again, but no one said anything about going to get another ice cream.

"Maybe next time I will," he replied.

They sat in silence for a moment, then Hattie blurted out, "You know everyone in town thinks you're grouchy." Okay, so she had been wanting to find a way to broach the subject with him, but this went beyond broaching. This was a downright attack.

He sat back a little on the bench seat, drew away as if she had threatened to smack him. "Why would anyone think I'm grouchy?"

"Well," she said, "mainly because you never smile."

He drew back again and frowned. "What does smiling have to do with anything?"

"It has a lot to do with it. Isn't that how you know someone is happy?" she asked. "That they're smiling?"

He shook his head. "You and Malinda . . ."

"Why? What did Malinda say?"

"It doesn't matter." But his tone had changed from that playfulness it had held earlier to a stern tone that she was more used to hearing from him. In fact, she hadn't realized that he had changed at all until it changed back.

"I didn't mean to upset you," she said.

"It would upset anyone, I suppose," he replied. "Wouldn't it upset you if someone said that you seemed grouchy?"

"Of course, because I'm—"

"Not grouchy," he supplied.

Hattie really didn't know what to say to that. She took another bite of her ice cream and savored it slowly. "What about that incident a couple of years ago? Do you remember? When that group of kids ran their buggies through your field. Well, one of your fields."

"I remember it well," he said, the scowl on his face darkening. "I had the right to be upset about that. They destroyed that field. It took a lot of work to get it prepared and ready to take crops again."

It was true that they had destroyed the field. The kids were racing their buggy, which was dangerous to begin with. They had wrecked his field, leaving deep skid marks, divots from the horses' hooves, and other gouges in the earth.

"But you had allowed that field to go fallow." Whatever had been growing in it the good Lord had put there. It wasn't like they ruined his crops or anything. It was just weeds, and yet he had had a fit over it.

Christian shook his head. "That's not the case at all." He dropped his spoon into his empty cup and sat back with his arms crossed. "There were dandelions in that field. I was growing them for salad and apothecary items. It might've looked like weeds to everyone else, but they were a planted crop. And those kids destroyed them."

Well, now that put a different light on everything.

"They were crops?" She had heard of people foraging for dandelions, but she never heard of anyone purposefully growing them. Though she supposed it could happen.

"They were crops. I lost a lot of money on that deal."

"But that field now has something else in it," she said. She remembered the kids had to go and replant it. At the time she had thought the punishment excessive, considering the fact that the field had just been full of weeds before and now they were planting tomatoes and watermelons.

"I moved the dandelion field back from the road so that people wouldn't think it was unattended." He still wore that angry scowl.

"Are you mad about it now?" she asked.

He shook his head. "It's over and done," he replied. "They helped me replant. We moved the crop that they had destroyed back and now everything is good."

And yet he still seemed angry.

"But if you're not mad about it," she asked, "why are you still frowning?"

His frown deepened, which almost made her laugh. "I am?"

She nodded. "I'm afraid so."

He shrugged. "Maybe this is just the way I look."

Hattie didn't know what to say to that. So she concentrated on her ice cream as he waited.

"I did have fun playing pickleball," he said.

She looked up at him and smiled. "Me too. Except for the points. I don't like the rules concerning scoring points," she said.

"I like it. I think it makes the game last longer since you can only score when you're serving."

"I guess I'm just used to tennis," she said. Even though it had been years since she had played. It was like that muscle memory that people were always talking about. She fell right back into the rhythm of tennis, with rules, the scoring, and everything else that she knew of the game.

"I think I like it better than tennis," he said. "In tennis the scoring happens so fast. This is a lot more fun to me."

She could understand that.

"Are you ready to go?" He nodded toward her empty cup.

"*Danki*," she said. "Let me get you some money for the ice cream."

He shook his head. "My treat," he told her.

She shook her head back at him. "No, I can't have you treating me if we are just going to meetings. In meetings, you go Dutch." Okay, truthfully she was making the rules up as she went along, but hey, she figured he could understand this one easily enough.

"How about you get the next round?"

She nodded. "Okay. I can get behind that."

They took their cups to the trash and started back toward her side of town.

"Why do you suppose they call it Dutch?" she asked. "Do you think it has anything to do with the Dutch? Or maybe it has to do with the Germans. you know like Pennsylvania Dutch?"

He shrugged. "I don't know. Maybe next time I'm in the library, I can look it up."

She nodded. "If you remember."

They walked for a while in silence.

"Is your buggy back at the park?" she asked him.

"*Jah*," he said with a quick nod. "I thought I'd walk you back to your house, then circle back and get my buggy."

"That's an awful lot of walking. You don't have to," she said.

"I want to. Even with meetings I think it's good to walk the woman home to make sure she gets there safe."

"Okay," Hattie said, ignoring the warm feeling she had inside.

He might be frowny, but he was certainly a gentleman.

Christian said goodbye to Hattie at the door to the popcorn shop. The outside one that led to the actual shop, not the one that led to her apartment. He figured that was good enough to make sure that she was home safe. Then he turned and walked stiffly back down the sidewalk.

He could almost feel her eyes watching him as if wondering what his expression was like as he walked away. People thought he was angry and grouchy? Why would anybody think that? Just because he didn't smile much? What was it about smiling? As far as he was concerned, smiling was overrated. Who wanted to go around showing everybody their teeth? When a dog showed you his teeth then you knew he was angry. Everyone thought he was angry because he didn't show his teeth. But he wasn't angry. It was just so darned perplexing.

He continued back to his buggy, wondering about the whole conversation. Pickleball had been great fun, and he had enjoyed himself immensely. But according to Hattie, he hadn't smiled once. Then she told him that the whole town thought he was a grouch. Well, that wasn't something worth smiling over for sure. And he wasn't a grouch.

Take the time those kids tore up his field of dandelions. That was a lot of money lost. And time that he had to spend to plow and plant both fields over again so he could move the dandelions back and put the tomatoes and watermelons over in their place. *Jah*, the kids helped. But that was expected. Still, he couldn't believe everyone thought he was upset about it. What was done was done. It was corrected and life went on.

But no. Everyone had to think that he was grouchy just because he didn't go around showing people his teeth. Maybe if only Malinda had said it, he wouldn't believe it. But now Hattie was saying it too. Malinda liked to boss him around, getting him to do what she wanted him to do. But Hattie, Hattie wasn't like that. She was only trying to help. She was only trying to make sure he was having a good time.

Strange as it was, he got the feeling that was why she had invited him to the whoopie pie benefit for Barbie Troyer to begin with. And that thought made him feel a little bit warm and fuzzy inside. But there was something else that plagued him.

He untied his horse from the hitching post and backed the gelding out of the spot where he'd parked him.

Christian swung himself up into the carriage and put his horse into motion toward home. He shook his head. So far he had gone to the whoopie pie benefit with Hattie, then had coffee at Perks of Paradise, then played pickleball and ate ice cream there in the park. And in all that time together, not once had he gotten around to asking her how she kept such a positive attitude all the time.

Hattie slowly climbed the stairs to the apartment above the popcorn shop. Her thoughts were still turning around and around over the news she had learned. She supposed it wasn't really news since it had happened a couple of years ago, but it certainly wasn't how she remembered the event to be. Had she been wrong?

Of course she had. Everyone in the community had been wrong.

"Did you have a good time?" Elsie asked as Hattie closed the door behind her.

Elsie was in the kitchen preparing supper, all the while nibbling on one of the leftover whoopie pies from the widows' meeting.

"You want one?" Elsie asked, nodding toward the container of sweets sitting on the kitchen table.

Hattie shook her head. She was pretty much on sugar overload after eating ice cream with Christian.

"Life is short. You should eat dessert first."

So says the skinny girl, Hattie thought. But she sat down and took one of the whoopie pies anyway. She wanted to talk. And eating a whoopie pie while Elsie cooked seemed as good an excuse to talk about Christian as any.

"He's not grumpy. No." Not exactly the best beginning to the conversation, but at least she had Elsie's attention.

"Who?" Elsie asked. "Christian?" She stirred the hamburger pasta mixture in the pan, then tapped the wooden spoon against the edge. Then she set it on the nearby spoon rest and turned to face Hattie.

"*Jah*," Hattie said. She had thought she could bring joy into Christian's life and that would make him more positive and in turn make him smile more and in turn make the community feel that he was positive and happy. But today she had learned that he was happy already.

Well, he hadn't said so in so many words. But he certainly wasn't as grumpy as everyone thought he was.

"Do you remember when those kids ran through his field? He got all upset and made them replant and all that business?"

Elsie nodded. "I do. That was quite the talk for a little bit."

"Everybody thought Christian Beachy was just being excessive and mean and grumpy. A curmudgeon, *jah*?"

"I'd say that's about right," Elsie replied. She took a step back to check the bread in the oven. "Almost ready."

Good. Hattie needed something to offset all the sugar, but still she continued to eat that whoopie pie that she really didn't want. "That's not what happened at all. He had planted that field with dandelions to harvest for greens for salads and for Betsy Stoll at the apothecary. The field wasn't fallow like everybody thought it was. He was actually growing—"

"Weeds," Elsie supplied with a chuckle.

"It's not funny," Hattie said. "All this time, we've had him wrong."

"That's just one incident," Elsie said. "Not that I'm saying it's not wrong, but there have been other times when he got upset over something that happened in the community. Every time couldn't have been completely justified."

"Maybe he had a reason," Hattie mused. "You never

know what a person is thinking. Unless they tell you, and then you still have to take their word for it."

She couldn't help but wonder if there were other times when Christian had taken the fall for whatever had happened. Times where the community had declared that he was the one to blame. That he was the rude and mean one in the whole situation. And Hattie, like everyone else, had given Christian a wide berth to avoid having to find out.

"He's delivered our vegetables for years," Hattie said. "He's been a member of our church just as long. We went to school together."

"What are you getting at?" Elsie asked. She pulled the bread from the oven, flipped the switch off, and propped her hands on her hips. The pot holders were still folded in half in each hand.

"It's not like anyone could say we're neighbors, but we're definitely more than passing acquaintances. Yet I've never taken the time to get to know him better." Not until now. "Nor have you."

"Nor have a lot of people," Elsie countered. "Because he tends to keep everybody at an arm's length with that scowl of his."

"Which is just why we came up with this bet. But now that I'm spending more time with him . . ."

"I can't believe what I'm hearing." Elsie tossed the pot holders onto the kitchen counter and flipped off the burner under their main dish. "Are you trying to slip out from underneath our wager?"

"No," Hattie said. "I'm not." Now more than ever, Hattie wanted to spend time with Christian. More time, not less. There was so much more to him than she had ever known. Plus he had promised to take her for an ice cream, and what was one more date? Meeting. That's what she would call it still, a meeting. An ice cream meeting. She had always been a fool for ice cream.

"Time's ticking," Elsie said.

Hattie rose from her chair and went to get the place mats to set the table. Time was ticking. But suddenly getting Christian to smile seemed less important than just getting to know him as a person, frown and all.

Chapter 8

Sunday morning dawned bright and clear, the perfect spring day leading into a beautiful Missouri summer.

"If you don't come on," Elsie said, "we're going to be late."

"I can't find one of my shoes."

"Wear another pair. You've got more than one."

"I don't want to wear those."

Hattie continued to rummage through the hall closet. They had to be in there somewhere. She always kept her shoes neat and tidy, but someone, a.k.a. Elsie, had dumped a whole bunch of miscellaneous stuff in the hall closet on top of her shoes.

"Where did all these things come from?" Hattie demanded.

Elsie waved a negligent hand at the mess spilling out of the hall closet. "I got it all out of the attic for Rachel. Her youth group is going on an overnight camping trip. So she wanted to borrow my camping stuff."

Jah, now Hattie could see. It was the tent, a telescope, the plastic box they stored the air mattress in, a sleeping bag, and various cooking utensils.

"Why didn't you go ahead and give it to her? Why did you just pile it on top of the shoes?"

"She's coming to get it tomorrow."

There it was. Hattie triumphantly pulled her shoe from the mess. Then she squished everything back into the hall closet and shut the door, praying that it would latch. God willing, of course.

Then she slipped on her shoes and they headed out the door. It was a short walk on a beautiful day down to Paradise Stables.

Jason Stoll was given special permission to open on Sunday mornings and Sunday evenings when they had the church service so everyone who lived in town could get their horse and carriage to attend. Jason was usually the last one to arrive at the service, but he was forgiven this lapse, considering the fact that he helped so many who lived in town.

Today's service was held out at Henry and Millie's. Hattie hadn't been out there since the wedding. But that had been over six months ago. Not that the place had changed all that much. Last year, Millie had made a few changes, just a measure of friendship with Henry and his grandfather, Vern, who had previously lived in the house. When Vern married Sylvie, the two of them being the older couple and childless, moved into the B&B, while Henry, Millie, and little Linda Beth, moved into the farmhouse.

Unlike some of the residents of Paradise Valley, Henry's farmhouse didn't have a bonus room for church. His barn was completely packed full of things. Understandable considering the fact that they blended four households into two. So they met in the house itself, just like the Amish used to do before everyone started getting fancy. Henry and Millie had moving doors and open rooms that allowed the house to hold all the people. Though Hattie heard them talking after the service about maybe building on a room where Linda Beth could play indoors during bad weather and they would always have room for church.

Truthfully that wasn't the news that Hattie was looking for. She really wanted to see if anyone said anything about Christian. About how happy he seemed. She hadn't been able to convince him to smile, so maybe everyone was thinking that he appeared happier in other ways. But that was a bust, and Elsie kept reminding her that time was running out.

"I know," Hattie said.

The thought didn't set well with her. Frankly she just wanted to flat-out ignore her cousin. She and Christian were friends. And there was nothing wrong with that. And yes, she and Elsie had a wager on this deal, but that's not why Hattie was doing it, trying to spend more time with Christian. She truly wanted him to smile. She honestly wanted to know that he was happy.

She looked over to where he stood talking to several other men.

"Did you have fun playing that tennis pickle game?" Katie asked, sidling up next to Hattie as she studied Christian.

Hattie averted her gaze as to not tip off Katie that she was staring at Christian. She'd been staring at him for a while now, almost willing him to smile. Exactly how could the man go through life and not be miserable and still not smile? She couldn't understand it.

"I would have a better time if I'd won, but the scoring is so weird. Not the same as tennis at all in that aspect."

"Pickleball," Callie said, with a shake of her head. "I don't understand how it got that name."

"Christian printed out some stuff from the Internet and apparently it was either named after the dog belonging to the person who came up with it or something to do with the pickle boat. I really didn't understand." And it really made no difference to the game, what it was named or how it got that name. And truthfully she'd rather play tennis.

"Are you going to play again?" This from Lillian Lambert.

"Maybe. I mean, Christian's got the equipment so he can surely play again." And she would surely go with him if he asked her again. As strange as it seemed, she actually enjoyed spending time with him. Surely she did.

"Looks like maybe next year we'll have to decide about another widow getting kicked out of the group," Katie said.

Hattie turned around and looked at all their faces. "Why would I get kicked out of the group?"

"You won't." Sylvie shrugged. "Unless we decide to just have widows. But of course that means Millie and I are out as well."

"But I'm not getting married." Not by a long shot. She was happily widowed. No, that didn't sound right. She wasn't happy about being a widow; she missed her husband every day. But living a single life, if that was what she had to live, was just fine with her. It was God's will after all.

"Not with the way you're looking at him," Katie quipped.

So much for hiding her gaze from Katie. "Marriages are not based on looks."

"Is that a pun?" Lillian asked.

"No pun intended," Hattie said.

This whole thing of trying to make Christian Beachy happy and smile was making her grumpy and frowny. Not exactly the way it was supposed to be turning out.

"I got a favor to ask." Christian cornered Hattie on the far side of the barn.

"What's that?" Hattie asked in return. She stopped and waited for him to continue. Everyone was almost done with the after-service cleanup and soon they would all be headed home. This was the first time that she had gotten to talk to Christian since their pickleball game. And surprisingly enough she found that she missed hearing his voice. Strange.

"I have a special errand to run tomorrow and . . . I would like for you to come with me."

"Of course," she said. She didn't even ask what the errand could be.

Okay, so the truth of it was she enjoyed spending time with him. And, even more truth, she wasn't even in the wager to win any longer. Unless you counted getting Christian to smile a win. It was true she didn't want to lose and have to clean the big copper pots at the popcorn shop. But making Christian smile and knowing for certain that he was happy, that was her true goal.

"I'll pick you up tomorrow at ten," he said. "Will that be okay?"

She would have to work something out with Elsie, and again her cousin would probably balk at the idea of her taking time off work. But she had to have some time to spend with Christian, and since he invited her to go, it just stood to reason that she should go.

"That will be fine," she said. And it was. Yet she couldn't

help but wonder what this errand could be. The ice cream day that he possibly was taking her on. The one to the place that was better than Paradise Cones? Maybe. That would be fun. So she was going to have to slow down on the sweets. She barely got her dress pinned today in time for church. Then she had to repin it after she had to dig around in the closet to find her shoes.

But still an ice cream with Christian sounded like a good morning to be sure. She didn't know what Christian looked like as he drove home, but she knew she had to hide her smile as Elsie might think something more was happening.

"We're going to Paradise Hill. Is that okay?" Christian asked.

"*Jah*." She'd just eaten a bowl of fruit for breakfast in anticipation of the ice cream. She had heard about a place in Paradise Hill that had incredible ice cream. Like Paradise Cones, the treat was made in small batches, made on-site, but this was made at the actual dairy where the cows were. It was amazing. And she couldn't wait to go there.

They rode across the line in companionable silence. It was funny how just crossing that invisible barrier made her feel a little bit of a rogue, a Springer all the way in the Hill. She mentally shook her head at her fanciful thoughts.

"Here we are." Christian pulled his horse to a stop in front of Hill Times and Chimes Clock store there on Main Street in Paradise Hill.

"Here?"

There was no ice cream shop in view. And certainly not one that had a dairy attached. They were still in town.

"*Jah*." Christian nodded. "Malinda's birthday is coming

up, and I would like for you to help me pick out a present for her."

Hattie nodded toward Hill Times and Chimes. "In there?"

"*Jah,*" he said again with another firm nod. "I think a clock would be a very good present for her."

Most women received a clock when they married. A beautiful piece to put on the mantel or even a large grand-father clock that could be had for generations to come. Hattie was ninety percent sure she had seen such a clock on the mantel at Christian's house the last time she'd been there for church, but that had been months ago, and she really hadn't been paying attention to the clock. She had been more focused on everything else that had been going on around her. Nothing special, just church stuff, the normal Sunday chatter. But perhaps Malinda wanted her own clock. Perhaps the clock that was currently sitting on the mantel at Christian's house belonged to his late wife. Perhaps Malinda didn't want Elizabeth's hand-me-down. Who knew?

"I'll help you pick out a clock," Hattie said. Though she didn't truly understand why he wanted to involve her in this situation. He seemed perfectly capable of picking out a clock by himself.

Or . . . Or maybe he liked spending time with her too. The thought warmed her from the inside out until she almost had to fan herself. She liked spending time with him and he liked spending time with her. That made for a perfect friendship.

"There is one other thing," Christian said. His words had turned so serious that some of that warm feeling instantly fled. But not all of it.

"What is that?" Hattie said, albeit a tiny bit warily.

"It's a big birthday for Malinda. And I want to do something special for her. But I think I need a woman's touch for this."

Now she was really wary. "A woman's touch?"

Christian nodded. "I want to have a party. But I don't know the first thing about throwing a party. I was hoping that you would help."

"Of course I will," Hattie said before she had time to stop herself. It wasn't that she didn't know how to throw a party. It was Malinda. Malinda was something of an outlier and had managed to upset every member of their district. And on more than one occasion. The woman was nosy and she was bossy and she was always into everyone's business even after they told her to leave it alone. She was not the most popular person in Paradise Springs. Probably not even in Paradise Valley. But if Christian wanted to throw a party for his sister and he needed Hattie to help, she was there. "You just leave it to me," she heard herself say. "I will take care of everything."

"One more stop," Christian said as he pulled his buggy into a parking place in front of the hitching post.

One more stop? She was starving. Okay, not really starving. Honestly, she hated when people said that. She was just very hungry. And she was ready to be home. Though part of her wanted to stay out with Christian a while longer. She needed to get something to eat. But as long as he was running her around Paradise Hill . . . Perhaps she should ask him if they could get something to eat after this. But then again, maybe he would just take her home and she could get something in Paradise Springs.

"Your choice," he said as they stood on the sidewalk

side by side. He pointed to the restaurant straight in front of him. An old-fashioned diner with booths, a few tables, and a countertop where people could eat and talk to the waitress all at the same time. The warm smell of French fry grease and onion rings wafted about and made her stomach grumble. "You have Gingerich Diner or"—he moved to point across the street—"Fiesta Cantina."

Hattie was too hungry to care. "I don't know what to choose. I've never eaten at either place."

"I can tell you that Fiesta Cantina has very good chips and salsa and their enchiladas are out of this world. But I can also tell you that Sal Gingerich makes a mean cheese-burger."

He said that last with such a touch of affection that made Hattie's mind up quick. "The diner," she said.

"The diner it is," he repeated, gesturing toward the door.

The place was lively, and a little loud with the noise of cooking and eating. Utensils against thick, industrial-white earthenware plates that a person usually saw in a diner. The smell of coffee was even stronger inside. It gave Hattie a warm feeling. She liked this place already, she decided. And that was even before she saw they had crinkle-cut French fries. Oh my, she loved crinkle-cut French fries.

"Do you want to sit at the counter or at a booth? There is one right over there." He pointed to the far corner of the restaurant.

"Booth," Hattie said without hesitation. They wound their way through the few tables scattered throughout the dining area and arrived at the booth just as their waitress did.

The young woman had clear green eyes and dark brown hair beneath her pristine white prayer *kapp*. Hattie had to wonder how she kept the thing so clean. She and Elsie had taken to wearing bandannas for the sake of convenience.

At the end of the shift, they could throw a bandanna in the washing machine. A prayer *kapp*? Not a chance.

"What would you like to drink?" the young woman asked as she set their vinyl menus down in front of them. "Just water for me," Hattie said. With a meal she was about to eat, she didn't need to be drinking more calories as well.

"Me too," Christian said.

"Hey, Christian." The young woman's face broke into a huge smile. "I didn't recognize you today. I'm sorry."

"It's okay, Rebecca," Christian said. "I'm usually at the back door."

"Your usual?" she asked.

He nodded, then turned to Hattie. "How would you like a cheeseburger with everything, including jalapenos and bacon?"

Hattie was about to reach for the menu when he said the words and she stopped. "I like a cheeseburger with bacon," she admitted. "I've never had one with jalapenos. But I'm up to try it." Or was it down to try it? She never could get that right.

He turned back to Rebecca. "Make that two," he said, and he picked up both menus and handed them back to the young woman.

"Two usuals. Coming right up. I'll have those waters out to you in a jiff."

"I take it you come here often," Hattie said, looking around the place as she spoke. It was busy, your typical diner atmosphere filled with black checks and red vinyl and the low hum of enjoyment.

"I deliver vegetables to them in the summer."

"I see." And she did. She wasn't one of those staunch Springers who felt it was disloyal to cross that line. Not that she did much. But she was busy with the popcorn shop; it wasn't like she could go willy-nilly all around the Valley.

Christian had it different. He was always out delivering something or another. Working on getting new accounts. She was sure that was the only way he would stay in business. She on the other hand had a store that was stationary. People came to her for a product.

"They're very nice people," Christian said with a frown.

"Why are you frowning?" Hattie asked. It wasn't the question that seemed to take him back, but her tone. She fairly demanded to know.

"Was I?" he asked. Maybe he hadn't noticed her tone. She hadn't meant to sound so sharp. It was just that, well, he was always going around frowning. And how was she supposed to get him to smile if he was forever frowning?

"*Jah*," she said with a quick nod. "Why are you frowning? What's so bad right this second that you have to frown about it?" The question was so impertinent she almost smacked her hand over her mouth. "No," she said with a shake of her head. "You don't have to answer that. I didn't mean to be nosy." Or for a word, hateful.

"I wasn't thinking anything bad," he admitted. "In fact, I don't remember what I was thinking about at all now."

He couldn't remember and all she could think about was the widows' group and what they would be thinking if they could see her now.

"I'm sorry." Her voice dropped to just above a whisper. Really, she should just give in and tell Elsie that she would clean the copper vats and be done with it. This whole event was making her squirrelly. And she didn't like it. She was grumpy and demanding and in general not having a very good time.

It seemed to be tainting the time she spent with Christian as well. And that time was something that she greatly enjoyed. She didn't want to ruin it by focusing on a stupid wager she'd made with her cousin. Or the other widows and what they would imagine.

He reached across the table and touched her hand in a comforting manner. "It's okay," he said. "You don't have to apologize."

Electricity shot from her fingertips all the way up her arm at his touch.

Hattie pulled away.

The residual sparks continued to ping in her arm even though he was no longer touching her. That in itself was proof that she had felt that connection. Had he felt it too?

No, she was just wound up, she thought as the tingles subsided. She looked at him, and he seemed like nothing was amiss. *Jah*, she had misinterpreted something along the way. Or maybe she was just too wound up from sitting in a Paradise Hill diner with Christian Beachy wondering what the Whoopie Pie Widows' Club would have to say about her sitting in a Paradise Hill diner with Christian Beachy.

He cleared his throat and sat back in his seat. "That was . . ." he said, then he shook his head. "I'm sorry."

"What are you apologizing for?" she asked.

"I shouldn't have tried to touch your hand."

Okay, so they weren't a couple and they were in public and they were both single. So no, he shouldn't have tried to touch her hand. But the look of misery on his face was so . . . well, miserable, that she wanted to reach out herself and smooth the frown from his forehead.

"How about we just forget the whole thing?" Hattie said. She shifted in her seat. This was making her uncomfortable. She didn't know how else to say it. She loved his touch, she hated his touch, his touch was too forward, and neither one of them should be here eating alone together. She just had to wonder if he was okay with parading her around Paradise Hill because he felt that no one would see them together. That thought really hit her hard so she pushed it away.

Thankfully Rebecca arrived with their burgers. They smelled delicious and just as Hattie had hoped there were crispy golden crinkle-cut fries on the side. But now the meal seemed tainted somehow, as if a dark cloud had descended on their day.

Rebecca took one of the plates off the tray and slid it in front of Hattie. The dark cloud was starting to lift. The meal smelled delicious and it wasn't just because she was so hungry. It really looked tasty.

"*Danki*," Christian said as she slid the other plate in front of him.

"Y'all want ketchup? Steak sauce?"

"Ketchup, please," Hattie said.

"Anything else I can get you?"

"I think we're good for now," Christian said.

"Enjoy." Rebecca shot them a dimpled smile, then carted the tray back to the kitchen.

"I really like the clock you helped me pick out for Malinda," Christian said after a big bite of hamburger.

Hattie was busy chewing and had to wait a moment before answering. "I think it was beautiful too. I hope she likes it."

He dragged a French fry through the puddle of ketchup and popped it into his mouth. "She's going to love it."

The black cloud that had been hovering about seemed to dissipate altogether. Or maybe she just had imagined it was there. Elsie was forever telling her she had too active of an imagination. Hattie didn't know. She was only months away from sixty years old and she only had the imagination God had given her. Since it was the only one she had, she had no idea whether it was overactive or not. Sometimes she just thought Elsie liked to fuss. Her cousin worried way too much about everything and anything. And sometimes Hattie found herself in that same cycle of worry.

Like now when she was worried about why Christian had brought her to Paradise Hill. And why he thought he could touch her here when he hadn't touched her at all in Paradise Springs. Hadn't even tried.

It was just an accidental brush of the hand. He was offering her a comfort. It was a sweet gesture. And it shouldn't be misconstrued into anything other than that. Besides, the hamburger was delicious and she didn't need to worry about ruining that.

"What do you think about the jalapenos?" Christian asked.

"It's a lot different than what I thought."

Christian frowned and took another bite of his cheeseburger before responding. "How so?"

"I don't know. I guess I thought they would be the pickled kind, like you get at the Mexican restaurant. Not these." She picked up one of the crispy strips of fried jalapenos. They were like those onions she put on the green bean casserole at Thanksgiving time. Except they weren't onions, they were spicy peppers. And they were delicious.

"I wonder if I can buy these someplace?" Hattie mused.

"Why would you want to buy them?" Christian asked.

"Can you imagine these mixed with French fried onions on your green bean casserole at Thanksgiving?"

He nodded. "I can. And that sounds very good."

"If I can get my hands on some, I might try it."

"I could ask Rebecca."

"I can do it," she said.

He nodded. "Just as long as you bring me some of that casserole when you get it done."

She smiled at him. "Done."

Chapter 9

They finished their meal in the same companionable conversation. But Hattie kept thinking about his request, that she bring him some of the casserole when she baked it at Thanksgiving. It was just now May, and they were making plans for six months from now.

It was as if they had truly become friends. It all started with a wager for her, but now it seemed to be about much more than that.

But not bigger than friends. They would never be more than friends. She couldn't imagine that. She'd been widowed for far too long. He had been widowed for even longer. Some habits were just too hard to break. But friends . . . she could do friends. So why did she keep imagining more?

When Christian asked for the check, Rebecca had just smiled and said that it was on the house. Hattie protested. She liked to pay her own way. Christian might be a vendor for the restaurant, but she wasn't. But Rebecca had smiled and said, "Any friend of Christian's is a friend of ours."

And that was that.

They were back to being friends.

Hattie hoisted herself up into the buggy and wished she

had gone to the restroom and loosened the pins of her dress just a little. The hamburger had been so tasty and the fries so yummy that she had eaten all but one little bite of lettuce. She would have to cut back to a half portion at suppertime. But it was worth it. So worth it.

"I have to tell you," she said as Christian pulled himself in beside her. He flicked the reins and started his buggy back toward Paradise Springs. "I thought you were going to take me to get an ice cream today."

He turned to her, mouth slightly open. "I'd forgotten about that."

He had forgotten? Now she really felt like she was being forward. He had forgotten and it was all she could think about.

"I mean not forgotten forgotten. I just didn't think about it for today. I guess I was so busy trying to get Malinda's birthday party stuff all settled."

"That's understandable." Hattie flicked his explanation away with a wave of the hand. She didn't need the ice cream, but there was a part of her that was disappointed. She had read too much into the situation.

"No," he said. "I haven't totally forgotten. Next time," he said with a small nod.

Hattie nodded in return. "Next time." But she had to wonder if there really would be a next time. By then the wager would be over as well as Malinda's birthday party.

Not that it should matter. It wasn't like they were dating. And once again she had to remind herself. This was all about trying to make him smile.

Friends. That's what she had told herself again Tuesday night at the Whoopie Pie Widows' Club meeting. She and

Christian were friends. And she would do what any friend would do when they had agreed to help out another friend. And that was to go to her circle of friends in order to get people to come to Malinda's party.

"When is it again?" Sylvie stirred the creamer in her coffee then sat down in the circle the widows had made from their chairs.

"Not this Saturday but the next," Hattie explained patiently. She had rushed through the introduction, the details, and the date of the party in an attempt to get it all out there in front of everybody. Maybe if she said it fast enough everyone would agree before completely understanding exactly what they were agreeing to.

No, she shouldn't think that. Malinda wasn't that bad. *Jah*, she could be a little trying, and *jah,* you had to watch what you said in front of her because if something you didn't want everyone in the Valley to know somehow escaped your lips, then it would be common knowledge come suppertime. But that didn't mean she was a bad person.

"Halfway between now and the Whoopie Pie Festival." Sylvie nodded knowingly.

"*Jah.*" Hattie smiled, hoping that her appealing facial expression did something to smooth out the rough edges of her initial request.

"And why do you want us to come again?" Callie asked.

Like the rest of them, Callie had brought whoopie pies for the meeting. Possibly, but maybe not, a new recipe that could possibly, or maybe not, be her entry into the festival baking competition. It was hard to say. And Hattie found herself wondering if she should enter her red velvet this year. Christian seemed to think that they were quite delicious. Was he just being kind or were they really that good?

Then again, what would Elsie say to her? As she told Christian, the red velvet recipe belonged to Elsie as much as it belonged to her, seeing as how they shared a grandmother and it was that grandmother's recipe. Maybe she should come up with something else.

"You know Malinda," Hattie said. She left it there. She didn't want to say anything derogatory concerning the woman. "Christian doesn't want it getting back to her though, this party. It's a surprise. So I am trying to make sure everyone knows that they're invited. He would like a big turnout."

Just a few people would be better than nothing. But she wasn't sure how many people she should recruit. There was more than a handful of widows. And if she could get all of them to come . . .

"I'll come," Millie said.

Sweet Millie. She'd been in Paradise Springs a year and had already fallen prey to the goodness.

"That would be terrific," Hattie said, not letting her smile drop once.

"A week from Saturday say?" Lillian asked. "I think I can make it then too."

"Me too," Katie said. "And I'm pretty sure I can get Imogene and maybe even Astrid to come."

Hattie felt relief flood through her. It seemed a good party could do wonders for overlooking a gossiping mouth.

"Me too," Sylvie said. "Do you need me to bring any whoopie pies?"

Hattie shook her head. "Christian has already ordered a birthday cake for her. And I believe he's going to buy ice cream to go with it." They had actually planned out the entire menu while driving home from Paradise Hill yesterday.

Hattie had promised to supply some cheddar popcorn,

and then they would have chips and dip, veggies and ranch dip and assorted nuts to go with cake and ice cream. Hattie thought that would be plenty. Sylvie would just have to find another outlet for the overflow of whoopie pies that occurred when she was trying to come up with a new recipe.

"What's wrong?" Elsie said. "We've all said we will come."

And they had. But Hattie still couldn't help but frown. "I just feel like it's a bunch of women. I mean, it's Christian's party for her. I think there should be some more men there."

"I'm sure Henry will come if I ask him to," Millie said.

"Vern too," Sylvie added.

Everyone went around the room talking about the male members of their family they could invite to make the party bigger and better. By the time they were done, Hattie realized everyone in the Whoopie Pie Widows' Club had promised to attend and bring at least one other person with them.

Christian was going to have a great turnout.

"You don't say," Christian said the following day.

He had met her in Perks of Paradise. Though she had no more than found his table that he stood and escorted her back outside.

"It's going to be great," Hattie said. And she meant every word. "Where are we going?" she asked as they stopped in front of his carriage.

"I want to check something out. Go with me?"

Now he asked. But Hattie didn't say that. "Of course."

She climbed up to the carriage beside him, and he started off toward Paradise Hill.

"*Danki* for all that work on the party," he said as they crossed the line from one city to the next.

"It's no problem."

"No, really," he said. "I do so appreciate it."

She smiled at him and resisted the urge to pat him on the knee to show her support. That would be just too familiar. "I'm happy to do it," she said instead. She really was happy to do for him and she was starting to feel such a connection to Christian. He might not smile much. Okay, he hasn't smiled once since she had started keeping track. But she enjoyed being with him all the same.

"Where are we going?"

"You'll see."

They drove in Paradise Hill with Christian waving at one person or another. It seemed he knew as many people in Paradise Hill as in Paradise Springs where he lived. Hattie found that a little peculiar, but she supposed it was because he delivered vegetables to several people in Hill as well.

They chatted about nothing and anything as they drove along. It truly was a beautiful day to be out and about. Though Hattie had heard it might rain that night. In fact, it was supposed to start raining at sundown and not stop until sometime Monday morning.

Thankfully this wasn't a church Sunday week for them. Hattie hated to even think that thought. It made her seem ungrateful. They needed the rain and the good Lord would provide it. She just hated driving in it and going to church in it and standing in the mud, etc. etc., as far as rain was concerned. And the worst part of all? This was the weekend that Rachel and her youth group were supposed to go camping. Too much rain and somebody was bound to pull out at the last minute. The kids didn't mind, but the chaperones hated it.

"Are you not going to tell me where we are going until we get there?" Hattie asked.

"You don't have very much patience, do you?"

"Christian Beachy, you have been driving me around for the last hour. I think I've shown more than patience."

He shot her a look that was almost a smile, but not quite. Yet it seemed they were at least getting closer. "Almost there," he said, and flicked the reins over the horse's back just to let him know he was still there.

Fifteen minutes later if it was a second, they pulled into Zooks' Paradise Hill Creamery.

"Ice cream?" Hattie asked, turning in her seat to look at Christian as they drove down the long, shaded drive.

"That's right," he said. "Best ice cream you'll ever eat."

"That sounds like a challenge."

"Don't start getting competitive with me, Hattie Schrock. This is one I'll definitely win."

"Truthfully," she said, leaning a little closer and wishing she hadn't as she could feel the warmth coming off his clothes, smell the fresh air in his hair, and her stomach gave a little pang of . . . something. She sat back straight. "Truthfully," she said again, "I hope you do win. I could use a really good ice cream."

Okay, so that last part wasn't exactly true. She didn't *need* ice cream at all. But she was having a good time running around with Christian. Except they seemed to be doing all their running around in Paradise Hill.

Still, she wasn't going to let that concern her. But the whole running around and spending so much time with him? It had her just a little bit concerned. "We're friends, right?"

"I thought we covered this."

Hattie turned back to face the front. "Right. Friends."

Christian pulled his buggy to a stop and tied it to the hitching post. "Do you want to get ice cream first or do you want to walk around and look at the grounds?"

The grounds were beautiful: sloping hills, green grass, tall trees that shaded the outbuildings. A beautiful cream-colored house set off to one side with a small sign in the front yard that read PRIVATE RESIDENCE. Behind that was a large barn and a path that led from it all the way up to another building, this one smaller, with a window on one side. It didn't take a genius to figure out that must be the ice cream shop. From there the hill sloped down to a beautiful pond where ducks of all colors, geese, and swans swam around, just waiting to be fed by happy ice cream patrons.

The customers themselves were a mixed lot, some *Englisch,* some Amish, though no one was there that Hattie knew. Everyone she knew went to Paradise Cones. Mainly because it was so much easier to stop at the end of Main Street than go all the way over into Paradise Hill to get an ice cream. But this place had more to do with atmosphere than just ice cream. At least it did for the moment. With Christian's promise of it being the best ice cream in Missouri who knew?

"Let's get an ice cream first," she said. That way when they walked around she could walk off some of those calories.

"Ice cream it is." Christian pointed the way toward the small building with a window in the side. They got in line behind a couple with a young son.

"Get anything you like," he told her. "It's all delicious."

That wasn't always the easiest route to go. She liked it all. "What are you having?"

"Ice cream," he said with a small frown.

"I meant what flavor?" she asked.

"Chocolate maybe."

"Christian," she explained, "you're in a gourmet ice cream creamery and you're going to get plain ol' chocolate ice cream?"

"It's better than getting plain ol' vanilla, right?"

"No." She shook her head. "Where's your sense of adventure?"

"I didn't realize that ice cream was adventuresome."

"It could be."

The people in front of them moved to one side to wait on their ice cream order to be filled and it was Christian and Hattie's turn. "Have you made up your mind?"

The girl in the window smiled and pointed to the chalk-board off to one side. "Pecan Praline is the flavor of the day. And then we have the flavors on the board to your right."

"What is an ice cream pie?" Hattie asked, studying the menu.

"We sell it by the slice or you can get the whole pie," the girl said. "If you buy the whole pie you can get whatever flavor you want. We just need a day's notice in order to make the pie fresh. Right now our pie is"—she turned away to look back at the sign behind her—"peanut butter chocolate chip."

"I love peanut butter," Hattie murmured.

"I love peanut butter too," Christian said. "But I never thought about eating peanut butter ice cream."

"There's your adventure," Hattie said. "Two slices of peanut butter chocolate chip ice cream pie."

"I don't get to even choose?" Christian asked.

"Just like the hamburger, you have to trust me on this one."

"But you have never even had their ice cream," Christian protested.

"If you say the ice cream's good, then this is our best choice. You're just going to have to trust me."

Christian shook his head as if she had lost her mind. This was peanut butter ice cream they were talking about.

He reached for his wallet, but Hattie stopped him. "It's my turn. I'll get the ice cream."

He shook his head. "I came here to order ice cream for Malinda's party. I didn't mean for you to buy our snack."

She shook her head. "I've got this."

It made her feel marginally better that she had paid for the ice cream since he'd paid for their lunch a couple of days before, but going out with Christian was starting to feel more and more like dates. And she couldn't have that.

They walked to the side and waited with the other couple for their ice cream pie to be ready. It wasn't long and the girl handed them two plastic plates and forks and two beautiful pieces of chocolate chip peanut butter pie in a chocolate cookie crust . . . Heavens.

The girl slid two coins across the counter toward them. "Have fun and thanks," she said, then turned to get the next customer in line. Hattie picked up her pie as Christian grabbed his slice and the two coins.

"There's a picnic table over there," Christian said, pointing off to the left. In fact, there were several picnic tables with brightly colored umbrellas hovering above them to shade happy ice cream eaters from the sun. It was already getting hot and it was promising to be the hottest summer on record. But for now it was still in the eighties and beautiful, perfect weather for ice cream. If there was such a thing.

"What are the coins for?" Hattie asked as they walked toward the picnic table. She sat on one side and he on the other as they settled in for their dessert.

"To feed the birds down at the pond. There's a machine down there. You put the coin in and it gives you some duck feed or whatever to feed them. The owners don't really like people feeding them ice cream scraps and stuff like that."

Hattie nodded. "Understandable." She picked up her fork and cut off a bite of the cool pie. So good. In fact she had to admit it was the best ice cream she had ever eaten. It might've been the best thing she had ever eaten in her entire life. Chocolate chip peanut butter was now at the top of her favorite things. Everything about it was perfect. The whipped cream on the top was fresh. Christian had told her that they made their own whipped cream fresh daily. The ice cream itself was delicious and creamy and thick. The sweet peanut butter flavor was perfect. The chocolate chips had just enough crunch as did the cookie crust. Honestly, it was heaven in a pie pan.

"You should get one of these for the party."

He shook his head. "Malinda hates peanut butter."

Hattie frowned. "How can anyone hate peanut butter?" Even dogs liked peanut butter. Everybody liked peanut butter.

"Sometimes I leave the jar open on the counter just because I know she'll come behind me and put it up. She can't stand the smell."

Like she needed any other reason to avoid Malinda. "Well, I love peanut butter, and this is awesome pie."

"I have to tell you I've never had their ice cream pie before. But I think I like it better than a cone."

"It seems to be more efficient eating this way. It doesn't melt all down your hand."

"*Jah*, very adult and grown-up."

She almost snorted. They were eating ice cream before going to feed the ducks. There was nothing very adultish about any of it.

"Do you need to get her ice cream today?"

"I was going to have somebody deliver it next week. But I do have a cooler in the back."

"We should just get it while we're here."

"I don't want her to see it in the freezer at home."

"You can keep it at my house."

They had plenty of room in the freezer, though she was certain to get teasing from Elsie if she was holding ice cream for Christian to hide for Malinda's party. But hey, that was what friends were for.

"You're sure?"

"Absolutely," she said. "Unless you just need to get it next week for financial reasons. There's no need to make somebody deliver it and have to pay that charge as well."

"They usually don't charge me," Christian said without a trace of smugness. "I deliver a lot of berries and such here."

Hattie shook her head. Was there anybody in the Valley that he didn't know? At this point she didn't think so.

They finished up their pie and Hattie hated to admit she was sorry to see the last bite go. She could've eaten that piece and another and still had room for some more. But there was no sense in making a pig of herself.

"Let's go get the feed for the ducks."

"Are they safe?" Hattie asked, following behind Christian down to the bottom of the hill.

"Of course they are."

Hattie wrinkled up her nose. "Don't ducks bite?"

"Not these ducks. They're used to people."

"But didn't Leroy Lambright have some ducks that attacked people at church one time?"

"You can't blame all ducks for the actions of just a few. Especially not ducks that belong to Leroy Lambright."

Leroy was the deacon for their district, a nicer man you wouldn't find. But he had a tendency to collect animals. Hattie supposed the best part of that was that he rescued a bunch of critters that otherwise might have died, but he tended to have too many at any one time. And his ducks . . .

Christian stopped at the food machine and put the coins inside. A cup appeared, like those vending machines at the hospital that spit out coffee. Instead of coffee, it spat out duck food. If there was such a thing. Was there such a thing? Had to be. She'd never seen anything like this before though. When she was coming up, they just fed the ducks corn. But this was something else entirely.

She looked down into the cup, then back over to the ducks that were already waddling in her direction. "Now what do we do?"

They were heading her way with purpose shining in their eyes.

"Throw something out for them." Christian poured a little of the food in his hand and tossed it in the direction of the ducks.

They waddled over to the food and started pecking the ground for it. All the ducks and geese were a little bit fat, even the swans seemed a little rounder than they should be, but who was Hattie to talk about such things?

She tossed some food toward the ducks, but half of it went into the water. A couple of swans swam over and picked it out with lightning efficiency.

"Okay, okay," Christian said, backing up as a swan started coming toward him. "Here." He tossed some more food in the swan's direction, but it still kept coming.

Christian backed up another step, then another as the swan charged. Christian dropped his cup of food and ran. The swan chased him clear around the lake snapping at the heels of Christian's boots before he finally gave up.

Hattie laughed as the ducks and geese pecked at the pile of food Christian had dropped.

Christian retrieved his hat from where he had dropped it in his haste to get away from the angry swan.

The swan, now having lost interest in attacking anything or anyone, wobbled over to the water and was now sailing across the lake, as peaceful and serene as a swan should be.

"That was the funniest thing I've ever seen." Hattie was nearly doubled over with laughter. Tears had already started to leak from the corners of her eyes. "Oh boy, what I wouldn't give to have a video recording of that."

"I can't believe you're laughing at me." Christian frowned at her. He smacked his hat against his leg to get the dirt off of it. Then he settled it back onto his head and crossed his arms.

"You gotta admit it was funny. And he didn't bite you, did he?"

"No," Christian grumbled. "I guess it would be funny if it wasn't me."

Hattie shot him a look. "It should be funny for you as well. Long laughs the man who laughs at himself."

"Is that some kind of New Age quote?"

Hattie shrugged. "Saw it in a gift shop."

"Of course you did."

But she thought she saw the corners of his mouth twitch as he said it.

Chapter 10

"Well, you're home."

Hattie let herself into the kitchen to find Elsie sitting at the table, a cup of coffee in front of her.

"I know it's my day to cook," Hattie said. "But I brought takeout from the Chinese restaurant."

Elsie harrumphed. But Hattie knew her cousin loved Chinese food. And she had filled the disposable container with all of Elsie's favorites. They usually got one takeout and shared it. But this time she got two. That way they could have leftovers for a day or two. There wasn't much better than leftover orange chicken. It just got stickier and tastier as it sat.

"It would've been nice to know where you had gone," Elsie said with a frown.

Hattie set the bag of Chinese food on the middle of the kitchen table, then opened the freezer.

"What have you got there?" Elsie asked.

"Ice cream. For Malinda's party."

"That didn't come from Paradise Cones." Elsie's voice was almost accusatory.

Hattie shut the freezer and turned back to face her cousin with an anxious smile. She wiped her hands down the front of her apron and tried to adjust herself so she didn't feel quite so uncomfortable. Because right now she did feel uncomfortable and it had nothing to do with that piece of peanut butter chocolate chip ice cream pie that she'd had today.

"Christian and I ran over to Paradise Hill to an ice cream shop out there. That's where I got it."

"Zooks'?" Elsie asked.

Hattie frowned. "How do you know that?"

"A girl hears things," Elsie said.

Hattie didn't have a response for that. Instead she said, "I'll get some plates, and we can eat."

Normally the person who was cleaning set the table, but Elsie showed no signs of getting up from her seat. Hattie wasn't sure what that was all about. If she didn't know better, Elsie was acting downright jealous.

"You've changed," Elsie said as Hattie set the plates in front of them.

"Me?" Hattie said. She was just about to ask Elsie what was wrong with *her*. "I've not changed one bit."

"You are always out with Christian Beachy these days. You barely leave me a note telling me that you're leaving or even where you are going. It's worrisome."

"Elsie, you knew that I was going to be spending time with him. How else can I get the man to smile and be positive?"

"I don't know, but you shouldn't worry your cousin/ business partner/roommate by running around and not telling them where you are."

"I'm sorry," Hattie said. And she was.

But Elsie was a worrywart.

"It's about positivity," Hattie explained. And it was. And that was all. It had nothing to do with that little jolt of electricity she felt when his leg brushed against hers in the buggy on the way home. It had nothing to do with the way his eyes crinkled even though his mouth remained stern. She had decided that perhaps that was a Christian Beachy smile. He was thoughtful, but it had nothing to do with that either. She just wanted him to be happy.

"Right," Elsie snapped. "Positivity. Got it. And what does positivity have to do with ice cream that now I have to have in my freezer until Malinda's party? The party that you have organized for Christian."

Hattie grabbed forks for them to eat with even though there were plastic forks in the bag along with a couple of napkins. She also grabbed a serving spoon before she returned to the table. She pulled out her chair and sat.

"I feel like you're getting upset about something else," Hattie said.

"Like what?" Elsie sniffed delicately and opened her container. She started dishing out food onto her plate. "Did you get egg rolls?"

"No," Hattie said, an apologetic tone threading her voice. "I forgot." She'd been in such a hurry because she knew she was running late, and it had just slipped her mind.

Elsie sniffed again. "Egg rolls are always my favorite."

"Yes," Hattie said. "I know."

But this didn't have anything to do with forgotten egg rolls. Elsie had buzzed into the Chinese food restaurant and forgotten plenty of things on her trips. This had to do with Christian and—heaven help them both—jealousy? No, that just couldn't be.

"Are you upset that I'm spending so much time with him?" Hattie asked gently. She waited until they had taken a couple of bites of their food before bringing it up.

"Of course not," Elsie said. "You're just doing a lot of things for him."

"He wanted help with the party because he didn't want Malinda to get word and blow the surprise. And well, you know Malinda." Did she really have to say it out loud? It was something they both knew.

Malinda was not the most popular person in their community. She wasn't the most popular girl to go to a party with or to have a party for, because she was so gossipy.

Both Hattie and Elsie knew for a fact that Malinda wanted to be a part of the Whoopie Pie Widows' Group so badly that she could probably taste it. Yet if she had truly known the cost of marrying and losing a husband, she would find herself not wanting to join at all. Though, Hattie had to admit, they did have a lot of fun in their group.

But there was no group for Malinda. She had outgrown her youth group and those who were still around and meeting did so casually. If rumors floating around were correct, and who knew if they were, they left Malinda out of that whenever possible.

"I feel a little bit sorry for her because she doesn't get invited anywhere. That's why I wanted to help get together a nice party for her."

"Are you sure it's not because you're falling in love with him?"

The words dropped like a bomb between them. It sent out shock waves upon shock waves that Hattie could physically feel in her body.

In love with Christian Beachy? How could that be? How could her cousin even think such a thing? She and Christian were nowhere near compatible. The only thing that she knew that they had in common was the love of peanut butter. And maybe horseshoes . . . and pickleball. But he had enjoyed pickleball much more than she had.

So, in love? That was insane.

"It's taking you an awful long time to answer," Elsie said.

Hattie coughed and managed to swallow the piece of orange chicken that she had in her mouth. She had stopped chewing when Elsie had delivered her little bomb. "No," she said emphatically. Maybe perhaps even too emphatically. "I am not and will not be falling in love with Christian Beachy. There is nothing between us but friendship."

"Huh," Elsie said.

Hattie had a weird feeling her cousin didn't believe a word she had just said. Unfortunately there was a piece of her that had begun to wonder if she even believed it herself.

"Where are you going now?"

Hattie stopped halfway to the door of the popcorn shop, all too aware that all the workers and half the customers were waiting for her to answer Elsie's question. "I got an errand to run." That was the most Elsie was getting out of her with everyone watching them for the latest bit of juicy gossip.

Elsie wiped her hands on one of the dish towels lying on the counter and jerked her head toward the back room, indicating Hattie to follow.

Hattie bit back an audible sigh and followed her cousin into the storeroom. She didn't want to. But it was the only way she was going to get out today and the only way she could explain to Elsie without everyone in town knowing by the time the sun set.

"If you must know," Hattie started, "I'm going with Christian to check out the chips and queso at the Mexican restaurant." He had stopped by Saturday afternoon and asked if she would take another trip with him on Monday. How could she say anything but yes? Yet now she was starting to rethink her quick decision. Only because she was going to have to explain it to her cousin. Strictly due to her recent comment.

That was the reason that Hattie had put off seeing Christian for a few days. It helped that it was a non-church Sunday for them, but truth be told, she kind of missed him and was happy to be going out with him today. Even if it was raining. Even if she had to tell Elsie and endure her cousin's speculative looks.

"We don't have a Mexican restaurant in Paradise Springs."

"I know," Hattie reluctantly admitted. "We're going over to Paradise Hill."

"Don't you think it's a little bit odd that he'll run you all around Paradise Hill, but he never wants to be seen with you in Paradise Springs?"

"That's not it at all," Hattie protested. But the thought had crossed her mind.

Every time he asked her to go somewhere, they ended up in Paradise Hill. He knew enough people in that town that she never felt like he didn't want to be seen with her by people he knew. However, since they were always in Paradise Hill, it seemed like he didn't want to be seen with her by people who knew him who lived in Paradise Springs. But that sounded ridiculous.

"You could've fooled me," Elsie said. "I didn't think you liked to get out in the rain."

The rain had started as the weatherman had predicted. Though it let up at times, it was a good soaking rain as if God were preparing the earth for the growing season to come. There were crops in the ground already sprouting, and this rain would just nurture them and help them grow even bigger. But no, she did not like to get out in the rain.

But in this case, she wouldn't be driving. And she did have an umbrella. And she had promised Christian that she would go with him to check out the chips and queso before she'd even realized that it was supposed to be raining at that time. Still, she had a feeling that Elsie wouldn't take any of her excuses for what they were, just mere explanations of her actions. Elsie would see them as . . . well, excuses.

"I won't be driving," she said. Let Elsie do with that what she would.

Hattie turned on her heel and walked out of the storeroom straight outside and down the street to where Christian was waiting.

He had parked his buggy on the side of the building that housed the popcorn shop. Not quite in front but definitely not in line of sight from the people who were inside buying their popcorn. But that wasn't saying anything at all either. That was the safest place for his horse and carriage to be parked as he waited for her to get ready and come out.

"Hey," he greeted, that small frown puckering the space between his eyebrows. "I was beginning to get worried about you."

"Just finishing up an order that I had to get out. Sorry if you been waiting a long time." She pulled herself up into the buggy and sat down next to him. Then she folded up her umbrella and shook it out before bringing it inside the buggy. Still, it was dripping on her shoes.

Christian nodded toward the back seat where a towel lay. "You can use that to wipe your arms off if you need to. And you can store your umbrella behind the seat."

"*Danki*," she said. See? It wasn't so bad out in the rain, especially not when Christian had been thoughtful enough to provide a towel to dry off her face and hands and even her shoes.

"Are you ready?" he asked.

She finished wiping off the tops of her shoes and tossed the towel back onto the rear seat. "Ready," she said.

She had expected things to be awkward between them today. After all, it had only been a few days since she just about convinced herself that she was in love with him.

Okay, she could admit that something was going on. Though she had mulled that over for so long that she couldn't quite figure out what it was. All the thoughts kept jumbling up inside her brain, confusing her even more. But just hearing her cousin say the words had been like a bucket of cold water on her face. Love? No.

Well, maybe. It had been so long since she had been in love that she couldn't even remember what it felt like. Love was never like the writers described it in books. Sometimes it was hard being with Christian and other times it was as easy as falling off a log. Even if he was acting grumpy. She had spent enough time with him to realize that frown of his was hiding thoughts, plans, and insight into what was coming next.

Christian's mind never turned off. He was always thinking about something or another. Someone or another. Maybe even a person who needed help. She had seen him run vegetables out to needy families and he was at every barn raising she had ever heard about. He was always lending a hand. And he really wasn't grumpy. He was kind, and like the towel on the back seat proved, thoughtful. So what if he frowned? Smiling for some could be overrated. Yes, she said it. Smiling could be overrated.

Then this morning when she had gotten up, Elsie had met her with a cup of coffee in the doorway to her bedroom and told her that they were calling the bet off.

To Hattie, agreeing to that was a lot like admitting defeat. Yet how could she carry through and make Christian smile? She wanted to make him happy. Though she wondered if it was possible to make a person happy who was already happy. So she told Elsie that her cousin wasn't getting out of this so easily and the bet was still on.

The problem was whether or not she loved Christian. She was really beginning to feel that she did. Yet what could become of it? Nothing. That's what. They were too entrenched in their own lives to change now. What would Elsie do if Hattie moved out? Where would they live if she and Christian got married? At his house? Where would Malinda live? There with them? It wasn't like they had a lot of choices the way Henry and Millie and Sylvie and Vern did.

No. And it would mess up too much if she pressed further. She needed to let it go quickly. Love or not, there was no future between the two of them.

She was jumping to a great conclusion to even think about where they would live when they got married. Who said they were getting married? She might think she was falling in love with Christian, but that didn't mean he was falling in love with her. He valued her opinion, that much she knew, and he seemed to enjoy spending time with her. She had learned early on that his facial expression didn't always reveal his true emotions. He would look stern and then say the sweetest thing. That was just Christian. But assuming that they would get married was a big assumption. There was no future in anything more than friendship between the two of them.

"You really want to get chips and queso from the Mexican restaurant for the party?" Hattie asked.

She probably shouldn't have asked, but she kind of wanted to know why. Why did Christian want to spend time with her? Maybe his answer would hold more than just the answer to the question.

"Malinda likes chips and queso."

"I don't know anybody who doesn't like chips and queso," Hattie replied.

"Fair enough," Christian said. "But I think we should go try it out before and make sure that we can get it on the day that we need it and all that stuff."

"You know they make phones now and you can call people up and ask them questions. You don't have to go out there."

"I know," Christian said. "But I'm a hands-on kind of guy. Plus, I want to ask them about this year's order. I grew some Roma tomatoes just for them and I'm hoping they will pick them up again to make fresh salsa."

Ah. It was about business. See? She had been jumping to conclusions about love and him adoring spending time with her, and it was just a business decision. Having her along was kind of a buffer to the situation. To make it look more casual. Like he was just driving by and Oh, by the way . . .

She was getting ahead of herself. And probably going down the road that she would never travel. There was not a "Hattie and Christian" and there probably never would be. And that was just the long and the short of it.

"So after chips and queso and potato chips with dip and veggies with ranch," Hattie said from beside him as they drove to Paradise Hill, "is there anything else we should serve at the party?"

Party party party. That was all she seemed to want to talk about. *Jah*, he had kind of put the responsibility off on her. *Jah*, she had said she would take care of everything.

But there were times when he just didn't want to talk about his sister. Or maybe it was his sister's party. Whatever it was. he just wanted to spend time with Hattie and enjoy the rain as it came down.

He'd thought there was supposed to be a break in the weather or he wouldn't have decided to come to Paradise Hill today. But the weatherman had called that one wrong and another chunk of rain had hit the radar. But at least his horse didn't seem to mind. In fact, Jefferson seemed to quite enjoy it.

"You have six girls, right?" He had been trying to re-member the names of all of Hattie's daughters. But there was one that just eluded him. Her youngest, he thought.

"That's right," she said. She gave him a curious look.

"And Sally's the oldest."

She nodded. "Then Beth, Hannah, then the twins Iris and Ada, and then Mary."

Mary, of course. How did he forget that name? And if he was really remembering right she was going to have a baby soon. Though he couldn't ask Hattie about that. That was too forward. Even between friends.

"And they're all married?" he asked. Even though he knew that the twins weren't married. Everyone in town knew about Iris and Ada. But anything could happen, he supposed.

"No," she said on a sigh. "Not the twins. When I moved out of the house and into town with Elsie, Mary and the twins took over the house. But now that Mary is married and on her own with her husband, it's just Iris and Ada in the farmhouse." Something in her voice sounded sad, maybe even melancholy.

"What's wrong?"

"I guess Elsie's rubbing off on me. She's such a worry-wart, you know."

"What are you worried about?" he asked. He took a moment to flick his gaze in her direction to see if she was okay. Her voice sounded all right, but with Hattie it was hard to tell. She usually sounded upbeat, regardless of the circumstances. Sometimes even when she was angry, she sounded happy. How was a guy supposed to figure that one out?

"The twins," she admitted on a sigh. "I'm just afraid they're going to be those twins. You know the ones that I think every community has that live on their own and never get married and smell like mothballs."

Christian frowned and cast another glance in her direction. "Why would they smell like mothballs?"

She flicked a hand as if to dispel his question. As if it didn't deserve an answer. "I don't know. They just do."

"If you're truly worried about that, why not try to find them a match somewhere?"

"And who would match them?"

"I'm a man," he protested. "How would I know about such things? I did hear about a matchmaker over in Paradise Hill."

"With all the people you know in Paradise Hill you should know that Astrid Kauffman is not a matchmaker."

"No," Christian agreed. "She's a romance writer. Tabitha Fisher is the matchmaker."

"Really?" Hattie shook her head. "I don't know a Tabitha Fisher."

"That makes sense considering how people in the Hill stay in the Hill and people in the Springs stay in the Springs, but there's a lot that goes on over in the Hill that's almost magical."

"Shut up, Christian Beachy. I don't believe that for a second."

He shrugged. "Suit yourself."

He didn't know much about matchmaking or romance authoring; he just knew what he heard. And word around Paradise Hill was that Tabitha Fisher could match just about anybody who asked her to. The only problem, according to the rumors, was she couldn't match herself.

"What about your kids?" Her words almost came at him like an attack.

"What about my kids?"

"Everyone's married and living away and it's just you and Malinda in that big old house. Ever thought about downsizing?"

He shook his head. "I bought the land from my neighbor about twenty years ago. So I got double the property I had when I first started out. I can't downsize. I won't have enough room to grow my crops."

"I hadn't thought about that," Hattie said. "When Elsie and I moved into town, it was just so much easier to stay above the popcorn shop than to try to drive in at all hours of the day or trying to get to the phone in the barn to check the messages. It's so much easier if people can just walk up the stairs and knock on the door if they need anything. Plus that gave Iris and Ada the house."

"Do you think you might have messed up in that aspect?" If she was so worried they were never going to get married and would end up smelling like mothballs, it might've been a better idea to kick them out of the nest instead of letting them have it. But who was he to say?

"Only time will tell," she said. "It's all in God's hands now."

And that was just Hattie: Give everything to God. God would take care of everything. God's hands were big and strong and capable. And Christian supposed that every bit of that was right. Thing was everyone knew to believe that. It was just that Hattie actually did. And that was one of the things he felt made her so special.

And maybe some of that had been wearing off on him lately. That nagging feeling that something was missing had gone. And he wondered if its disappearance had anything to do with Hattie. He had started feeling that way; then he begun hanging out with her, and the feeling was gone. Seemed like more than a coincidence to him. But how was a guy to know?

Like how was he to know if he was missing out on anything? Or that he might have forgotten how to live?

Just like this party. It was really no big deal but coming up with the idea of giving something back to his sister was completely rewarding. And that was why he was feeling better about life in general. It really had nothing to do with Hattie Schrock. She was just incidental in the whole thing. Or at least that was what he was going to continue to tell himself. Because otherwise he might just find himself falling in love with her.

That thought was sobering. He didn't need to be falling in love. Falling in love was for young people. He'd already had love; he'd had a family and kids. And now he had grandkids and a farm and a sister whom he looked after. He didn't need anything else in his life. His life was full. And it had been. That feeling that things weren't quite right? Well, that just had to have been some sort of glitch in his faith. He was back now and he wasn't letting that go.

While at Fiesta Cantina, Christian ordered extra chips and queso so he would have enough to take to the men's meeting that evening. He really didn't want to go. He had to endure so much ribbing about all the time he was spending with Hattie Schrock. And they didn't even know the half of it. Sometimes he parked around the corner so people wouldn't see them together. It wasn't that he was ashamed to be seen with her, but if word got out that they were hanging around together, it might get back to Malinda. Then she might figure out that they were having a party for her. He wanted this birthday party to be a surprise. It was a big birthday. So he wanted it to be kind of a big deal.

"Where'd you say you got these?" Vern asked, shoving another chip covered with queso into his mouth.

Christian had no idea how the man ate so much and still managed to stay so wiry. "There's a place over in Paradise Hill."

Everyone grew quiet.

"Paradise Hill?" Felty Lambright stopped, chip halfway to his mouth. "Why Paradise Hill?"

"Do you see a Mexican restaurant on this side of the line?" Sometimes Christian got a little annoyed with this competition between the two cities. Without the orders he had from Paradise Hill, his business wouldn't be as successful as it was. He needed their business and they needed his vegetables. As far as he was concerned, that was a match made in heaven.

Rufus Metzger shook his head. "I guess it's all right then. It is pretty tasty."

And it was. But Christian had had it before. And yet he had taken Hattie this morning to try it out for herself. Just as he thought would happen, she had declared the chips and queso the best she'd ever had. They bought extra, ordered some for the party, and he got a second order to bring to the men's meeting tonight. It was as if he was coming up with excuses to spend time with her. Which was ridiculous. He had plenty to do with and without her. There was no need to come up with extra reasons.

"So what's this I hear about a party?" Vern asked.

"It's supposed to be a surprise, so everybody keep it a secret," Christian said. "And I hope to see everyone there."

"It's next Saturday?" Felty asked.

"*Jah*." Christian nodded. "No gifts. Just come and celebrate Malinda and eat and have fun." *And leave your secrets at home.*

"So what's it with you and Hattie Schrock?"

Really. Someone just had to bring it up again. This time it was Titus Troyer. Titus who was still tan from his trip to Florida and still seeming as carefree as a *youngin* on *rumspringa*.

"I thought we were here discussing the next pancake breakfast?" Christian countered. He did like pancakes. In fact, he made awesome pancakes. And he loved making pancakes for the pancake breakfast.

"I'd rather talk about you and Hattie." Felty smacked his lips and shoved another chip with cheese into his mouth.

Of course he would. "There's nothing to talk about. She's helping me plan the party. Don't say anything to Malinda or Hattie about it and just let it be." Because if they let it be, it would die down. If it died down, then he didn't have to think about it. And he didn't have to think about how after this party was planned and executed, he'd have no excuse to spend any time at all with Hattie. And that just wouldn't do.

"We get it," Henry said. "No one can say anything in front of Malinda."

Leave it to the youngest in the group to be the voice of reason.

They had started off as a widowers' group just like the ladies, but somehow it had grown past widowers to anybody who wanted to come and help support the community. They did a lot of talking amongst themselves about problems in farming, things that they could do to help their neighbor. Just like Felty's son Benjamin.

Benjamin never got to attend because he was just so overworked. Frannie Lambright, Leroy's wife and Benjamin's sister-in-law, took care of Benjamin's new baby girl, Diana. She had been born and her mother had died and Benjamin's life had fallen apart. He had four other children who had gone to live with his mother-in-law because he couldn't care for all of them at once. That was something Christian couldn't imagine: being a grieving widow trying to care for young children. At least he'd had older children to help with the young ones when his Elizabeth had died. It had made it that much easier. Even though, he still missed her like crazy. Sometimes he still woke up in the middle of the night and reached over to see if she was there. She wasn't. But at least they'd had each other for a time.

Nowadays when he saw Benjamin, the man looked sadder and sadder. Christian couldn't help but wonder if he would benefit from having his children back with him under the same roof. But who would take care of them all then?

"I guess the next big thing is the Whoopie Pie Festival," Thomas Kurtz said.

Thomas was the local handyman and unofficial leader of the men's group. He did his best to keep everyone on track, but since they were completely unorganized, they spent a lot of time getting off track. And they enjoyed that just as much as they enjoyed helping their community.

"Are we going to have a booth again this year?" Felty asked.

"We need to start selling tickets for the ice cream social Memorial Day weekend," Thomas said. "We got to give the *youngins* something to do so they don't go out and . . . well, do things they shouldn't be doing."

The men chuckled.

"Christian, can you run the booth again this year?" Thomas asked.

"Of course." Because he always ran the booth. And he never did anything else but run the booth.

Truth be known, he wasn't the biggest whoopie pie fan out there. It was just cake with frosting in the center. And sometimes it tended to get dry because it wasn't wrapped like a cupcake in a wrapper to keep it moist. He'd just as soon have a piece of chocolate chip peanut butter ice cream pie, but he was getting off track.

"We really appreciate you doing that for us," Rufus said.

Rufus was the local beekeeper and harvested the best honey in three counties. His sister, Katie, always baked a honey whoopie pie for the festival. Even though she didn't win, they gave away the extras to promote their business. As far as Christian could see, that was a pretty good marketing plan. Because that honey was good. Katie also made candies and sold them in the stores. Small batches, just enough to make everybody want more. And again, another good business plan.

"I guess that's it for tonight," Thomas said. "Unless somebody has anything else."

Everyone shook their heads and looked around to see if anyone else was nodding. But they were all in agreement. The meeting was over.

They bowed their heads and said a small silent prayer. Then everyone rose and started moving their chairs back to where they belonged.

They didn't have a place like the B&B as Sylvie did for her widows. But they got by just fine in the community theater. They put their chairs away and cleaned up their messes every Monday night without fail.

Vern went over to the refreshment table. The men were gathering up the food, putting what wasn't eaten into trash bags or saving it for later. Vern grabbed another chip, dipped it in the cheese sauce and shoved it in his mouth as if his life depended on it.

"What are you going to do with this cheese sauce?" Vern asked.

Christian shrugged. "I don't know. Do you want it?"

"I'll take it," Vern said. "*Danki*."

"You're welcome," Christian replied. It would be good to have chips and queso for a late-night snack but having that in the house just made him think of Hattie. And he didn't need to think of her any more than necessary.

Chapter 11

"So you and Christian went over to Paradise Hill yesterday," Sylvie said to Hattie as she reorganized the order of the whoopie pies on the dessert table.

Sylvie did like things a certain way. Though Hattie had a feeling she had to touch every plate of whoopie pies just to see exactly what they were. She was nothing if not serious about this competition. Though last year's loss to Sadie Yoder had really been hard on her.

"How did you know I went with Christian to Paradise Hill?" Hattie asked.

Sylvie smiled. "I didn't. But now I do."

She walked off without another word. And went to perch on her chair.

Hattie followed behind. "And how did you know that Christian even went to Paradise Hill yesterday?"

"Vern brought home chips and that cheese sauce from the Mexican restaurant that Christian took to the men's meeting last night."

Of course Vern did. The man loved to eat. And she could just imagine how he would dig in to chips and queso.

"It's for Malinda," Hattie said. Looking at the curious

and smiling faces of the rest of the widows. And former widows.

They all nodded and smiled and smiled and nodded and Hattie felt like a bug on display in the classroom.

"It was. We're going to serve that at the party."

She turned back to Sylvie. "Speaking of which," she said hoping to switch the subject a little off of her and Christian and a little more onto the party. "We can still have it here, right?"

Sylvie nodded. "Of course. It will work better to have it here in town. A more central location for everybody."

That was true, but Hattie figured Sylvie just liked being the hostess. Another reason why she held the Whoopie Pie Widows' Club meeting at the B&B every week. But now that Vern had moved in, Hattie had wondered when they would start having the men's meetings there as well. Not that it was any of her concern.

"We really appreciate it," Hattie said.

Katie elbowed Elsie in the side. "Do you hear her? We?"

Elsie frowned a bit and nodded. "I hear her."

The widows were still nodding and smiling and smiling and nodding, and Hattie knew the whole thing was useless. She could crow about it 'til the cows came home, and no one would believe that there was nothing more than friendship between her and Christian Beachy.

Any feelings that she might have were strictly one-sided, and were most likely some weird infatuation that came with just spending so much time with someone. Even though she still hadn't managed to get him to smile. Not even once. She had come close though; she had come close.

Deciding to cut her losses, Hattie gave Sylvie a quick nod and headed for her own seat.

"Who brought these red velvet?" Lillian asked, picking

up the cake and studying it critically. "I think this is the best recipe I've ever had."

Beside her, Callie nodded. "I agree. They are scrumptious."

"I brought them," Hattie said. "It's my grandmother's recipe. I mean, mine and Elsie's grandmother's recipe," she backpedaled.

"You should definitely enter these into the competition," Katie said.

Directly across from Hattie, Sylvie frowned. Perhaps *serious* was not the best word for how seriously she took the competition.

"I could never make them for the baking contest," Hattie said. "It's not my recipe."

"It's your recipe if you make them," Callie protested.

Hattie shook her head. "It's not as simple as that. The recipe belonged to our grandmother. As far as I can see, it belongs to Elsie just as equally as it belongs to me. And how weird would it be if she and I both entered the same recipe?"

Elsie turned toward her. "Is that why you've never entered it in the competition?"

"Well, *jah*. I mean, she was your grandmother too."

Elsie scoffed. "Yes, she was my grandmother. But I never baked whoopie pies with her like you did. We were always out gardening together."

Somehow as the years had passed, Hattie had forgotten that little detail. But she shook her head. "It wouldn't be right," she said.

"What's not right about it?" Elsie asked.

What wasn't right about it? If Hattie wanted to enter the competition and use that recipe and Elsie didn't mind, and didn't want to enter the contest and bake that recipe, what was the problem with the whole idea?

"Are you saying you don't care if I enter the competition and use our grandmother's recipe?"

"No, go right ahead," Elsie said. She patted Hattie on the leg reassuringly.

Hattie's heart melted a little for her cousin. They were truly as close as sisters. And she would never do anything to upset Elsie. Doing so would break her own heart.

"If you're certain?" Hattie said.

Elsie nodded emphatically. "One hundred percent certain."

"You better get a move on if you want to enter though," Callie said. "Registration ends Friday."

Hattie wasn't certain but she almost thought she saw Sylvie shoot Callie a *be quiet now!* look but that couldn't be. Sylvie was serious about the competition but not that serious. Plus Hattie was looking at her out of the corner of her eye. Must've been an eyelash or something in the way. "I'll do it then."

Everyone clapped, and Hattie could feel herself blushing. Just what she needed: one more thing to do between now and the competition. She had to go down and register to enter. She had to go with Christian to the party store. She had to finish organizing the party and decorate the inn.

Oh, and don't forget. Most important of all, she had to find some way to make Christian Beachy smile.

"What's the matter with her?" Hattie asked the following day.

First thing that morning she'd gone down to register to enter the Whoopie Pie Bake-Off for the first time ever. It felt weird to do it and still she had the slight feeling that she had betrayed her cousin. But Elsie assured her that everything was fine. Now it was done. She was entered.

"I don't know. She just sort of came in in a bad mood today."

Rachel Lehman was normally a happy person. Hattie knew not to look at someone's life and think that they should have everything peachy and rosy. Rachel had lost her mother at a young age, had gained a stepmother in Joy Lehman. But still she couldn't figure out what Rachel had to be so unhappy about.

"Have you asked her?" Hattie asked.

Elsie shook her head. "I figured it probably had to do with boys, and I wasn't sure I was up for that today."

Hattie frowned at her cousin. "Up for it or not, you should've asked."

She moved away from Elsie over to where Rachel was restocking the bags of white cheddar popcorn. "Rachel, dear, is something the matter today?"

"I'm sorry," Rachel said. Her expression crumbling from irritation to remorse. "I'm trying but it's just so hard. So. Hard."

Hattie gave her a reassuring smile. "What's so hard?"

"Joy and Dat." She briefly closed her eyes and shook her head. "They were supposed to come on our camping trip tomorrow night."

"I thought you were going camping last week," Elsie called from across the shop.

Rachel looked even more miserable if that was possible. "No one wanted to go because it was raining. Well, that's not exactly true. None of the chaperones wanted to go because it was raining. So that meant none of the kids could go. Now Mamm and Dat are sick and—" She broke off with a shake of her head. "And I feel terrible because I'm upset with them for being sick, but it wasn't like something they could have changed. It wasn't like they did it on purpose."

"So you don't have a chaperone, and you can't go camping tomorrow," Hattie repeated just to make sure she understood.

"It's postponed again. I so wanted to go. I've been waiting on doing this stuff for years. I got to watch Rebecca do it for years, and I know I'm not supposed to be envious, but I was. I was so jealous. For years she got to do all the fun things and now that I've finally turned sixteen, every time I turn around something gets canceled because of something else. It makes it even worse than not being able to go at all."

"What if I came?" Hattie said. It was a very impulsive suggestion.

"It has to be a *mamm* and a *dat*," Rachel protested. "But it's sweet of you to offer."

It wasn't that Hattie was trying to be sweet. She liked Rachel and she just hated to see the young girl so upset when surely there was something that could be done.

"Elsie and I can be a *mamm* and *dat*."

"Only if you get to be the *dat*," Elsie quipped.

Hattie shot her a look. "I'm sure the bishop would be okay with that. I mean it's tradition for a *mamm* and a *dat* to go, but what happens when a *mamm* and *dat* get sick?"

"Another *mamm* and a *dat* from the youth group takes their place," Elsie supplied.

"That's the problem," Rachel cried. "None of the other *mamms* and *dats* can go. Except for the other couple who's already coming."

That was right, Hattie thought. It was usually two couples who escorted all of the kids in the group. Out of any given youth group, there usually were plenty of couples to choose from. But there were times when a youth group had several kids that belonged to the same family. That seriously cut down on the numbers of *mamms* and *dats* available for such activities.

"I'm sure Zebadiah would make an exception this one time and let me and Elsie come and chaperone."

Elsie came around the counter like lightning and bumped Hattie's elbow. "Cousin, can I talk to you for a second?"

Hattie frowned. "Can it wait? I'm trying to do something here."

"No, it cannot." Elsie pulled her to the side, then turned Hattie so she blocked Rachel's view. "I don't want to go camping. I didn't want to go camping when we went camping as a youth group. And I was young then. I'm fifty years old."

Hattie propped her hands on her hips. "I'm fifty-nine, and I don't mind going."

"Good for you," Elsie snapped. "I don't want to go. So come up with another plan or tell that poor girl you can't help her."

"You should be ashamed of yourself," Hattie whispered, then moved around to go back to Rachel.

Her steps slowed because she was so close. The shop was small. It wasn't like they were yards from each other. And she didn't have time to think of something else as she approached. She wanted to help. But she couldn't imagine that Zebadiah would make an exception for just her to be the chaperone. He would at least need the substitution to be a couple of people. Two people to take the place of two people.

"She doesn't want to go camping," Rachel said intuitively. Or perhaps she had heard Elsie's words.

Hattie didn't know what to say. "Well, surely we can come up with—"

She had been about to say "another idea" when the bell

on the door to the popcorn shop rang, and Christian Beachy stepped inside.

"Christian!" Hattie said. "How do you feel about going camping?"

"Did you really just talk me into that?" Christian asked.

They were on their way to the party store over in Paradise Hill.

Jah, there was a perfectly good party store there in Paradise Springs. But Christian was worried that if he bought supplies there or even at the variety store, it would get back to Malinda and she would know what he was planning. No, this was a much safer course of action.

"As I recall," Hattie started, "there wasn't much talking into that was needed."

Okay, so that was true. She had asked, *How do you feel about camping?* and he had wanted to say it was great when I was young, but I don't feel like doing that anymore. Then something in the sparkle of her eyes stopped him from saying those words.

So he had said camping was wonderful and the next thing he knew they were calling down to Zebadiah's, leaving a message at his phone shanty about the two of them being chaperones for the youth group going on the camping trip the following evening. Of course, they mentioned that they would be staying in separate tents.

Christian just hoped he could find his tent when he got back home. Of course, getting it out would alert Malinda to a change in the air, and he might have to explain to her what he had been doing at the popcorn shop to begin with.

He supposed he would cross that bridge when he got there.

"I couldn't tell you no in front of that girl."

For all that he could see, Rachel Lehman was a sweet person and Hattie was just as nice. Rachel was in need and Hattie jumped in and Christian somehow managed to do everything Hattie wanted him to do. It was a vicious circle. But it would be ending soon. Just as soon as Malinda's party was over.

But instead of feeling light, the thought sat like a stone in his middle. It weighed him down.

"Well, that girl really appreciates it. And now she's going to help us decorate the B&B for Malinda's party."

"That's another thing. We're going to be gone all tomorrow night and half of Friday."

"Which is the exact reason why I said Rachel had to help us."

He supposed *us* included him and Vern and possibly even Henry because the men could reach higher spots even from a ladder. And he supposed that was a small price to pay for his sister.

"I want to put balloons all over the place," he said. "Malinda loves balloons."

Hattie smiled. "Who doesn't?"

Her smile was beautiful. It turned that weight in his gut into a heart with wings.

"I don't know if I told you this, but I really do appreciate you helping me." In fact, he didn't know what he would've done without her.

To his amazement she turned bright pink. "You're welcome," she murmured. Her voice was thoughtful and quiet. Not at all like her normal Hattie voice. He wondered if something was wrong.

They rode the rest of the way to Paradise Hill in silence. That was typical for Christian. He'd been accused his entire life of being too thoughtful, but he was used to Hattie chattering away about one thing or another. Now with a camping trip looming on the horizon, he figured she would talk about nothing else. Yet she sat silently next to him.

"Is everything all right?" he asked after he pulled into the parking lot at the party store, Party on the Hill.

She seemed to shake herself out of her stupor. "*Jah*," she said a little too enthusiastically. "Of course. *Jah*. Of course everything is fine."

But it wasn't. He didn't know how he knew, but he just knew it wasn't. And he really didn't know how to broach the subject with her.

Had he said or done something? He didn't see how. One minute she was fine and the next minute she wasn't. One minute he was thanking her for helping him with Malinda's party, and the next she was as quiet as a church mouse. It was about the weirdest thing he'd ever experienced.

"Shall we go in?" she asked, gesturing toward the building.

The parking lot was around back and had a space for horses and buggies like most stores did when they were close to an Amish community. The back of the building was painted bright yellow with a rainbow and clouds and balloons and that magical creature called the unicorn. He wasn't sure what a rainbow and unicorns had to do with parties, but he wasn't the one that designed the painting.

"*Jah*." He set the brake and got down. Then he tied Jefferson to the hitching post, and he and Hattie walked side by side around the corner of the building.

Each outside wall of the building was painted a different color. The side they walked on was bright blue with more balloons which made perfect sense and another had unicorns which didn't. The front of the store was painted red with hearts and flowers and peace signs.

Again, he had no idea what that had to do with a party supply shop, but he just had to go with it.

The mood inside the party store could only be described as festive. Upbeat music played a little too loudly, as far as he was concerned, and everything inside seemed to be bright and shiny and glittery. There was ribbon and those shiny balloons blown up and waiting for the party. Stacks of brightly colored paper plates, all sorts of napkins, little toys to give away, he supposed, at the children's birthday parties, and more colors of forks and tablecloths than a person could shake a stick at.

"Do you want to go with a theme of some sort?" Hattie asked.

Christian frowned "Theme? What does that mean?"

She nodded. "You know like a Hawaiian theme or a unicorn theme."

He scoffed. "No unicorns."

Aside from the fact that Malinda was a grown woman, unicorns didn't exist.

"Well, you could do a theme or you could just do a single color. Does Malinda have a favorite color? We could do all yellow."

"Define 'all yellow,'" Christian said. He had no idea what that really meant. Was she talking about a yellow cake or was she talking about yellow things that he hadn't even thought of? And come to think of it, Malinda hated yellow.

"No yellow," he said.

"Right. Check. No yellow. But we can do shades of pink or shades of blue or all one color pink and all one color blue."

The truth of it was he was way out of his depth.

"I'm feeling a little overwhelmed here," he admitted.

Aside from the fact that he was still reeling from Hattie's jarring change of mood.

"You want me to find some things perhaps and to show you what I'm talking about?"

"Are you sure you own a popcorn shop and you're not a professional party planner?" Christian asked. He wanted so badly to put that smile back on her face.

A ghost of one hovered about her lips. "I'm sure. Stay here, and I'll show you what I'm talking about. She gestured toward the chair that most likely had been left for other males who had no idea how they had gotten into a party store and what to do about it now that they were there. He sat down and waited.

She was gone for just a few minutes, and Christian kept himself busy watching other people bustle around, gathering all sorts of things, from piñatas and candy to huge bouquets of balloons so large that he had to wonder how they would be getting them home.

Finally Hattie returned with a stack of paper plates each neatly wrapped with ten others just like it.

"Here's what I thought might be good." She held them up one at a time. "Okay, you have something that looks like a quilt. We've got puppies. We've got kitties. We've got balloons. We've got just happy birthday. And we have hearts. These last ones are for Valentine's Day, I think, but I like the red so I brought them over."

He liked the red too, but they did look like something for Valentine's Day and not necessarily appropriate for his sister.

"Can we get some of the blue ones and some of the happy birthday ones?" he asked.

Hattie turned them where she could see them, examining the colors and seeing how they went together. At least that's what he suspected she was doing; he truly had no idea. He wasn't the party planner here.

"We can," she said. "The colors are kind of primary with basic pink, basic green, and basic orange. We could do multicolored balloons, bowls of jelly beans, and all different colors of crepe paper. We could have different colors of plates, plastic ware, and napkins."

She continued on, but to Christian it just started to be a drone in his head. The more excited she got, the more he had trouble concentrating on her words. Of course she was speaking faster and faster, getting into the idea of decorating the B&B.

"I need to get a shopping cart," she said. She bustled over toward the door, grabbed one, and went back to where he was sitting. "Are you coming?"

He'd actually like nothing more than to sit right where he was, but it was his sister's birthday, after all.

"I'm coming," he said.

He was glad that the old Hattie was back, he thought as they went up and down each aisle loading the basket cart with multicolored streamers, multicolored balloons, the jelly beans she promised, different colors of everything that somehow matched the plates. At least that's what she told him she was doing. At this point he was merely along for the ride.

She went to go down the next aisle. "Hup," she said, and immediately turned around. "This aisle has wedding stuff on it."

"Do you ever think about getting married again, Hattie?"

He had no idea where that question had come from. And he had no idea why he felt it necessary to ask her. It just wasn't done. Men, whether single or married, did not ask single women when or if they ever thought about getting married again. It was just not done.

She turned that shade of bright pink again, just about the exact color of one of the packages of forks they had loaded up into the cart for the party.

"No." She turned away then, and he couldn't see her eyes. But he could tell in her tone. She had no plans of getting married again.

But that didn't bother him. It didn't bother him at all. It wasn't like he was going to ask her to marry him. It wasn't like she even wanted him to.

Still, he couldn't help but imagine what was going to happen when this party business was over. They might find an excuse to hang out at some point during the Whoopie Pie Festival. But he was running the men's group booth to collect tickets for the ice cream social in a few weeks. So there was nothing.

Of course, he could invite her to the ice cream social. Even though that was more for the *youngins*. And he wouldn't be able to spend any time with her because he would be handing out scoops of somebody's homemade strawberry banana ice cream, wishing it was pistachio with almonds and cherries. And wishing he had an excuse to spend more time with her.

Chapter 12

"Thank you so much for agreeing to come with us," Rachel said as the group finished setting up their tents.

Their hired driver had dropped them off with promises to return the following morning after breakfast. Just long enough for all the adults to be tired of dealing with kids and ready to get back home.

There were ten teenagers in all: four boys and six girls. The other couple chaperoning were Dave and Patty Brenneman, parents of Evie Brenneman who was possibly dating Johnny B Lehman.

Hattie was secretly grateful that Johnny B had begged off coming on the trip. He had fallen a couple of years back and damaged his spine. There were always rumors about whether or not he would walk again, but so far he was confined to his wheelchair. It would've been hard to get him up and down and help him with everything. And Hattie felt a little bad about it. Johnny B might've fallen, but that didn't mean he didn't deserve all the fun that the rest of the kids were having. But truthfully it had nothing to do with her. She was just here to help out Rachel.

"I'm glad to help. We're glad to help," she said, dragging Christian into the reply whether he wanted to be there or not.

She still wasn't sure how Christian felt about coming camping. He seemed to be enjoying himself. Not that they'd been out there very long. Just long enough to find a campsite, set up their tents, and start collecting things for a campfire. Tonight they were supposed to roast hot dogs and marshmallows and tell ghost stories until everyone either got too scared and went into their tents or fell asleep out in the open. Then tomorrow morning, they would pack it all up and head back to Paradise Springs. Then her good deed was done for the week.

"We really do appreciate it though," Evie said, coming up beside Rachel and linking her arms with the other girl. It seemed that the two had become quite close since Rachel's dad had married Johnny B's mom and Evie was dating Johnny B. Or at least that was how Hattie saw it.

Still, she couldn't get behind rumors and she shouldn't be spreading them herself. That was Malinda's job.

And no more uncharitable thoughts, she told herself.

"Okay, everybody, start collecting firewood. You three, start getting kindling. And you three, we need some rocks for the campfire. Just about this size." Christian held his hands out about six inches apart. "Not too big, not too little. Just enough."

"That was clear as mud," Hattie said.

The girls giggled in return but did as Christian requested.

"Did you get your tent set up?" Christian asked.

Hattie nodded.

Since she and Christian would not be sharing a tent, she was bunking with Rachel. Christian had brought his own tent, a small thing that was supposed to only house one person. But she couldn't see how his tall frame would fit inside without his feet sticking out of the opening. The thought made her smile.

"What's so funny?" Christian asked.

"Aren't you afraid that the bears might nibble your feet during the night?" she asked with a nod toward his tent.

"Are you making fun of my tent?"

"Is that how they sell them? As a whole tent or a half of one?"

"You just wait," he said. "I have a fine tent, and it will be just perfect for tonight. I will be incredibly cozy, with no worries whatsoever."

"With your feet sticking out six inches."

He turned back toward the tent, then he looked to Hattie once more. "I did buy it when I was a teenager."

Hattie shook her head and laughed. "I hope you brought an extra blanket for your toes."

"That's everything," Dave Brenneman said, brushing his hands as if dusting the matter away. He had just finished unloading the van of all the food and such that the campers would be sharing.

Beside him, Patty smiled. Hattie knew that they were old enough to be parents. Or they wouldn't have a child who was almost eighteen. But they looked no more than twenty-five themselves. Or maybe Hattie was just getting old.

"What's next on the agenda?" Patty Brenneman asked.

"I heard the kids say they wanted to go swimming down in the lake, but I told them they need to get a campfire going first."

Dave nodded knowingly. "You're right. Firewood first, then they can go swimming."

"That water is going to be freezing cold," Hattie said.

Patty shrugged. "They're kids. They will get in it regardless. Don't you remember doing that as a teen?"

Hattie wasn't sure how to take that remark. Was Patty

calling her old? Or was she just merely trying to get Hattie to recall?

Hattie decided that she was going to take it as the latter. Otherwise she might take offense. "I guess there's nothing like being young and . . ." She didn't finish the sentence. It wasn't a positive statement.

"Stupid?" Christian asked. He had no qualms about it though.

"We'll go down to the lake with them," Dave said graciously. "We don't mind."

Hattie had to wonder if they might take a dip themselves. There was no way she was getting in the cool lake water. It was hardly warm enough come July.

"You can stay up here," Patty added. "In case any of the kids don't want to swim. You can read."

There was a part of Hattie that wanted to protest.

It wasn't that they were old. Never mind that most of her hair was shot with gray and that she couldn't help but notice years of smiling had put crow's feet at both sides of her eyes. Not that she would go back and change that. She liked smiling. But the world considered that an indication of advancing age. It might be noble in their community, a badge of honor to grow old, but when it came to hanging out with young people, not so much.

"*Jah*," Christian said with a firm nod. "Y'all go ahead and we'll stay up here and make sure nothing happens to the campsite."

The young couple smiled, linked arms, and headed off toward the lake.

"Stay up here. Read," Hattie grumbled. "They act like we're a hundred years old."

"You want to go get in that water?" Christian asked.

Hattie shook her head. "No way."

"I'd be grateful that they think you're old."

Had he read her thoughts?

"Do you think so?" Hattie asked. "Do you think we're getting old?"

Christian scoffed. "Is that a trick question? Of course we're getting old. Every day you get a little older. They are getting old. Nothing wrong with that."

"*Jah*, I suppose so." And who was it that said that getting old just was testament of days serving the Lord? Her. That was who. Right now though, she didn't quite feel that way. "You know what I wish sometimes," Hattie said.

Christian sat down on top of the cooler. It was the large kind the young kids could fit into easily. He patted the spot next to him.

Hattie perched on the edge.

"I wish I had appreciated my youth when I had it."

"I did," Christian said.

"You didn't wish your early teen years away thinking about going on *rumspringa* and then didn't wish your twenties away waiting to get married and then all the wishing for your children to walk and talk. We just wished them to go to school and the next thing you know they're all grown and married and on their own and you're old."

"No. I had a great time on my *rumspringa*. I had a great time raising pigs before that. I enjoyed my childhood immensely."

That was not the answer she had been expecting from him. He always was going around scowling and frowning. And if he wasn't scowling and frowning, he surely wasn't smiling. And yet he seemed to have enjoyed his life till now. There wasn't anything he regretted. How was that possible?

"It's the little things," Hattie said. "I guess, anyway."

"Like?"

"Like I never would wear the color green."

"If that's all you have to be sorry for your life, I say you did quite well." Christian shook his head at her as if she were unbelievable.

"I wear green all the time now. I think it looked good on me when I was young, but every time I wore green, all anybody could talk about were my eyes. And I wanted them to notice more than my eyes."

Christian just shook his head again. "I suppose to some youth is wasted on the young," he said.

"I guess," Hattie replied. But she had always thought she was overweight. She wished she were that fat now. Not that anybody around her cared. But she sort of did.

She wasn't about to go on a diet and try to lose a bunch of weight. She kept it in check just enough that she didn't get roly-poly fat. She had a feeling, though, if she ate all the desserts she wanted, she would have to be rolled out of the B&B after a widows' club meeting.

But it was more than that. She hadn't run and jumped rope and played with the other kids the way that she should have. She was always a little self-conscious of her size. Now she wouldn't let that hold her back. It was funny how a person can look back on their life and see the mistakes they made as clear as day. And yet at the time that stuff seemed so important.

"So," Hattie said, "did you bring a book?"

The next time he was asked if he would go camping he was telling them no. Absolutely, one hundred percent, no. There'd been a time in his life when he enjoyed camping. But he had decided that now was not that time. Not now when he had barely gotten any sleep because his feet stuck out of his tent along with about six inches of his legs. Thankfully the weather was nice, and the temperature hadn't dropped too low. He kept his socks on so his feet weren't frozen. But no. He did not like camping.

He hadn't brought a clock or watch with him, but he could tell by the position of the moon that it had been well past midnight before the last couple of kids crawled off into their tents.

Hattie was almost asleep sitting up in front of the fire, doing her best to chaperone these young people. She was entirely too nice. But it was something he liked about her.

Now it was morning and breakfast time. The boys had managed to somehow convince the girls to cook breakfast for them, and the girls had fallen for it, hook, line, and sinker. Of course they had when Christian had been that age too. But he liked to cook. He liked to cook breakfast anyway.

"You want me to make pancakes?"

All heads turned in his direction.

"You can make pancakes out here?" one of the kids asked.

Christian shook his head at them all staring like he was about to perform a magic trick. "Of course I can make pancakes out here."

He gathered the things he needed from the cooler. And the milk. He wished he had buttermilk, but this would have to do.

"Did you bring any flour?" He looked from Hattie to Patty to see which one might answer.

"I don't have flour," Patty said. "But I brought a box of baking mix."

"Good, good," Christian said. It would have to do. It wasn't really *good*. He prided himself on his pancakes. But making pancakes on an open flame was something of an art and he had mastered it long ago.

"Do you need any help?" Hattie asked.

"Not with this," Christian told her. "But if you could get me the butter . . . I forgot to get it out of the cooler."

Christian put the iron skillet on the rack they had set up above the fire. The kids watched in awe.

While the pan heated, he mixed up the batter, then tossed a pat of butter into the skillet. It sizzled deliciously.

He waited until the edges of the butter turned brown, then took a spoon and dipped some batter into the skillet. At home he used a ladle that held about a half a cup. Maybe a little more. It made perfectly beautiful pancakes. These were going to be smaller. But they would still taste good.

"Who wants to go first?" Christian asked, looking from one to the other of the kids. He flipped over the first set of pancakes and waited as the teens decided who would get the first taste. It ended up being Evie Brenneman.

He dished the two pancakes onto her plate next to her bacon and eggs, then tossed another pat of butter into the pan.

"Too bad we don't have any syrup," Evie said, looking a bit forlornly at the pancakes.

"They're good dusted with powdered sugar too," Christian suggested. He hadn't thought about syrup out here, and there was nothing better than a pancake cooked in butter and covered with maple syrup. Yum. Yum.

"We've got some icing left over from the cupcakes last night," Hattie suggested.

Patty had brought unfrosted cupcakes along with a plethora of sprinkles and a can of store-bought icing. The kids had had a great time after supper decorating the cupcakes and otherwise keeping themselves occupied with nothing more to do than spend time together.

Evie shrugged. "Works for me."

Hattie went to retrieve the icing and a plastic knife. As

Christian served up two of the silver dollar pancakes to each of the teens, Patty smeared them with frosting and everyone sat down to enjoy their breakfast.

"You're a really good pancake maker," Hattie said. She'd taken one bite of one pancake, and it was made from store-bought mix at that.

"Why are you trying to flatter me?" Christian asked.

"No, you really are good. They're the perfect size and even with store-bought icing on them. I mean, if they had some maple syrup and some fruit like some peaches or some pecans or even sprinkled with bacon . . ."

He made a face. "Peaches and bacon?"

She shook her head at him. "Don't knock it until you try it. Restaurants and cafés are adding bacon to everything. We've been trying to figure out how to add bacon to our popcorn."

"Okay, I'll give you that," Christian said. "Everything is better with bacon. Everything except maybe peaches."

"I'll have to make it for you. Just think about it: Take marshmallow cream and puréed peaches, then mix it with a little bit of maple syrup. Top that with a sprinkle of bacon."

He had to admit it sounded pretty good. But the whole thing gave him a niggling of an idea. It just stuck in the back of his brain. Pancakes and peaches and bacon and icing. It just hovered there, circling around but not landing so he could fully grab hold of the idea. Oh well. Like it mattered.

Everyone enjoyed the pancakes, even if they were made from a box and served with store-bought frosting. It was a good breakfast and before long they were clearing up the mess, cleaning up their campsite, and waiting for the van to head back to Paradise Springs.

"Do you need some help decorating tonight?" Evie asked as they rode back to the Valley.

The kids had all brought some sort of road trip scavenger hunt and most were busy looking for dogs, certain road signs, and car tags from different states. Evie, it seemed, had grown bored with hers and instead had turned her attention to Hattie.

Christian was in the seat behind and couldn't help but hear. It wasn't that he was trying to eavesdrop, he was just easily within earshot.

"For the party tomorrow night, you mean?" Hattie asked.

Evie nodded. "I overheard Rachel saying something about it. That you guys came to help with the youth group and she was helping you to decorate. But you helped me as well so I would like to return the favor," Evie said.

"We can always use help," Hattie replied.

"I'll help," one of the guys behind her said.

"Me too," another added.

A chorus of offers to help went up in the van.

Christian hadn't spent a great deal of time in the main room of the B&B, but he couldn't imagine ten people crammed in there, much less ten people crammed in there while trying to decorate. Thirteen if you added in Millie, Sylvie, and Hattie. Millie might beg off, but he couldn't imagine Sylvie just letting anyone run around the place.

"That's really nice of you," Christian said, "but we don't need that much help."

It was just too many people and too much of an opportunity for someone to get hurt.

The kids started to protest, claiming all the reasons why they needed to help, each one talking over the other. The crazy amount of noise was beginning to give Christian a headache.

"Stop," he said. He wouldn't say he yelled. But his voice did grow louder. It was the only way to get them all to be quiet. "I appreciate it very much. Rachel's coming to help and that is that."

He expected another chorus of complaints, but no one said a word. In fact, no one said anything the rest of the trip back to Paradise Springs.

The driver dropped them off at the community center. Most of the parents were already there waiting. Those kids whose parents weren't expecting them had left their horses and buggies down at the stables. They said bye to everyone and started walking down there to get their rides. Before long everyone had cleared out except for him and Hattie.

She frowned at him.

"What's wrong?" He could almost see the steam coming out of her ears.

"You didn't have to do that, you know," she said. Her voice was a little bit shaky on the end.

"Do what?"

"Yell at everybody. They were just trying to help."

"I didn't yell at everybody. When did I yell at everybody?"

She shot him an incredulous look. "Really? You don't call that yelling? What you did there in the van? Telling everyone to stop, that you didn't need any help tonight decorating for the party?"

He frowned at her, mulling over the situation and what had happened. "We don't need that many people decorating. We'll just be tripping over each other. There's not that much room. And there aren't that many decorations. I appreciate the offer, but it's not necessary."

"That didn't give you call to yell."

"I didn't yell!" Now that time he had.

Hattie crossed her arms and glared at him. "You don't scare me, Christian Beachy."

"What?" What did she mean he didn't scare her? Why would he want to scare her?

"I know beneath this grumpy exterior there's a heart of gold. I just don't know why you won't let anyone else see it." Her piece said, she grabbed her gear and headed for the popcorn shop, leaving him staring bewilderedly behind her.

It was almost suppertime when she climbed off the ladder at the B&B. Hattie stopped and looked around.

"It looks great, *jah*?" Rachel asked. Hattie could see the tired lines around her young mouth. She was exhausted. After staying up half the night, then the ride back from the camping trip and now decorating for the party. The poor girl was worn-out. "You can go on home now, Rachel. Do you have a ride?"

She jerked her head in the direction of the street. "Vern said he would take me."

Sylvie looked around for her husband. "Where is Vern?"

Sometime after all the streamers were hung and the banners in place, the men seemed to have disappeared. Thankfully all the stuff that needed to be hung high was done, but still.

Hattie was also still a little upset with Christian. How was anybody supposed to see what a great and happy person he was if he kept fussing and yelling and scowling and frowning at everybody and keeping them all at an arm's length?

Sometimes she felt he wanted the same for her. That she would just go away and leave him alone. But if she asked him, he would tell her "of course not." Because he didn't want to hurt her feelings? Or because he really wanted her around? How was a girl to know?

Okay, so she wasn't exactly a girl.

As if he heard his name, Vern came out of the door that led to the kitchen. He had a whoopie pie in one hand, the other hand cuffed underneath to catch any crumbs. "You need me?"

Sylvie looked back to the other women, pressed her lips together, and shook her head. "I should have known." That was one thing everyone knew about Vern King. He loved to eat.

"Are all the rest of the men in there with you?" Millie asked. Her job had been blowing up the many different colored balloons that were pinned all over. Hattie had gotten a little overzealous with the balloons and Millie had just kept blowing them up. So now they were all lying around the floor like happy bubbles.

"*Jah*, all the men are in here."

"It's time to take Rachel home," Sylvie said.

"*Danki* again," Rachel said, "for helping us with the camping trip."

Hattie smiled and she felt the tiredness in her own face. Thankfully the day was just about over. "It was my pleasure." And it had been. It was. And if she had to do it all over again, she would. Mostly because she liked to help, but also because she would love to eat more of Christian's pancakes.

Something about them just kept sticking in her mind. And she couldn't imagine why he couldn't see bacon and peaches together. That sounded like the perfect combination, the sweet of the peaches and the salty of the bacon. Yum. Or maybe she just needed to eat something. It was getting quite late.

"You ready to go, girl?" Vern asked.

Rachel nodded and gave Hattie a hug. Then she followed Vern out the door.

"Why don't you and Christian stay for supper?" Sylvie asked.

Hattie jerked her chin in the direction of the door where Sylvie's husband had just disappeared with Rachel. "Aren't you going to wait for Vern?"

Sylvie shook her head. "Vern eats constantly. Missing one mealtime ain't going to hurt him. He can eat when he gets back."

"I can't speak for Christian," Hattie said. Mainly because Christian seemed so moody, she wouldn't know how to answer for him. "But I can say for myself that I would love to."

"Good then," Sylvie said.

"Let me call down to the popcorn shop and tell Elsie I'll be staying here." Hattie started toward the phone.

"I had a feeling we'd be running late," Sylvie said. "So I made a casserole this morning. It's in the refrigerator. All I have to do is pop it in the oven to heat it up and we'll be eating in no time."

"Perfect," Hattie said. That was Sylvie always making sure everybody had something to eat.

Half an hour later they were all seated around Sylvie's large kitchen table. It was a homey piece of furniture with scratches and dents that made it look like it had been through generations of family. Which couldn't be right, considering that Sylvie didn't have any children. But the table still represented life as far as Hattie could see.

The weird thing was that they were coupled together. Sylvie and Vern. Millie and Henry. Hattie and Christian. But then not. There was no Hattie and Christian. And there wouldn't be a Hattie and Christian. He might have asked her if she wanted to get married again, but he certainly hadn't given her that information concerning himself.

And she had told him flat-out no. What could she say? That *jah*, lately she'd been thinking about getting married again a lot more than she had ever thought about it before. Ever. In fact, she hadn't thought about getting married again until now. That was all Christian Beachy's doing. And yet . . . And yet he continued to resist her attempts to make him smile.

Even if he wanted to get married and even if she wanted to get married again, how could she marry someone who never smiled? She wasn't sure she could take it. At least that was what she was going with now. It was about the only reason she could find for not marrying Christian Beachy. He was handsome enough. He had his own farm. He was a successful businessman. And he was a loving, caring person. Even if he had a hard time showing it, that was one thing she knew about him for certain.

Chapter 13

Finally it was time to get ready for the party. Thankfully Hattie had had too much to do that she couldn't stop and have a conversation with Christian. Because right then she really didn't want to talk to him. She didn't know what she didn't want to say, but she just didn't want to say it. There was no need for him to go around being grumpy all the time. How was anybody supposed to know what was truly in his heart if he went around acting like a curmudgeon?

Once everything was in place, and guests started to arrive at the B&B, Christian headed after Malinda. He had come up with some story about bringing her into town for dinner for her birthday. If Hattie was hearing right, he had suggested they had a reservation at Paradiso Italiano.

Of course there were guests from the B&B poking around as well. It was something that Sylvie had warned them about. But as far as Hattie was concerned, the more the merrier. Except she wasn't feeling very merrier at the time. At least not as merry as she wished she was feeling.

But she had done what she said she was going to do. She took care of Malinda's party. It was going to be a great party. Perhaps the best party Hattie had ever thrown for anybody. The entire front area of the B&B was decorated in multicolored balloons and streamers, glittery banners and all sorts of other party paraphernalia.

She'd help Christian pick out a cake at Joy's bakery. Rebecca Lehman, Uriah's oldest daughter and Rachel's sister, had been taking cake decoration lessons. It was the most beautiful cake that Hattie had ever seen. It seemed Rebecca had a touch for art in icing. She had gone to work at the bakery sometime last year. Before Uriah and Joy decided to join their families.

The best part of all was that everyone hid when they heard Uriah whistle as Christian pulled into the B&B.

Hattie didn't know what Christian told his sister about why they were making a stop there, but it didn't matter. She was completely astonished when everyone jumped out, yelled "Surprise!" and started honking party horns. Actually that's what it was all about. Surprising Malinda, giving her something to remember. A special birthday.

Though Christian had told everyone not to bring gifts, there were gifts galore. Some as small as a paper and pen set and others as large as gift certificates to local stores and restaurants. But Christian's gift was the best of all. Tears rose in Malinda's eyes when she saw the beautiful clock.

Hattie mentally patted herself on the back for helping him pick it out. But the final decision had been his. Hand-painted roses on smooth lines and a clean big face. Instead of regular numbers it had Roman numerals, which gave it a look of elegance. At least Hattie thought it did. And unlike some of the other models with curves and corners and crannies formed out of the porcelain, this one wouldn't be a pain to dust. All in all, if Hattie had been choosing one for herself, she would've chosen that one. And she hoped truly that Malinda loved it as much as she seemed to when she opened her gift.

Once all the birthday traditions had been dispensed

with and everyone had moved from the chips and dips to eating cake, conversation around the party shifted. Most now were talking about the upcoming Whoopie Pie Festival.

Hattie was too tired to join in any conversation. She had such a time the last few days between running around with Christian, going camping with the youth group, and then finishing up the final touches on the party. She was exhausted and wanted to do nothing more than climb into bed and go to sleep for an entire day. That wasn't going to happen.

Tomorrow was a church Sunday and she would have to be up before the sun to make sure everything was in place before they left for the service.

She wandered out of the common room and over to the staircase in the foyer. She just needed a little bit of time alone. Just a moment to decompress a bit, she supposed.

She eased down on the second step and stretched her legs out in front of her. She rotated her ankles and feet, giving some relief to the tired muscles.

It was worth it, she told herself. For Malinda to be so happy, and Hattie to have had a part in bringing her that happiness. All the effort, all the trips to Paradise Hill, all the decisions had been totally worth it. But in no way was she ready to take up a job as a party planner anytime soon. It was exhausting.

"What are you doing out here?" Christian frowned as he came toward her.

Great. The last person she wanted to see. She had come out here to get herself back together. And the one thing that continually bothered her was now standing in front of her scowling and wanted to know what she was doing.

She sighed. "I just came out for a little bit of quiet."

"Thank you for all your help," he told her.

She nodded. "Of course." What else could she say? It wasn't like she would've turned him down. The time she spent with him, even if it was in an attempt to get him to smile and be more positive, was enjoyable. They had become friends. And friends helped each other.

He nodded toward the step where she sat. "Do you mind?"

She scooched over closer to the wall and patted the wood next to her.

Christian came closer, eased down on the step brushing against her leg as he did so.

Really, the staircase was too narrow for two large adults to sit there. Unlike her, Christian wasn't chubby; he was just solid, thick, and broad.

"You're upset with me," he said. He was sitting a hair-breadth away, and she could feel the rumble of his words as his shoulder touched hers.

They had sat this close together in the buggy. Maybe not quite *this* close, but close to it. Yet there was some-thing a little more intimate about sitting on this step while a party raged in a nearby room. And they weren't in a buggy.

She started to tell him that it wasn't true, that she wasn't upset with him, but she couldn't bring herself to lie. "You're a very special man, Christian Beachy," she started slowly. "But if you go around frowning at everyone and scowling all the time, well, no one will know that you're as wonderful as you are."

He seemed at a loss for words. So Hattie continued. "I know you're just thoughtful. But the world doesn't know that. They would have to spend a great deal of time with you to really understand." That was what she had done. She had spent a great deal of time with him these last couple of weeks, and in truth it only made her want to spend more time with him. Regardless of what she told herself.

"Perhaps you worry too much about what other people think," Christian said quietly. There was no accusation in tone. But Hattie felt the barbs. It was true. Perhaps she did care a little too much about what others thought. Not in the aspect of what she did for her community and how she behaved toward her fellow man. But in other aspects, such as her weight and her graying hair.

She told herself daily that she accepted both, but she didn't. She fought them. Tooth and nail. Not that it did much good. Her weight seemed determined to remain the same, and her gray hair . . . ? It was only going to get grayer as time passed. "Maybe," she murmured. "But—"

Christian shook his head. "There are no buts. I know I'm a good person, and I think people around me know that I'm a good person. I help. I do my part for my community. I always have. So why do you care if people think I'm grumpy?"

Because she was falling in love with him, and she wanted everyone to see him as special as she did. That was a silly dream. No one would view him with the same eyes that she did.

Some might understand his stern demeanor. Others might be able to look past his grumpiness to what he did for his fellow man. But no one was going to see him the same way she did because she loved him. Not that it would do either of them any good. But there it was. The truth laid bare. At least in front of her.

There was no way she was admitting her love to Christian. Not that it was a bad thing, but she had gotten to know him. She had gotten to know what a kind and caring person he was. He wouldn't want to break her heart if she told him that she loved him, and he didn't love her in return. She didn't want to lay that on him. Obviously he didn't care for her that same way or he would've said something by now. They had spent ample time together.

"Hattie."

Christian spoke softly next to her.

She raised her gaze to his, only then realizing that she had been looking at him as she mulled over her unrequited love.

"Hattie," he murmured again. Then he lowered his head toward her.

There was a split second when she realized that he was going to kiss her. A split second where she might have moved away, but she didn't have it in her. This might be the only kiss they ever shared. And though it was forward of him to give it and it was even more forward of her to accept it, she wanted it. She wanted this kiss, this touch of his lips, this possibility of his caring. It was going to keep her warm in the nights to come, as she grew old without him.

The kiss was wonderful, his lips searching hers, as if mapping them out for future reference. It had been a long time since Hattie had been kissed. It had been a long time since Hattie even thought about being kissed. She decided then and there that it was perhaps the most precious gift that Christian could have given her.

All too soon he lifted his head. But he stayed close, looking at her as if searching for something long-lost.

She stared back into his beautiful blue eyes, searching for love, for signs of something more. But she was only being hopeful. Just like her, Christian seemed as if he didn't want to get married again. It wasn't a necessary part of his life. And that made her label this as "the kiss to nowhere." Because there was nowhere for it to lead.

Without a word she pushed to her feet and headed back to the party.

"Hattie," he called after her.

She didn't stop.

Katie Hostetler loved parties. She loved the party atmosphere. She loved seeing people standing around chatting, eating junk food off paper plates, and otherwise suspending their normal lives for a bit to celebrate something. Celebrations . . . That was what life was all about.

Despite her love for the whimsical, she had been accused more than once of having a no-nonsense attitude. But that's what happened when you had ten children. Or perhaps it was being married four times and widowed just as many. Now at seventy-two, she was done with all that. She was perfectly content to live with her brother Rufus, to make her candy and taffies from the honey he harvested, and to live out her days with the celebrations of others.

She was kin to about everybody in Paradise Springs by blood or marriage. So she had plenty of opportunities to celebrate the good fortune of others. And truthfully it wasn't a bad way to go. Sometimes celebrating your own life meant cleanup afterward. This way was so much nicer.

Of course Rufus, her brother, had been talking lately about their mother's ninety-fifth birthday coming up this fall. You couldn't let ninety-five slip by without an acknowledgment of some sort. Perhaps Hattie would organize a party for their mom, Lolly Metzer.

As expected, Lolly was stooped and arthritic. She lived in the *dawdihaus* of her great-grandson's farm, and most considered her a stay-at-home busybody. Even though she rarely left the *dawdihaus*, she somehow managed to know more gossip than Malinda Beachy herself.

It would be a chore to keep news of a party from her mother, Katie mused. So perhaps Hattie was the way to go. She had obviously managed to keep this one a great secret from Malinda, who somehow managed to ferret out every bit of gossip and news that the community had to offer.

Katie made a note to talk to Hattie about that the next time she had an opportunity. Maybe Tuesday at the Widows' Club meeting.

Katie made her way over to the food table. Most everyone had already had a piece of cake and had started in on the coffee that Sylvie had made. Katie had noticed a few minutes ago that Sylvie had bustled back into the kitchen; she was certain to start another pot. With this many guests, coffee didn't last long.

"There's the birthday girl," Katie said as she gathered up her second round of snacks. She supposed at her age she should eat the vegetables, the tiny carrot sticks and the little trees of broccoli with ranch dip on the side. But she would much rather have the chips and queso. Or even good old potato chips with French onion. Bah. She could eat vegetables tomorrow. She loaded up her plate with chips and dips.

"I can't believe this party," Malinda said. Her blue eyes sparkled, and for a moment she almost looked as if she were about to burst into tears again.

In fact, most the time that Katie had seen Malinda this evening, she looked like she was on the verge of tears. Like she couldn't believe so many people had come out to celebrate her or that somebody would take the time to make such a wonderful party just for her.

Katie didn't point it out, but it must've taken the better part of the day to merely get the balloons blown up. They were everywhere. Guests were kicking them to the side, moving them off of furniture so they could sit down. It was like having bubbles all over the place. Katie liked it. She would have to remember that idea for Lolly's party.

"Are you having a good time?" Katie asked.

"A wonderful time," Malinda gushed. "I still can't believe he did all this for me."

"He" being her brother Christian, Katie supposed. "Hattie Schrock helped him a lot," Katie said. She wondered if Malinda had any idea how much time Hattie had been spending with Christian.

Maybe she did. Maybe she didn't. They were adults. They might share a house, but Katie was certain they didn't check in with each other like an old married couple. They were siblings. Just because they lived under the same roof didn't mean they divulged all the details of their personal lives and whereabouts every moment of the day.

"I must remember to thank her," Malinda said.

Katie glanced through the crowd. "She should be around here somewhere." But she didn't see her right away. Maybe she had stepped out to get a breath of fresh air. It was quite warm in the common room.

At least that's what Katie thought Sylvie called this room. She should know; she heard her mention it a hundred times if even once. This was the same room where they held their Widows' Club meetings.

"I'm not going to worry about it tonight," Malinda said. "I'll write her a thank-you note tomorrow."

"Give it to her at church?" Katie asked, though she really didn't expect an answer. Everyone was going to be exhausted tomorrow when it came time for the sermon. She just hoped no one fell asleep.

Though most people managed to stay awake, there were a few who dozed off from time to time. It was going to be more than a few tomorrow if the party didn't start winding down.

"I wonder why Christian went to Hattie for help," Malinda mused. A small frown puckered her brow, and she looked so much like her brother that Katie almost laughed.

"I guess because they've been spending a lot of time together," Katie explained, taking a quick bite of chip before continuing. "Ever since Hattie decided that she was going to make Christian smile."

"What?" Malinda turned toward Katie, a light of interest in her eyes. "She's trying to make my brother smile?"

Perhaps Katie had said too much. But she was already in it this far. "Apparently Hattie and Elsie have some sort of wager that Hattie can get your brother to smile, I guess, and have a more positive attitude."

Malinda pressed her lips together before responding. "My brother is plenty positive."

Katie shook her head. "You don't have to convince me."

"Then I should go talk to her." Malinda made as if to walk across the room in search of Hattie.

Katie grabbed her arm. "You can't tell them I told you. I should've never said anything. It's just some little friendly thing they've got going on between the two of them. And you have to admit your brother rarely smiles."

"He gets a bad rap in this community," Malinda said. "He always has."

"People think he's grumpy," Katie said. "But everyone knows that he's got a good heart. Everyone sees the things that he does for his community and his fellow man. So please . . . you cannot say anything to Hattie and Elsie or anyone that I said this to you. Especially not Christian. Because truthfully it might hurt his feelings." And Katie was certain that neither Elsie nor Hattie wanted to hurt him in any way. It was really all done with a good heart. And some things should just be left alone.

"I can't promise that," Malinda said.

"You have to," Katie returned. "If you tell them that I told you what they've been up to, they're going to be mad at me."

For a moment she thought Malinda was going to shrug off her protests. The thought made Katie feel slightly ill. She didn't want to hurt anyone with her careless mouth. Surely Malinda could understand that.

Once again the other woman pressed her lips together, then gave a nod. "Okay," she finally said. "I won't say anything. I won't tell them that you told me."

Chapter 14

It was perhaps the most subdued church Sunday Hattie could ever remember. Even the church leaders were dragging a little bit, as of course, they had also attended Malinda's party. But she was glad everyone had such a good time.

All the memories of the party were so sweet, as long as she blocked out that kiss from Christian. A kiss. What had he been thinking? What had she been thinking to let him kiss her?

Aside from the fact that they were sitting in the foyer at the B&B and anyone could've come through and seen them, it just wasn't done. Neither one had any sort of intentions on the other. If they had been dating, the bishop would've come out and demanded that they get married immediately. It would've been a scandal. And she had sat there and calmly leaned into him as he leaned into her. Shameful.

That's what it was. It was shameful. Shameful to care about someone so much that you put all of your good sense aside. Shameful to not care enough about what those around you might discover about you. Shameful that it had nowhere else to go.

That kiss had haunted her all through the night. She was dragging a little bit more than everyone else, simply because she'd gotten less than an hour and a half of sleep the entire night. Coupled with the sleepless night of excitement over the party and the sleepless night with all of their camping antics, she felt like she could go to bed and sleep for a week. But that was no reason to let a man kiss her. Out in the open. Where anyone could've seen.

But of all the things about the kiss that bothered her, it wasn't those that concerned her the most. What worried her was that she had loved the feel of Christian's mouth on hers. She loved the way he tasted like cake and coffee, making the kiss even sweeter. She had loved the scent of him that she breathed in as he came near. The smell of man, good earth, and soap that seemed to follow him around everywhere he went. It was the knowledge that it was the first time and the last time he would ever kiss her.

"You're nothing but an old fool, Hattie Mae Schrock," she scolded herself as quietly as possible. But somehow she had said the words too loudly.

"What was that?" Katie asked.

"Nothing," Hattie muttered.

"Is everything okay?" Elsie asked. It was perhaps the hundredth time that Elsie had asked her if she was feeling all right since she had come back into the party after kissing Christian. And for the hundredth time Hattie told her she was just fine. And for the hundredth time Elsie didn't believe her. Hattie could see it in her cousin's eyes.

Elsie pressed her lips together and turned away.

"Is there any more pie?" Callie asked.

"It's an Amish church service," Katie started. "Do you honestly think we would run out of pie?"

Callie propped one hand on her hip. "So I guess the question is where are the other pies?"

"Just inside the house," Hattie said, and started in that direction, toward the back door of the deacon's house, where they were having church today. Frannie and Leroy Lambright had a built-on, screened-in porch with high tables, just perfect for storing pies during the church service.

Hattie made her way up the porch steps and swung open the creaky screen door. Her thought had been to get a couple of the pies and come back. But it seemed Callie had followed her.

"Here we go," Hattie said, grabbing a couple of the pies.

Callie grabbed a small cardboard box that contained two others. "That should do it."

Hattie waited for Callie to get the door since she had one hand that could be freed. But instead of reaching for the small handle, Callie studied her face instead. "Are you all right today, Hattie?"

Hattie scoffed. "Of course I'm okay."

"You just seem sort of . . . off."

She had no idea. "I'm fine," Hattie said. "I'm fine, everything's fine, all of it is fine."

The words rushed from her mouth without any warning from her brain. Hattie shook her head. "I'm fine," she said again, this time in a more calm and controlled voice. "I'm just really tired. It's been a very busy week."

Callie nodded. But Hattie could still see the concern in her friend's eyes. Though truthfully, what could Hattie say? *Christian Beachy kissed me last night and now I'm even more than halfway in love with him and there's no place for that love to go?*

Nope. Definitely not something she could admit to now. She would just have to go on pretending she didn't love him. Go on pretending they hadn't kissed and go on pretending that everything was fine. Just fine.

"I know we haven't always been the best friends," Callie said. "Not real close anyway. But I wanted to tell you that if you need to talk to someone—maybe someone other than Elsie—I'm here for you. Just let me know. Maybe one day you could come down and we can have a slice of pie at the buffet."

Callie's concern brought tears to Hattie's eyes. She blinked them back so the other woman wouldn't see how touched she was by the small gesture. It might be small looking on the outside, but to Hattie it was large, as big as the Grand Canyon. Bigger. It was good to know that she had friends who cared. It would get her through.

"I really appreciate that," Hattie said. "But truly I'm fine."

How easily that lie slipped from her lips.

They went back out with the rest of the churchgoers who were milling around and eating. Talking and visiting. Hattie took the opportunity to glance Christian's way whenever she could. But every time she looked at him, he was looking someplace else. Talking with Felty Lambright, or Henry King, or even sometimes Vern King. It seemed he had no shortage of conversationalists on this day.

Hattie wondered what they were talking about. Most likely the things that men talked about—manure, farming, fertilizer, horse tack, dog feed, men stuff. But she was sure they were also talking some about the party and how he had surprised his sister and how much fun everyone had. It wasn't that she wanted to know anything about the conversations he was holding with other people. She just didn't want to feel ignored.

Yet that was exactly how she felt as she watched him.

If she hadn't known any better, she would think that he was purposefully trying to disregard her. That he was purposefully looking the other way whenever she decided to look toward him. But that couldn't be. First, he had no idea when she was going to look at him. But if that weren't the case and it was simply by chance, then it seemed to reason that at some point she would glance his way and find him looking back at her. But it never happened.

He dismissed you, she told herself. And he had. He kissed her and had found her somehow lacking. She wasn't sure in what. Or maybe it was true and he just didn't want to get married. He had enough of a life, even as a widower. He had five children. He had seven or eight grandchildren. He had a big farm, practically a double farm, and he had his sister. He didn't need a wife to cook and clean. He didn't need someone to help raise his children. He didn't need anything like that. And obviously he didn't need her.

He could almost feel her gaze land on him, as soft as butterfly feet. Just the thought made him shake his head at himself. Butterfly feet? He was losing it. He was losing it over someone who said they never wanted to get married again. Who had said it in such an offhand manner that he had no choice but to believe it.

Perhaps if she had looked him dead in the face and with a stern growl had declared that she never wanted to get married again, he could believe the opposite. But she had practically skipped down the aisle saying she had enough in her life and didn't need a man. What choice did he have but to believe it?

Yet no matter how badly he wanted *not* to believe it,

he knew he should. Then he had gone and done the most stupid thing a man can do when a woman was not interested in him—he kissed her.

It wasn't planned. He hadn't intended to kiss her when he followed her out to the foyer at the B&B while the party raged on inside the common room. He hadn't planned to kiss her as he gestured to the space at her side and wedged himself between her and the railing. He hadn't planned to kiss her at any time until he found his lips on hers. It was as if his body had taken control without any say-so from his mind. Or maybe it was his heart that had led.

Jah, it was true. Hattie Schrock—always positive, always smiling, always sickeningly happy—had managed to capture his heart.

She wasn't really that bad. At least she hadn't been as bad as he had thought originally. In fact, she wasn't bad at all. And in further fact, he really did enjoy spending time with her. He wanted to spend more time with her and more time with her and share more kisses with her. And perhaps even a little more. But that was wholly impossible without marriage vows. Vows that she vowed never to vow again.

This whole thing was making his head hurt. Or perhaps that was the sleepless night he had spent reliving that kiss over and over again. Trying to figure out what he had done wrong. Why had she looked at him with such betrayal and jumped up and immediately fled back into the party? Even if she didn't want to get married again, she didn't have to be so angry about one little kiss.

Okay, so he was making complete light of the situation. That kiss had been dangerous. What if the bishop had walked out of the party at that exact moment? What if anyone had walked out of the party at that exact moment? They were too old to be carrying on like that, and they would have had a lot of explaining to do. Explaining that would have ended up with them married, most likely. Even if Hattie's uncle was the bishop.

Perhaps that's why he had done it. Perhaps that's why he had taken the chance. That it would've been out of both of their hands and he would have had to make a decision. And she wouldn't have been allowed to tell him no. It would've just been done.

Was he that . . . What was the phrase? Passing aggression? No, passive aggressive. He wasn't sure what the words meant by themselves, but as a whole, the best he could figure in listening to other people use the term, it meant that a person did what they could to get what they wanted without really taking a firm action at all. But he had taken action. He had kissed her.

But he kissed her instead of being forward enough, brave enough to just go up and ask her to marry him. When in truth, that's what he really wanted.

"You okay?" Vern clapped him on the back as if he had swallowed something wrong.

"I'm fine," Christian managed to choke out as Vern continued to whack him.

"You just went all pale there for a moment."

Christian stepped sideways out of Vern's reach. For an old guy he sure packed quite a wallop. "If I'm pale, why are you pounding me on the back?"

"I thought maybe you were choking."

Better just leave that one alone. This was Vern King they were talking about. And though Christian really enjoyed Vern and his quirky ways, sometimes they were a bit hard to fathom.

"I'm fine," Christian said, somehow managing to stay out of Vern's reach.

Vern studied him with a critical gaze. He might be quirky and he might be getting old, and according to the rumors in town he might be getting a little forgetful, but there were parts of Vern that were sharp as a tack. Like his intuitiveness when it came to someone else. "I don't think you're fine at all," Vern said. "In fact, you have all the makings and looks of a man in love."

This time Christian did choke. But instead of it being on a piece of cheese or a bite of pie, it was on his own spit. He couldn't even swallow correctly after Vern's revelation. "Love," he sputtered.

"That's what I said." Vern nodded.

Christian continued to sputter though he kept telling himself to get it together. What would old Christian do? What would the Christian who wasn't in love with Hattie do? He would frown.

He put on his best scowl. "That's the most ridiculous thing I've ever heard," he said. Then he turned on his heel and marched away. Case closed.

To Hattie, it felt like the longest church day in the history of church days. And truthfully that made her feel a little sad. She should love going to church. She should love time with her community and worshiping God and all the other beautiful things. The singing, the prayers, and the fellowship afterward.

But all she wanted to do was go home and lie down in a dark room by herself. Elsie was always accusing her of being too positive. Well, she didn't feel so positive now. She was only positive that she was not positive about anything anymore. She wasn't positive about anything other than she was positive she should not have kissed Christian Beachy.

"You want me to make us something tonight?" Elsie asked.

On church Sunday, they normally just grabbed a snack around suppertime. Maybe a piece of leftover pie and some cheese. Any lunch meat they could find. Nothing big, just something to keep them from being hungry and help them get through the night till breakfast in the morning.

Hattie slipped into one of the chairs at the kitchen table. She propped her elbows on the tabletop, her chin in her hands. "If you would, that would be great."

"Is your head hurting?" Elsie asked. "I can grab you some aspirins if you want?"

No, Hattie didn't have a headache. She had a heartache.

"It's over," Hattie said. She lifted her head and turned her sad gaze to her cousin.

Elsie frowned. "What's over?"

"The bet. I want out. I'll clean whatever for however long. I don't care. But I can't do it anymore. I thought I could make him smile, but you know, I just don't think it's in his makeup. He seems perfectly happy, and all I'm doing is messing in his life." *And messing in my own.*

Elsie slipped into the seat across from her and reached for her hands. "Let's just call the whole thing off. We don't have to have a winner or a loser. We should've never come up with the stupid bet." She shook her head. "Let's just forget it ever happened. *Jah?*"

Hattie tried to give her cousin a smile, but her lips trembled and tears leaked from the corners of her eyes.

"Hattie," Elsie crooned. She scooted her chair around one side and did her best to hug Hattie across the corner of the table. "It's all going to be okay. It's not a big deal.

It wasn't like you guys were dating or anything. I mean, not really."

Hattie prayed that her cousin would be quiet. She didn't need any explanations of hers in Christian Beachy's relationship. She didn't need anyone recounting it. She just needed to let herself know that it was over.

Any association she might have with him concerning the wager? That was over too. She had lost, Elsie had won, yet they had called it a tie and quit. But even if she had gotten Christian Beachy to smile, Hattie knew that she had lost. Because she was hopelessly in love with him.

Tuesday at the Whoopie Pie Widows' Club meeting, things were tense. It was the last meeting before Friday when the baking of the whoopie pies would begin. Of course everyone had once again brought whoopie pies for their refreshments, most in flavors that would not be present as their whoopie pie entry. No, these almost served as decoys for the real entries. The only thing that the collection of whoopie pies showing at the refreshment table would tell the other contestants was what that contestant *wouldn't* be bringing.

Apparently Callie Raber wouldn't be bringing her French vanilla with raspberry filling. Lillian Lambert would not be bringing chocolate chip with peanut butter filling. Katie wouldn't be bringing strawberry strawberry chocolate chip. Millie had brought vanilla, though if she was entering, that would be probably her flavor of choice, seeing as how she didn't hardly eat anything but vanilla whoopie pies when whoopie pies were available. And everyone knew that Sylvie would not be bringing double chocolate devil's food with creamy marshmallow filling.

Hattie had wanted to make her red velvet, but she was just so tired. And if she were entering them in the contest, she shouldn't be parading them around under everyone's noses so they could determine her secrets. So instead she made banana nut whoopie pies and had just been done with it.

Not that it truly mattered what she brought or what she even planned to enter. It wasn't like she would win. Not with the way Sylvie Yoder King baked. And then there was Sadie Yoder. She had won last year with an innovative whoopie pie made with brownie instead of cake.

Hattie, of course hadn't gotten to try one. After the competition was over, the volunteers handed out samples of the entries in little cups. It was first come, first serve, and the brownie concoction went fast. But she had heard people talking. It seemed that was the thing to try.

She could imagine. She loved brownie. And it was very clever to substitute brownies for the cake. It was almost a natural choice. And she knew some women who baked their whoopie pies with an almost cookie-like recipe for the sandwich halves. Hattie couldn't say if she liked one better than the other. She was definitely up for giving equal rights to all desserts.

"I don't think she'll do it again this year," Katie was saying.

It seemed she might've missed something important.

"I don't know," Sylvie said with a mysterious smile hovering around her lips. "Good is good. And that was obviously very good." She didn't need to finish and say because it beat her world-famous whoopie pie baking and cut her streak short at seven.

So Hattie was getting a little ahead of herself. Sylvie's

whoopie pies weren't exactly world-famous, but they were definitely southwestern Missouri famous.

"You really don't think she would enter the same winning recipe as last year?" Lillian was shaking her head the whole time she spoke.

Sylvie shrugged. "Why not? We're all expecting her to do something different. And perhaps we might imagine that she would do something even more different than a brownie, but . . . what if she just enters the same old thing?"

And this was why Hattie rarely entered the competition. There was too much strategy in this part of it. If people just baked and tasted, voted on what was good, and that was the end of it, she might could handle it. But for Sylvie, it was more serious than that. She picked out a strategy, tried to determine her competitors' moves. She thought it through. Maybe thought about it too much. But that was just Sylvie. And perhaps that was what made her great.

"That would be a bold move," Callie said. "Entering your same recipe as last year seems to indicate that you think your recipe is superior and that no one else can come up with something better."

Sylvie nodded, but she still had that look on her face, like she knew a secret that no one else knew and she was just dying to tell it. Or maybe that was Hattie reflecting her own feelings onto Sylvie's expression. Hattie was the one with the secret. Hattie had been the one to kiss Christian. Hattie was the one who had gone and fallen in love. But Hattie didn't want to share that with anyone else. It was obvious that Sylvie couldn't wait for the whoopie pie competition to arrive.

"How's her fabric store doing?" Katie asked.

Sylvie shook her head. "I for one still go over to Hill Fabrics to get any material that I need."

That was a drawback to Paradise Springs. Up until recently there had been no independent fabric store in town. You could buy a few bolts at the variety store where Lillian worked, but they didn't always have a large selection of colors and fabrics for them to choose from. More often than not, they ran out of black for everyday aprons. So if the women of Paradise Springs needed fabric, they were forced to drive into Paradise Hill.

The women didn't talk about it much. It was just one of those dirty little secrets of their town. But now Sadie Yoder. She had opened a store right there on Main. And yet these women seemed too jealous, too envious to take advantage of the location. Hattie had never given it much thought until now, and it seemed petty and wrong. And it was something she was going to correct as soon as possible.

"Is she married?" Callie asked.

That was the other problem with trying to get to know Sadie Yoder. She lived in the other church district there in Paradise Springs. It was smaller and held church on the alternate Sunday because they used the same bishop. Plus, it was hard to get to know folks who lived that far out. The church district didn't have its own elders. Just a deacon to help run things. If they needed the bishop's counsel, they called Zebadiah. They shared the bishop, the preacher, and the minister, but not much else. So it wasn't like they could've seen Sadie at church with her husband or even an intended.

"She's fifty years old if she's a day," Katie said. "If she's not married, then perhaps she's a widow? Maybe we should invite her to come to one of our meetings."

A cloud of noise rose above the women. It was hard to tell who was saying what. But there were choruses of *What do you mean? That's a terrible idea!* And *Why would we do that?* that went up all around.

"Hear me out," Katie said. "What if you were new in town and no one welcomed you?"

They all sobered at that thought. Hattie herself felt rightly chastised and she hadn't been purposefully avoiding Sadie Yoder. Hattie hadn't made herself a new dress in a year or so. And when she needed fabric she picked it up at the variety store. But now . . .

"Maybe," Sylvie finally said. "It might be good to get to know her." Learn her secrets. Sylvie didn't say it, but it lingered in the air around her.

Hattie could only hope that Sadie could hold her own with this group.

She thought back to the confident woman she had seen accept the award check and trophy after the judging last year. *Jah*, she could take care of herself. No problem. Even against the likes of Sylvie King.

"It just goes to show," Sylvie said later in the meeting, "it's not enough to have a tasty recipe. You have to be creative. You know, think outside the box."

Think outside the box. Those words stuck with Hattie all through the evening and into the next day.

It made her wonder why she had even bothered to register for the whoopie pie baking competition, because she wasn't the kind of person who naturally thought outside the box. Until she was forced to. She could be innovative and resourceful when called to, but just to come up with creative ideas for the sake of creative ideas? No, she couldn't do that.

Elsie. She was the one who came up with the crazy popcorn flavors and the ideas for new candy glazes, like root beer. It was basically root beer candy melted onto popcorn. As far as Hattie was concerned it seemed like the most disgusting thing on the planet. And aside from cheddar candy and dill pickle candy it was the best-selling flavor. Go figure. So no, thinking outside the box was not Hattie's strong suit. But those words just kept going around and around in her head.

It was just like the other day during the camping trip when everyone wanted pancakes but there was no syrup. She was the one who suggested they eat the icing on them. The perfect sweet to cover a pancake if there was no syrup available.

In the end it had been fun to start brainstorming on what would be good on those silver dollar pancakes. Like peaches and bacon and maybe even some marshmallow cream. Whipped cream or pecans. So many yummy things that could've been put between two little silver dollar pancakes . . .

. . . that were just about the same size as the halves of the whoopie pie cakes.

Hattie dropped the large spoon she held that they used to stir the popcorn with. It clattered on the tile floor and sounded as bad as a car wreck.

"Have mercy, Hattie," Elsie said. She pressed a hand to her heart. "You just about scared the life out of me." She stopped and looked at Hattie. "Are you okay? What's wrong?" The words were flung at her with bullet precision.

"I think I might need to leave," Hattie murmured.

"Okay. Are you going to the doctor?"

Hattie shook her head. "No. I'm fine."

Elsie frowned at her. "You don't look fine. You look like you've seen a ghost."

"No, no, no. Nothing like that. I just got this idea."

Silver dollar pancakes toasted to perfection filled with peach-flavored buttercream frosting and sprinkled with pecans and bacon. And maple syrup. Don't forget the maple syrup. She would get that in there somehow. How about peach maple syrup buttercream frosting? *Jah.* That was it.

This was a winner. It was unique. It would be tasty and it could also be for breakfast. No one could argue with the whoopie pie for breakfast. Not when it was made from pancakes and bacon.

"An idea?" Elsie parroted.

"Elsie," Hattie started once more. "What if I didn't enter Mammi's red velvet recipe in the competition?"

Elsie scoffed. "Seriously. What is wrong with you today? Why would I care what you enter in the competition?"

"So even though we've already discussed it, it's okay if I enter whatever recipe I want?"

Elsie all but rolled her eyes. "Yes, I do not care. Or no. Whatever the answer is. I don't care. Enter what you like. Don't enter anything at all. It's up to you."

It was up to her.

Her and Christian Beachy.

"Can you take care of things while I run out to talk to Christian?"

Elsie's forehead lined into a frown. "What do you need to talk to Christian about?"

Hattie smiled. "Whoopie pies," she called, as if that was the most logical answer she could give.

Elsie shook her head. "I've got it here. You just be careful."

Hattie started for the door. "I will," she called as she rushed outside and down to the stables.

It seemed to take forever to get her horse hitched up.

As usual, Jason wanted to talk about the good weather they were having and the Whoopie Pie Festival coming up, and Hattie just wanted to get out to the farm and talk to Christian. They had a great idea and together with that idea they might just be able to win the whoopie pie baking competition. Well, she would do all the cooking. She wasn't sure Christian was up with something like that. But the whole pancake idea was his, and she just didn't want to take it and run with it and not let him have some piece of the action.

She set her horse at a pace as fast as he could go and still pull the carriage safely. Though she wanted to just race the horse like she was in her *rumspringa*, somehow she managed to control herself until she got all the way out to Christian Beachy's house.

She pulled to the front, hitched up her horse, and rushed up the stairs. She knocked on the door, hoping Christian answered and not Malinda. Of course now she realized that she hadn't seen him since the kiss. Well, church the following day didn't really count. She had seen him there but she hadn't talked to him. She hadn't been close to him. In fact, she kept as far away from him as she possibly could. And it seemed like he did the same. Like those science models of planets orbiting the sun she had seen once at a museum. Only worse because this involved a kiss.

"What is the matter?" Christian said as he flung the

door open. Okay, so she had been knocking rather loudly. This was exciting.

She pushed past him into the house.

"Come in," he said. He shut the door behind her.

"Christian. Forget everything else. Listen to me. We're going to win the whoopie pie competition."

"What? You and me. We're going to win the competition? We're not even registered."

"I'm registered. You're going to cook the pancakes, and I'm going to make the filling, and we're going to make the best breakfast whoopie pies this Valley has ever seen."

Chapter 15

The following afternoon, Hattie felt as if they had been working for days. They had truly been working for hours on end, that was sure, and still, she was no closer to the perfect combination of peach and maple in her buttercream frosting.

She kept adding ingredients. A little more maple syrup but too much and she had to add some more peach purée. Too much of that and more vanilla had to go in. A little more powdered sugar, a little more butter, and the process started all over again.

Now she had the largest mixing bowl that Christian and Malinda owned, almost full to the rim of still-not-perfect peach frosting.

But she was getting closer.

"Here, try this," she said, smearing frosting on another of the silver dollar pancakes Christian had been making all morning.

"You know, I liked to make pancakes before this," he grumbled.

"Stop complaining and eat it." Hattie shoved the makeshift whoopie pie in his direction, then waited, hands on her hips as he ate the newest effort.

"I can't tel—" He stopped. "That tastes good, Hattie."

"Just good?" It couldn't be just good. It had to be fantabulous. If they were going to win this competition— and they were going to win this competition—it had to be better than just *good*.

"It's incredibly delicious," Christian said. He watched her, waiting expectantly.

Hattie frowned at him, then took one of the little pancakes, tore off a small piece, and dipped it into the frosting mixture.

She put it in her mouth, rolling it around on her tongue to get all the flavors. It was good. But was it good enough? That was the thing. It had to be better than just good enough. It had to be good enough to win.

"Do you think it needs more peach?" She turned to get some more purée, only then realizing she had used all she had. She would have to make some more. In order to do that she would have to go to the store and buy some more frozen peaches, since there were none currently available from the trees.

"Where's my purse?" She really didn't want to run to the store, but what choice did she have? They couldn't leave it needing peaches. That would just be unacceptable. She started toward the front room of Christian's house hoping to find her purse.

Christian snagged her wrist in his warm grasp. "Hattie, it's good. We don't need any more peaches. What we need is a break."

She shook her head. A break would get them nowhere. "If we're going to win this competition, it has to be perfect."

"Is that what you need from me?" Christian asked. "To say it's perfect? It's perfect. Besides, you haven't even tried it with the other flavors. If we put pecans and bacon on top, that will adjust everything."

Hattie's eyes grew wide. "You're right. We need to fry up some bacon. Now."

Christian frowned, shook his head, and tugged on her arm until he got her out onto his back porch. "We're taking a break before we do anything. I haven't been in the kitchen this long since—" He stopped. "I've never been in the kitchen this long. You may not need a break, but I do."

Hattie relented. How could she not? Everything could wait ten or fifteen minutes, she grudgingly supposed.

She plopped down on the back porch steps and surveyed Christian's impressive backyard. Three large greenhouses took up most of the space. Hattie knew he owned the property on both sides of the house. On one side was a crop of fruit trees and pecan trees, while on the other, the delicious vegetables he grew. There was also a goodly sized shed where she supposed he kept all his farming tools and equipment. But to one side she thought she saw . . . "Is that a bicycle?"

Christian eased down beside her on the steps. "*Jah.*"

She turned to him in surprise. "Christian Beachy. You rebel, you."

"I'm not rebelling. Zebadiah said that bicycles would now be allowed in the district."

"*Jah*, but that was like four days ago, and you've already got a bicycle?"

He at least had the decency to color a bit. "I may have known that he was going to make that decision beforehand. And I may have bought the bicycle at a garage sale during that time."

"Why would you go and buy something like that? You

can't even ride the thing." She drew back in further surprise. "Can you? Can you ride it?"

He nodded. "*Jah*, I can ride it."

Would the surprises stop coming? "When did you learn to ride a bicycle?"

He cleared his throat. "Maybe on my *rumspringa*?"

"'Maybe,' my foot. You are a rebel," she said.

"I am not a rebel. But it was allowed when I was running around so I did it."

"You know I heard that the reason they got rid of the bicycles to begin with was to keep Paradise Springs kids in Paradise Springs and not going over into Paradise Hill and falling in love while they were running around."

"That doesn't make any sense," Christian said. "If you could ride a bike on *rumspringa* you can get to Paradise Hill."

"I guess I hadn't thought of that," Hattie said.

"I guess the leaders saw all the people on bicycles that can ride across the country and figured some Amish might get industrious and try it too."

"Or maybe it just fell victim to the no rubber tires?" Hattie knew that a lot of districts didn't allow rubber tires, no exceptions, which tossed bicycles out of the mix for travel as well as recreation. But then she also heard of several districts that allowed tractors! And not just the kind with metal wheels. Real tractors just like the *Englisch* had.

"I'm guessing you don't know how to ride a bike?" Christian said.

Hattie shook her head. "Unlike you, I was a good girl during my *rumspringa*."

"Of course you were," he said. His words held no

teasing, so why did she feel like he was ribbing her? "You want to learn how to ride it?"

"Are you kidding?" He went around frowning all the time and she couldn't tell if he was joking with her or not.

"No. I'm not kidding. I'm offering to teach you how to ride a bike."

She still couldn't shake the feeling that he was somehow poking fun. "I don't know for certain that you can ride it," she said. "So I would like to see you demonstrate before I agree to any lessons."

Christian pushed himself to his feet, dusting off the back of his pants and heading over toward the shed where the bicycle waited.

It wasn't one of those sleek models with the curved handlebars that looked like rams' horns and had the skinny, skinny tires. This one had a more old-fashioned look, with fat tires and something akin to a fender curving over them. It was chunkier, sturdier, and a beautiful shade of blue.

She watched in awe as Christian rolled the bike toward the hardpacked space just in front of the greenhouses. He threw his leg over the bike and before she knew it, he was zipping back and forth in front of her.

"Satisfied now?"

She laughed as she watched him. How glorious! "Satisfied," she called in return.

"Then get over here." He motioned her over, then miraculously stopped the bike. He was still straddling it when she got there.

He swung his leg over and leaned the bike in her direction.

She looked at the handlebars and the seat and the wheels. She had never realized until that moment what a complicated mechanism a bicycle was. "I don't know where to put my hands."

"For starters, put them right here on this rubber part."

Hattie did as he instructed, and he released the bike into her grasp.

"Now swing your leg over."

She did as he told her, the skirt of her dress bunching up in the middle.

"Now remember, it's all about balance."

Her head swung in his direction. "Balance?" She was a chubby, middle-aged woman. How was she supposed to balance on this little metal contraption?

"Maybe this isn't such a good idea." She shook her head.

"So you're just going to give up?"

It was as if he knew exactly the right thing to say to kick in her competitive nature. "No," she countered. "I'm not going to just give up. I'm merely saying that I'm not sixteen anymore."

"Of course you're not. That doesn't mean you can't learn to ride a bike."

"Okay then." She exhaled slowly. She could do this.

"Now I'm going to hold onto the bike while you get up on it. I'll help you balance, but you have to pedal. Keep pedaling. You need the momentum to keep your balance, okay?"

"Momentum for balance. Keep pedaling. Got it." She put her feet on the pedals and hoisted herself up onto the seat while Christian held the bike.

"I'm going to walk with you. Here we go," he said as he moved her forward. "Start pedaling."

Her heart was thumping in excitement as the bike

moved underneath her. Even though Christian had ahold of the bike, she could still feel herself wobbling.

"Hold her steady," Christian said.

"Steady. Got it." But holding it steady was harder than it looked. When Christian had zipped back and forth on the bike, it had looked so easy. Was that why they said just like riding a bike? No, that was about remembering things.

"Hattie. Focus," Christian commanded.

"Focus," she repeated.

"Keep pedaling. The slower you go, the harder it is when you're first starting out," he told her.

"Pedal fast," she said.

"I'm going to let go now."

"No!"

He had been jogging beside her, keeping her upright as she had pedaled.

"*Jah*," he returned. "Get ready."

She wanted so badly to close her eyes. Her hands were getting sweaty on the handlebars and her heart had moved from thumping in her chest to beating rapidly in her throat. She was too old for this sort of thing.

"I'm not ready," she protested.

"Now or never," Christian said.

She wasn't sure the exact moment he let go of the bike, just that one minute she knew he was there and the next he was gone. And she was pedaling, still wobbling back and forth, but pedaling on her own. It was a thrilling thought, perhaps even more thrilling than driving the buggy for the first time. Except now that she was going, she really didn't know how to stop!

"Christian!" she called just before she fell.

* * *

"Hattie!"

Christian rushed across his backyard to where Hattie lay in a crumpled heap of bicycle and blue dress. "Are you okay?"

She pushed herself into a sitting position. "I don't think anything is . . . broken." She seemed to assess herself, then looked down at one knee. It was smeared with blood.

"Ouch," she murmured. "It stings."

Thank heavens that was all that had happened. Perhaps he'd been wrong to tease her about riding a bike. But it was so much fun and he had a feeling Hattie would love it just as much as he did. And then maybe they could go bike riding together and—

You're getting way ahead of yourself, old man.

And he was. It was just that he had sort of gotten used to spending time with Hattie. Once upon a time, he had thought her almost annoying. But now . . . now she seemed a little bit fun. Except when she was trying to perfect peach maple icing to go in between pancake whoopie pies. They had needed a break, and this had seemed like the perfect distraction.

"Come on," he said, straightening up and reaching a hand out to her. "Let's get your knee cleaned up."

She didn't protest, just allowed him to hoist her to her feet. Then she walked beside him silently as they headed into the house. He left his bike where it lay. He could get it later.

He instructed her to sit down at the kitchen table while he went to the bathroom to gather up some sort of antiseptic to clean her wound.

Wound. That seemed so dramatic. The cut. *Jah*, that seemed better. It wasn't like she was maimed in battle or anything.

"My goodness," Hattie exclaimed when she saw the armload of supplies he had gathered.

"Can't be too careful," he told her. "There's a flesh-eating virus and stuff going around."

"*Jah*, I know. But I don't think I need all that." She waved a hand toward the bundle he carried.

"Well, this is to clean it." He held up a squirt bottle of hydrogen peroxide. "And then we'll follow it up with this." He held up a bottle of spray alcohol. "Then we have antibiotic ointment, antibiotic cream, a roll of gauze, some adhesive tape, a couple of self-stick bandages, and—"

"Give me that," she said, pointing to the hydrogen peroxide. "And a Band-Aid. I'll be fine."

"Are you sure? It's still bleeding a bit."

"I'm fine," she returned. "Now give it here and give me a Band-Aid so I can get back out there."

"Out where?" he asked.

"On the bike, of course." She looked at him, a perplexed expression across her face. "One lesson isn't going to teach me how to ride that thing."

"And you want to get back on it?" He looked down at her knee. "Even after that?"

"Of course." She waved her hand in the general direction of her knee. "It's just a scratch. And I want to learn how to ride. That's sort of fun."

Christian nodded understandingly. "*Jah*," he said. "It is sort of fun."

Two hours later Hattie was laughing and winded, but she could finally ride a bike. In those two hours, she

scraped her other knee, along with one of her elbows, and
she was certain she would have a bruise the size of the
state of Missouri on her hip come morning. But she could
ride a bike.

"You got your bike at a garage sale, you say?" Hattie
asked him. She had to get one of those. It would be so
much easier to buzz around town on a bike instead of
walking. And she might even could make some shorter
trips that normally she would have to use the horse and
buggy for. *Jah*, she liked Zebadiah's decision to allow
bikes in their district.

But she really just wanted to go on a bike ride for fun.
She loved the feel of the wind on her face as it pushed her
prayer *kapp* strings behind her.

More than anything, she wanted to take that bike ride
with Christian. And why not? She and Christian were
friends. The silly wager was over and done; why couldn't
they remain friends?

There was no reason at all. So why didn't they? Why
wouldn't they?

"*Jah*, I got it in the garage sale. But I've heard that Karl
Lambert is going to start stocking some at the variety
store. Russ Campbell has some over at the hardware store
too. Most of those are for kids, but I'm sure he could order
one like this if you really want one."

Hattie nodded enthusiastically. "*Jah*," she said. "I want
one."

She might even buy Elsie one for Christmas.

"You're welcome to come out and ride this one anytime," Christian said.

Hattie wasn't sure who was more surprised, her or him.

"That would be . . . fun," she replied. Not quite knowing what else to say. Yes, it would be fun. But it would be
more fun to ride together. And yes, she would love to

come out and spend more time with Christian. He was a lot more fun than she had given him credit for.

He was looking at her, his expression intense. It was almost as if he wanted to say something more. Something to her. And she waited. She waited for him to say something. She held her breath, not wanting to miss even one word.

The screen door slammed at the back of the house, and they both jumped and turned. Malinda was standing on the back porch. "What are you doing out here?" she called to them.

"I'm teaching Hattie how to ride a bike."

Hattie propped her hands on her hips. That competitive nature just wouldn't go down. "I'm practically an expert now."

Malinda nodded. "Should I call an ambulance for standby?"

"Very funny," Hattie returned. "Come join us."

Malinda shook her head. "He tried to get me to do that when we were teenagers. I wouldn't do it then, and I'm not going to do it now."

"See what I'm up against?" Christian said.

Hattie wasn't sure how to take that so she just smiled. "The struggle is real."

"What about the mess in the kitchen?" Malinda called.

"The whoopie pies!" Hattie had forgotten all about it. How could it be that one minute it was the most important thing in the world and the next she had forgotten? That didn't make any sense at all.

"Sorry," she called to Malinda while Christian said, "We're coming now to clean it up."

"But—" Hattie laid a hand on Christian's arm to stop him from going into the house. "But we haven't perfected the icing yet."

"Hattie," he said. "It's fine."

She shook her head. "First we've got to cook the bacon."

And then they had to get the pecans and then they needed to make some more pancakes. . . .

Christian sighed. "I'll cook the pancakes and bacon," he said. "You clean up the icing mess. But no more experimenting until we get it all together, okay?"

Hattie nodded even though she wanted to experiment immediately. She wanted to run to the store and get those peaches she hadn't gotten before she got distracted by the bicycle. Fifteen minutes! Two and a half hours was more like it. Like they had time to waste.

But she did have fun.

"Okay," she reluctantly agreed. "No more experimenting. I'll clean up the mess. You cook the bacon and some more pancakes."

Christian nodded. "Good girl."

And she could only pray and hope that their recipe was ready in time for the competition on Saturday.

"What happened to you?" Elsie demanded the minute Hattie walked into the door. She looked down at herself. Her apron was covered in powdered sugar and smears of butter. She was certain there was some peach juice mixed in there as well. And then all the popping grease from the bacon they had fried after the bike riding lesson. So *jah*, she was a mess. But it had been a good day. A really good day.

"I told you, we're trying to get the recipe together," Hattie responded.

Elsie marched toward her, then turned her arm around

where Hattie could see the blood on her elbow. "That's the danger of cooking."

"Well, that wasn't from cooking," she started. "Christian taught me how to ride a bike."

"Land sakes! Are you kidding me? Please tell me that you are kidding me. This is all a joke. At your age? On a bike?"

"At my age? What's wrong with my age?" She was only ten years older than Elsie. Well actually nine and a half. But who was counting?

"Lucky you didn't break something."

Hattie shook her head. "You worry too much, Elsie."

"So you think God's going to protect you on a bicycle?" Elsie asked. "That's what helmets and elbow and knee pads are for. And I'm guessing you didn't have any of those."

Hattie was glad that her dress covered up her bruised and scabbed knees. *Jah*, she was a little bit of a mess. *Jah*, she had skinned places that she hadn't even seen in a long time. And *jah*, she was going to be sore tomorrow. But she had had a great time.

"I learned to ride a bike today, Elsie." Hattie crossed her arms and smiled, completely satisfied with herself. She had done something new. And she had enjoyed doing it. When was the last time she had done anything new?

"*Jah, jah, jah,* you learned to ride a bike."

"Zebadiah said we could have bikes. We could go riding together. It would be fun."

Elsie shook her head. "There's not enough prayer in the world."

"Seriously," Hattie said. She walked to the refrigerator and got out a pitcher of water. She poured herself a tall glass and one for Elsie as well. Hattie slid them both onto the table and eased down into her chair. "When is the last time you've done something new? Or even learned something new?" It had never even occurred to Hattie until now. She thought her life was completely full. She had everything she needed. She had friends, her cousin, her shop, the church, even the widows' group. Funny how one new thing comes in and all of a sudden you're young again.

No, that wasn't exactly right. She still felt her age. She still had aches and pains and creaks and everything else that came with being almost sixty years old. But doing something new made her feel young. Learning. It was sad that people stopped learning about things when they were young and didn't continue.

She had learned to drive a buggy one time. She had learned to roller skate once. She had learned to bowl once, and since then she hadn't done much. She made popcorn in different flavors, but this was something else entirely.

Elsie shook her head and slid into her seat across from Hattie. "I want you to be careful," her cousin said.

"I am being careful. Careful enough."

"Promise me that the next time you get on Christian's death bike that you wear a helmet, elbow pads, and knee pads. Maybe even shin guards like the soccer players wear."

Hattie shook her head and laughed. "That's not necessary. Now that I've learned how to ride, I'll be fine. And I can't wear a helmet with my prayer *kapp*," she pointed out. "Everything will be fine."

Elsie made a face. "You're going to make me gray before my time."

"Sure. You say that when it is your time, then you're

going to blame it on me. That's not fair at all," Hattie said, mimicking Elsie's face. "And you're so worried about this, I didn't even get to tell you about the whoopie pie we made."

Elsie shook her head. "I still can't believe you're not entering the red velvet into the competition."

Hattie made a face. "Are you sure you're okay with that? Me not entering the red velvet? It's just this idea is so different." She hadn't told anybody except for Christian, of course, and possibly Malinda knew. But Hattie was certain the town gossip had been sworn to secrecy. Thank goodness it was only a few more days before the competition started. Otherwise the whole county would know.

"Different enough to take on Sadie Yoder and Sylvie King?"

"*Jah*," Hattie said. And it was. She still would like to add a little more peach purée to the icing mixture that they made today, but Christian had told her it was perfect and they weren't going to worry about it anymore. Now they just had to wait until tomorrow to make the ones for the judges to eat.

Elsie sat back in her seat and studied her cousin closely.

Hattie shifted under that scrutiny. "What?"

Elsie shrugged. "I don't know. You just seem different."

"Different? Different how?"

"I don't know. Just different."

"Good different or bad different?"

"Good different, of course." But Elsie said the words a little too quickly. They rushed from her mouth so fast that they almost tripped over themselves. A sure sign they weren't the truth.

But Hattie didn't call her out on it. She felt different. Riding a bike was almost life-changing. Life-affirming. Learning something new. Maybe she should take a class or something to learn more, to keep her brain going. But unlike her cousin, she knew in her heart, the difference she felt, it was all for the good.

Chapter 16

They couldn't have asked for a better day to hold the Whoopie Pie Festival. To say the atmosphere was upbeat and positive would've been an understatement. *Festive* was the only way to describe it and what better attitude for a festival than a festive one?

The thought made Hattie smile. Yesterday all day long she had worked on the pancake whoopie pies. She and Christian had stayed side by side in his kitchen making the perfect pancake that would taste good even cold because the whoopie pies wouldn't be served warm like a pancake would. A little bit more sugar, a little less buttermilk, and they came up with the perfect recipe. Then Christian had made four dozen sets while Hattie began to perfect the filling.

It took several tries and a pound of bacon, but they finally got it right. Just the right amount of bacon, just the right amount of pecan, and just the right amount of maple syrup.

"I still think we should make it with apple," Christian had said, taking a bite to sample.

"Save that idea for next year," she had told him. "Maybe we could make almond flour pancakes or oat pancakes." She shook her head. It was not a good time for her creative brain to finally kick in. "This is our idea for now. This is what we're sticking with. Stop coming up with variations."

He had shaken his head at her then. "You stop coming up with variations."

"Fair enough." Hattie had smiled at him and, surprise surprise, he had smiled back.

It wasn't a smile like other people had, big, showing teeth, laughing, mouth open. It was just a small curve of the lips. But it was a smile all the same. And it had warmed Hattie from the inside out.

Then Christian picked up another of the samples and tasted it. "We're going to win this thing," he said in awe.

Hattie had laughed then. She couldn't stop it. "I just think we might."

"Have mercy," Christian had said. "What's that going to do to Sylvie King?"

But Hattie didn't have an answer for that then. She didn't have an answer for that now. As everyone was buzzing around wondering exactly who had entered what in the competition.

Everyone at the Whoopie Pie Widows' Club thought Hattie had entered the red velvet cake recipe. No one knew that she had developed this new idea with Christian Beachy. Not even Elsie. Hattie had told her that she and Christian were working on something special, but she hadn't told her what. She hadn't wanted to share that information with her cousin. That was just for her and Christian. And if they didn't win, they sure had had a lot of fun.

She had finally managed to get him to smile. Not that there was a bet going on any longer. Nor had anyone been around to see it. Now it was just all about being happy. She knew that Christian was happy, and she was happy. And who knew where it would go from there? She could worry about that later. Right now there was a Whoopie Pie baking competition to win.

As usual there was a parade with the high school band marching around and playing the school's fight song along with other songs that Hattie didn't recognize.

Sammie Franklin, the mayor, always dressed up in an outfit from the 1900s—*the* early *1900s*, Hattie thought—with a monocle and striped pants and those white things to cover her shoes. To Hattie, and most of everyone, she supposed, the mayor looked like the little guy on the Monopoly board. Not that Hattie played Monopoly much. She was just too competitive to enjoy a game like that. It was a strange way for a woman to go around dressed, even on such a special occasion, but Hattie supposed to each their own.

The downside of the day was that Christian was stuck behind the booth selling tickets to the ice cream social that was supposed to happen in a couple of weeks. She would've loved to have walked around with him regardless of any stares or questions or whispers behind their back that they might have gotten. She would love to be standing by him now as the judges were coming out to announce the winner.

She looked over and saw Sylvie standing with Millie, Henry, and Vern. Of course, Millie had Linda Beth on one hip. The pair were wearing matching peach-colored dresses.

Suddenly Hattie felt just a little bit bad for Sylvie. Hattie sort of wished that she hadn't entered the competition at all. It meant so much to Sylvie to win and it really didn't mean anything to Hattie but another notch on her belt for something she could say that she had conquered. She wanted to withdraw immediately. But it wasn't just her whoopie pie entry; it belonged to Christian too.

Sylvie glanced at something on the other side of Hattie. She turned as well and noticed Sadie Yoder standing on the far side of the crowd. She was tall and almost regal waiting there, in a beautiful teal-colored dress that made Hattie wish she'd gone into her shop and bought some new material for a new *frack* to wear today.

Sadie must've felt their gaze for she turned and gave them *both* a small wave. Hattie waved back not knowing whether Sylvie did the same or not. When she turned back around, Sylvie was facing toward the front once more, waiting for the winner to be announced.

"Now I know this is what you've all been waiting for." Sammie Franklin held up an envelope in one hand. "I have here the judges' tally for this year's whoopie pie baking competition."

Hattie knew she was dragging out each word on purpose, trying to prolong the suspense before announcing the winner.

"Are you guys ready to hear who won?"

"Yes!" the crowd cried in unison.

"Okay." Sammie looked up from the paper with wide, almost comical eyes. "There's a note here from the judges. Let me see . . ." Again with the prolonging of the suspense. Truthfully Hattie about had enough of it. Her heart was beating so quickly in her chest, and her mouth had gone dry.

She wanted to win. But she also wanted Sadie to win, to get the crown back for one more year. Hattie wanted Sylvie to win because Sylvie lived for it. It was a very confusing day for a nice and empathetic competitive person.

"After the tough competition we had last year, the judges decided to add a new prize to the contest. There is one First Place and an Honorable Mention. The Honorable Mention can be for creativity, taste, or even presentation. This year that award goes to Hattie Schrock and Christian Beachy! You girls come on up here."

The Amish in the crowd laughed. They all knew that Christian was a male.

Hattie couldn't believe it. They got an Honorable Mention? They got an Honorable Mention! How she wished Christian could be there with her!

"Go on," Elsie nudged her, setting Hattie's feet into motion.

Hattie rushed up to the stage and stood next to the mayor. It was very uncomfortable with everybody's eyes on her. For once she wished she hadn't won anything at all. She would much rather be back down there, lost in the crowd.

"The judges said you presented them with the most unusual and delicious whoopie pie they have ever seen, made with pancakes, maple syrup, and bacon."

Hattie leaned over toward the microphone. "And peaches."

Sammie Franklin laughed. "And peaches. Don't forget those. Here's your trophy and your check for a hundred and fifty dollars. We appreciate your entering the contest this year with such a creative creation."

Hattie nodded, then not knowing what else to do, she took a step back.

"And this year's winner is . . . Sylvie King."

Everyone cheered as Sylvie, who had turned red as a

Valentine, made her way through the crowd and up onto the stage.

"Now, Sylvie, you had a very unique whoopie pie as well. Can you tell us what kind of cake you used?"

"No cake," Sylvie said. "They were baked beignets, with cream cheese and raspberry filling."

"What an interesting concept," Sammie Franklin said. "And very creative of you as well."

"*Danki*," Sylvie replied.

"Here's your check for three hundred dollars and the trophy for winning this year's Whoopie Pie baking competition." She turned her attention to the crowd. "We hope everyone has a wonderful rest of the evening. Don't forget your tickets to the ice cream social, and if you see some trash, pick it up. That's all. Thank you."

Sylvie shot Hattie a look. "Pancakes?"

Hattie smiled. "Beignets?"

"Vern's addicted to them. I figured if he liked them so much, there might be something to it."

"I'd sure like to try one," Hattie told her.

"There's none left at the tasting table," Sylvie said. "But I'll make sure you get some of the next batch. Maybe I'll even make some for the widows' meeting. But only if you bring some of your pancake ones."

"That's a deal," Hattie said.

Together the women walked down the steps where they were met by Sadie Yoder. She was really a striking woman, tall with dark hair and, like Katie said, she had to have been fifty years old if she was a day. But she carried her age well. Or maybe it was just her stature. Shoulders thrown back and a prideful look that somehow didn't seem too prideful. Just prideful enough.

"Congratulations, ladies," Sadie said.

She gave them each a bright green flyer with the name of her fabric store across the top.

"Bring this in and I'll give you twenty-five percent off your first purchase."

"*Danki*," Sylvie and Hattie said together.

"I hope to see you there," Sadie said. Then she gave them a quick nod and blended back into the crowd.

"Was that weird or was it just me?"

Hattie shrugged. "I don't know what to think anymore. I just won a hundred and fifty dollars."

"You need to go tell Christian about that before someone else spills the beans."

Hattie's eyes got wide. "Of course I do." Christian! She had almost forgotten.

She all but ran over to the booth where he was selling tickets for the ice cream social.

"Christian," she hollered as she got close. "Look! We won an Honorable Mention."

She didn't even think about it once, much less twice. She launched herself at him in her excitement, knocking his hat sideways with the little trophy. Luckily he caught her.

It was amazing having him hold her, and thrilling and . . . wrong.

She pulled away from him and smoothed her hands over herself. She had lost control and forgotten herself for a moment. Forgot that she and Christian were no more than partners in a contest. Maybe . . . *maybe* they could call themselves friends, but that was pushing it at best.

Yet she felt like more than his friend.

And he had kissed her. Surely that counted for something.

Or maybe not. . . .

If he felt the same—or anything at all—she couldn't see it in his expression. He was frowning at her as if she had just told him his popcorn was going to cost double the normal amount.

"Honorable Mention? Isn't that like fourth place or something?" His frown deepened.

Hattie pulled her thoughts back to where they needed to be. She had brought this on herself. And she would get through it. "First of all, wipe that frown off your face. There was only First Place. So this Honorable Mention? It's kind of like second place."

"I was hoping we would win," he said.

Somehow this seemed better than winning to Hattie. Sylvie got the win, and Hattie and Christian were acknowledged for their creativity. They couldn't get much better than that.

"We won a hundred and fifty dollars."

That smile toyed with the corners of his mouth once again. "Sweet," he said, and it sure was.

Chapter 17

"What are you doing in here?" Christian startled as Malinda came in the dining room behind him.

Since he had more room in his house, Hattie told him he should take the trophy home. Plus, she had said, the whole idea of substituting pancakes for the cake was his idea. He protested a bit but finally relented. Now he found himself going to the dining room just to look at the trophy. Just thinking about it made him smile.

See? He smiled.

He was smiling a lot these days. And it was all because of Hattie Schrock.

They truly were a team. Yes, he might've come up with the pancake part, but the filling was all hers. Winning the whoopie pie baking competition was a great surprise, but it was definitely something they had done together. Looking back, those might've been the best two days of his life as they developed the perfect filling to go inside his perfect pancakes. Of course they adjusted that recipe as well to make it more palatable as a dessert, but still it was all breakfast. And in his head, he was coming up with variation upon variation. What about a dash of cinnamon? What if they'd added a little more vanilla? He had never been one to cook much before, but now it seemed to be all he could think about.

"You're supposed to be resting today." Malinda shot him a look and walked on through to the kitchen. *Jah*, it was their off church Sunday. It was supposed to be a day of rest and reflection. Well, he was reflecting. Reflecting on how they had won yesterday and how Hattie had thrown herself into his arms and how he had hugged her tight for just a moment before realizing that he needed to let her go. It was not appropriate, not okay, and not something they needed to be doing anywhere, much less in public. But there for a moment, he wanted to hold her forever.

Forever? His knees grew weak, and he found himself sinking into one of the dining chairs. Forever moved toward . . . love.

It took a second for him to catch his breath. It took a moment for him to realize that his thoughts were indeed the truth. And it took a full minute for him to accept. He was in love with Hattie Schrock.

He mulled the words over and around in his head, almost said them out loud just to see what they would sound like. Somehow he managed to control his tongue. He wouldn't want Malinda knowing too much too soon. He hadn't even told Hattie yet. Shouldn't she be the first to know? The first to know that he had done the impossible and fallen in love again. And he had fallen in love with her. And her bright smile and her nearly nauseating positivity, and her spunk and her bravery, and all the other little facets that made her who she was.

There was a part of him that wanted to keep all that to himself, all her good qualities, all her sweet qualities, everything about her. He wanted to keep it to himself and hold it close as if somehow that would make everything work out. Then there was a part of him that wanted to run through the streets, shouting her name, telling everyone how wonderful he thought she was. It was like being sixteen all over again and falling in love with Elizabeth.

"Are you going to sit here all day and just look at the trophy?" Malinda pushed her way back from the kitchen into the dining room.

"No." He said the word, but it was weak at best.

"It's a beautiful day. You should get outside."

And he would. He still had to go and water the plants in the far greenhouse. But for now he just wanted to sit and kind of settle into this new idea. This idea of being in love once more.

"Are you okay?" Malinda marched toward him and placed the palm of her hand on his forehead. "You don't feel feverish."

He pushed her hand away. "I'm not feverish."

She propped her hands on her hips and twisted her mouth into that look she got when she didn't believe him. "Something's wrong with you. Sitting around in here moping."

He scowled. "I'm not moping. I was simply thinking about yesterday and—" He couldn't tell her what he was really thinking about. He couldn't tell her how thrilled he had been to hold Hattie for just a moment in time. And she really didn't need to know that he figured out that he loved her. *Her* being Hattie, that was. But he supposed if things were about to change in their household, that he needed to tell Malinda sometime.

He cleared his throat. "What if I told you that I'm in love?"

"So you admit it?" She grinned at him. "I was wondering how long it would take."

He frowned. "You were wondering?" He shook his head. "I didn't even tell you who I am in love with."

"You don't need to. Everybody in town knows that you and Hattie Schrock have fallen for each other."

Were they really that obvious?

Surely not. It was just his sister had a hard eye on everything, all the time. She knew when most people in town changed their shoelaces. He should have expected that she would figure out that he had fallen for Hattie Schrock.

"I think . . . I think I'm going to ask her to marry me." He hadn't meant to even say those words. They hadn't come to him first so he could weigh them out. It was just one minute he was talking to Malinda and the next minute he was telling her that he was going to marry Hattie. The thought settled around him like a warm blanket in the wintertime. He would marry Hattie Schrock. The rest they could work out later. Where they would live. What they would do. What would become of Malinda. All of that could be figured out later. Just for now he was going to marry Hattie.

The thought of not spending the rest of his life with her . . . He couldn't stand it. He wanted to spend every minute from here to eternity with her. And he wanted to get started now.

He stood. "I need to go talk to her," he said. He would hitch up the buggy and head into town. He didn't think there was anything in the *Ordnung* about asking someone to marry you on Sunday. And people went visiting all the time on Sunday, so it was no problem for him to hop into his buggy and head into town to see her. It was just that somehow it didn't seem quite right to bust in on a Sunday and hit her with all this news. They had once talked about the future, but not about love. And they had talked about the fact that she didn't want to get married again.

He shook his head. "I'll just have to talk her out of it."

Malinda stared at him as if he had grown another head. "What are you talking about?"

"Hattie," he started. "She said she didn't want to get married again. I'll just have to talk her out of that." Because he was planning on marrying Hattie Schrock.

They were perfect for each other. Absolutely perfect. It was amazing to him that a person walked around with someone who was potentially the love of their life, or even the second love of their life. How they could walk around with them for years and not realize it until one day . . . Bam! You were in love.

Malinda smiled, her eyes filling with tears. "I think that's beautiful."

"I'll be back later," he said.

He looked down at himself. He wasn't certain, but that looked like a mustard stain on his shirt. He couldn't ask Hattie to marry him with a mustard stain on his shirt. He'd have to change. And the bottom of his pants were dusty from going out and watering this morning. He was wearing chore clothes. He couldn't ask someone like Hattie to marry him when he was in his chore clothes.

"I need to change," he said, and he headed up the stairs.

Malinda was right behind him. "I'm so happy for you," Malinda said.

Christian stopped midway up the staircase and turned toward his sister, a grin on his face like he'd never felt before. "Me too," he said. Who knew at his age that he would find love again?

He headed on up the stairs and into his room. Then he closed the door firmly behind him. There were times when boundaries definitely had to be set with Malinda. This was one of those times. He could hear her outside his door as he rustled through his closet to find a clean shirt and clean pants. He wished he had a minute to brush off his shoes. Maybe he would stop at the kitchen sink before heading out.

"I think it could be so amazing. The stories you are going to get to tell your grandkids. Though I guess it's a little sad that you won't have grandkids together but . . . whatever." He could almost imagine Malinda waving a hand in the air as if dismissing what she had just said.

Christian finally found a suitable shirt and a clean pair of pants. He ran a comb through his hair, not allowing himself to look too closely at the gray. He was going to ask Hattie Schrock to marry him. It was perfect. He couldn't think of anything he wanted more from life than to join his life with hers. They could work out all the details later, but he just had to know that she loved him as well.

He opened the door to his bedroom and rushed back down the stairs, Malinda right on his heels. "It's just going to be so much fun to tell everybody how the two of you came together because of the bet."

He was just about to put his hat on his head. Then her words sunk in. "The bet?" What was she talking about?

He almost discounted it as Malinda just being Malinda. But she did know what was going on in the community. Probably better than even the bishop did.

"*Jah*," she said. "Hattie and Elsie's bet. And if it hadn't've been for it, you two might not be together now."

He could feel the joy slowly seeping out of him. He mentally tried to gather it back. Somehow he knew this was not going to turn out well.

"What bet?"

Malinda paled, and he figured she had just realized that she had said too much. "You don't know about the bet?"

He pressed his lips together and breathed out his nose, feeling a little like a bull snorting. "What bet?"

"Now, Christian," Malinda started. "Maybe I shouldn't have said anything."

He twirled his hat in his hand. "Maybe you shouldn't have," he said. "But you did. So tell me . . . what bet?"

Malinda took a deep, fortifying breath. "It seems that Elsie and Hattie had a bet that she . . . Hattie . . . couldn't bring a smile to your face. Something about having you be more positive in your life."

"Elsie and Hattie?" It was almost a question. "So Hattie had to come to me?" *Please say no. Please say no.*

Malinda shook her head. "All I know is that they had a bet and Hattie had to make your life more positive some way."

"And if she won?" He was trembling with an emotion he couldn't name. Rage? Disappointment? Self-loathing?

"Something about cleaning up the shop. And those copper vats they have. I don't know for certain."

"How do you know this?" he asked. He didn't want the answer. And yet he did. He wanted her to tell him something bizarre so that he could discount it all.

"I just know what Katie told me."

"Katie Hostetler?" he asked. Katie was no-nonsense. She wasn't one to gossip. So if she had told this to Malinda . . .

"You can't tell her that I told you this. She made me promise to keep quiet, but then when you were talking about being in love—" She broke off, shaking her head. "I don't want Katie mad at me. Or Hattie. Or Elsie."

Christian hung his hat back on the wall. "They're not

going to be mad at you," he said. The dejection had set in. Hattie hadn't cared about him. She had only been trying to win some kind of cleanup bet with her cousin. She hadn't come to him and ask him to the Sadie Hawkins Whoopie Pie thing because she wanted to spend time with him. She had been trying to get him to smile.

He thought about all the times that she had asked him why he didn't smile. All the times she told him so sweetly, so candidly, that the people in the community thought he was grumpy. That she knew he had a bigger heart than that. All those times he had believed her. She had played him through and through, trying to get him to believe something about himself that perhaps wasn't true. And all because she didn't want to clean the copper vats at the popcorn shop? It was incorrigible. Unbelievable that someone would do another human being that way.

He walked over to the staircase and sat on the third step up. He braced his elbows on his knees and put his head in his hands.

"Christian?" Malinda started hesitantly. "Are you not going into town?"

He shook his head without lifting it. Without meeting his sister's gaze.

"What I said," Malinda began, "don't let that . . ." She trailed off then, obviously to find her footing once more. "Don't let that change your mind about her."

It didn't just change his mind about Hattie. It changed everything. She was not who he thought she was. First of all, making a wager. Even if it didn't involve money, it didn't seem like something the bishop's nieces should be engaging in. But even putting that aside, manipulating someone's life. Pushing her way in and making him fall in love with her. It was just . . . He didn't even know the word. It was more than he could express.

But there was one thing he knew without a doubt. His heart was broken. He wanted to go into his room and crawl on his bed and just lay there for a bit, try and get himself back together. But he was a man. He couldn't engage in that kind of behavior. The plants in the far greenhouse needed to be watered once more, and he should go and check on the corn. He'd seen some deer roaming around. Sometimes they were bad about digging up the seeds and eating them before they even had a chance to sprout.

He pushed himself to his feet.

"Are you going to see Hattie then?" Malinda said.

"No." Christian grabbed his hat off the hook by the door and started outside. "Christian," Malinda called after him. "You should go talk to her. Find out all of the story. Not just what I'm telling you."

Christian turned and could feel the sad droop in his face from the heartbreak that was coursing through him. "One thing I know from being your brother, Malinda. You know everything that goes on in this district. And I've known you my entire life. Why should I believe anyone else?"

He had been in love before. He had lost love before. So he was in love and losing love once more. It wasn't anything new, just another lost love in his life. At least that's what he told himself all through the night. He slept fitfully, waking up too many times thinking about Hattie, wanting to talk to her, knowing it would do no good. Too much damage had already been done.

Malinda did know practically everything that went on in their district. If she said Hattie and Elsie had made a wager, then chances were Hattie and Elsie had made a wager. Even if Hattie told him no now, there would still be a big cloud of doubt hovering over him. He didn't think it would ever go away. How could he marry someone with a cloud of doubt between them? It just was not going to work. As much as he wanted it to and as much as he re-arranged it in his thoughts, in his mind, and in his dreams, the fact remained that he couldn't rewrite this. Heartbreak was heartbreak, and it always would be.

But after getting up in the morning, scrubbing his face and splashing cold water on his cheeks, after eating break-fast and finishing up the morning chores, he knew what he had to do.

He found Malinda in the kitchen, reorganizing her can-ning jars.

"I'm going into town. Do you need anything?" It was a question he had asked her countless times over the years. But when she turned around and looked at him, it was as if his sister knew. Maybe it was because he was wearing the same clothes he'd been wearing last night. But he was only wearing them now because he put them on last night. Or at least that's what he told himself.

"Christian," Malinda breathed. There was so much weight in his name. That one word heavy with things unsaid.

"Nothing?" he asked. "Anything?"

Malinda rinsed her hands and wiped them on a dish towel. "You're going in to talk to her."

No sense avoiding the truth. It was certain to get back around to Malinda sooner or later. And knowing Malinda, most likely sooner.

"*Jah*," he said.

"Christian, I'm sorry."

"You have nothing to apologize for."

Even if she did, she had apologized countless times last night, calling through the door like she had when they were children. "But if I hadn't said anything—"

He shook his head. "I'm glad you did." He was glad his sister had told him the truth. He was glad that it came out when it did and not a couple of years down the road when he and Hattie had merged their lives.

"Are you going to talk to her? Work things out?"

He didn't know about all that. But he had to hear her say it. He trusted Malinda explicitly. She was his sister. And they were closer than most brothers and sisters, he felt. Especially in large Amish families were there might be ten or twelve children running around. It was just he and Malinda and their younger brother David. They seemed closer than most. But he had to hear Hattie say it. He needed her to admit this deception so he could start to move on. It was all he wanted. Then the rest would just have to come with time. And in time he knew that he wouldn't be so excited to see her every chance he got. His heart wouldn't beat a little faster. He wouldn't look for her in the crowd. In time, he would forget that he loved her. And right now that was all he could ask for.

The trip into town seemed to take forever. He wanted to slow the horse. He wanted to speed him up. He wanted . . . something. He wanted to not feel this way.

Hearing Hattie say that she had deceived him would not make him feel any different. In fact, he was preparing himself for it to make him feel worse.

He waved to a few people he passed in town. Vern was out on the porch of the B&B watering the flowers that added charm to the old house.

All too soon Christian was at the popcorn shop. He

parked around the side where it was easier to leave his horse and carriage and made his way into the small shop. There was the customary bell over the door that told everyone that he was there. The inside of the shop smelled sweet and salty and of popcorn all at the same time. His stomach rumbled a bit thinking it was about to get a treat. But his heart knew different.

A couple of people were looking at bags of premade popcorn in varying flavors. A young Amish girl was at the counter and he could see Elsie behind, stirring something in one of those large copper vats. He figured it was some sort of candy to coat the crunchy popcorn with. The girl behind the counter, she looked familiar. He thought she was a Yoder, but he didn't have any kids running around now and she was a bit younger than his brood.

He got in line behind two people at the cash register. He just wanted to talk to Hattie. Just for a minute. He had to hear her say it.

The girl rang up the first customer as Christian shifted uncomfortably. The next customer wasn't so easily taken care of, and before long Elsie was over at the register. She called back to Hattie. She turned and smiled at Christian.

Hattie bustled out of the back, wiping her hands on a dish towel. "What is it now?" she asked. She hadn't seen him standing there.

Elsie waved her away from the cash register and pointed to Christian.

Her eyes lit up as she saw him. But he knew that was his own false hope. She might be happy to see him, but she wasn't going to be happy to see him. Not if what Malinda had said was true.

He wanted to doubt his sister now that he was looking at Hattie and her sweet face and her loving eyes and her spunky dimples. She just didn't look the part of someone who would deceive another person that maliciously.

"Christian," she breathed his name like a prayer.

His heart skipped a beat. He had to remain strong. This wasn't the time for caving in and allowing his emotions to take over. He cleared his throat, crinkled his eyebrows into what he hoped was a convincing frown. "Can I talk to you for a moment?"

She seemed to sense the seriousness of his attitude. Her smile fell, the corners of her mouth drooping. "*Jah*. Sure."

She turned to Elsie.

Her cousin nodded. "Go on. I've got this."

Hattie walked them over to a display of varying name-brand candy mixed with popcorn. But this wasn't private enough. People were still milling around. Some not paying them any mind. Mostly the *Englischers*. But the Amish were craning their necks to see what was going on between the two of them.

"Maybe outside?" he asked.

Her expression seemed to grow darker. Sadder. "Sure." She pushed out of the popcorn shop and onto the warm street. There was a bench at the corner of her shop attached to one of the old-fashioned light poles that dotted Main Street. It sat back off the road just a bit and had a planter filled with petunias on one side. The flowers were bright and colorful—red, hot pink, purple—and the exact opposite of how he felt in that moment.

"Why do I get the impression that something's wrong?" she asked.

He couldn't answer that.

She settled down on the bench, but he couldn't sit next to her. He couldn't be that close to her and say what needed to be said. So he hovered above her doing everything in his power to keep his tone even and less accusing than he wanted to sound. "Did you make a bet with Elsie about making my life more positive or something like that?"

She just stared at him. Then she swallowed hard.

"Hattie?" he said when she didn't speak. "Answer me."

It started in her toes and her fingertips and worked its way up her arms and her legs until it went to her very core. A tingling feeling that seemed to paralyze her as she searched her thoughts for the right thing to say back to him. *Jah*, he normally scowled, and *jah*, he normally looked generally unhappy. But this was different, this look on his face now. This was true emotion and not a neglect of smiling. He really was upset. He really was on his way to anger. She needed to say something, anything to him to wipe that look away. But what could she say other than the truth? And she had to tell him the truth.

"It's not what it sounds like," she said. Her voice broke on the end. It was exactly what it sounded like. She had manipulated him, she had pilfered in his life, she had played with his emotions. And it was wrong from the word go. She had only been thinking about herself. She had only been thinking about how it would affect her life if she got Christian to be more positive. How it would affect Elsie if she had gotten Christian to be more positive. But she hadn't thought about what it would do to Christian if he ever found out the truth, and the truth was that she and Elsie had made a bet.

"I think it's exactly what I think it is."

She stood and swayed a bit. Her toes still a little numb. She needed to say the right thing, but she couldn't grab the words from her brain. Everything was just swirling around inside her head like it was caught up in a tornado. She had to say the right thing. Because if she said the wrong thing she might alienate him forever. "I just wanted you to smile. I just wanted to know that you were happy."

"What gave you the right to play in my life?" he asked.

"I'm sorry." It was all she could say. She was sorry that she hadn't thought this whole thing through. She was sorry that she had let it go a long time ago when it looked like she wasn't going to even be able to get close to him. And then she found a way and she got close to him. She'd gotten so close to him that she had fallen completely, head over heels in love with him. But she should've led with that. Or rather she should've said that yesterday. Yet what Amish woman goes around declaring love for a man who hadn't confessed his love first? And why would he? It wasn't like they were dating. She had just been a fool and gotten her heart tangled up in a man who for the most part seemed misunderstood by the people around him.

"I know now that you're happy. And I'm glad that you are happy. And I didn't mean to—" Her voice broke completely down. She swallowed back a sob and tried to get herself together. If only she'd had some idea that he knew. Maybe then she could come up with something to say. But then she would've been manipulating him once more. That was the last thing that she wanted to do.

"I'm sorry," she said. "For the record, I didn't mean to hurt you."

With nothing more left to say, she turned and bustled back into the popcorn shop.

She hadn't meant to hurt him.
It was all he could think about on the way home.
She hadn't meant to. But she had.

He had acted like an idiot. Had he not seen this coming? She practically told him. Sitting at the picnic table telling him how everyone thought he was grumpy. How he should smile more. It just all fell into Malinda telling him basically the same thing. What were the chances of that happening? He had no idea, but it had happened. It had led him to believe that maybe she was something different. Maybe she truly did care about him.

He was glad old Jefferson knew the way home. He couldn't pay attention to the road and what was going past him. Everything was on automatic.

Malinda rushed out onto the porch the minute he pulled the carriage close to the house.

"Christian," she called, her voice full of questions.

He shook his head, unable to answer anything. He still hadn't gotten his mind completely around everything that had happened. Hattie had deceived him. She had tricked him. She had made the bet and played with his emotions. It was more than he could take in at one time, and he couldn't talk about it until he absorbed it. Until he came to terms with it on his own. Until he could accept it as the complete truth.

He knew it was the truth, he thought as he unhitched Jefferson and led him to the barn. Now he just needed to *know* that it was the truth.

"Christian?" Malinda called tentatively behind him. He raised one hand in an indeterminate gesture but didn't turn around as he led the horse into the barn.

She had known about the bet. A part of him wanted to be angry with her for waiting this long to tell him. If he hadn't said that he was going to ask Hattie to marry him, would Malinda have ever told him about the bet?

No. He couldn't allow his thoughts to go in that direction.

This was not Malinda's fault. It was his fault for believing Hattie. And Hattie's fault for lying to him.

But did she lie to you?

A lie of omission. A lie of deception. But she hadn't really lied to him. In truth, she had brought a lot of joy into his life. And in a time when he thought his life was growing stale. Perhaps he needed a change. He had been envious of Titus Troyer.

Well, this just showed you what envy would get you. It had left him open and ripe for the picking.

That's how he wanted to see Hattie. He wanted her to be manipulative and rude and a bunch of other bad things. But all he could remember was her telling him that she was sorry. That she hadn't meant to hurt him. But he wished he had stopped and asked her: If she didn't mean to hurt him, what did she expect the outcome to be?

He gave Jefferson a scoop of feed in his feed box. Then Christian grabbed the brush and began to smooth his shiny chestnut coat. He had work to do and the horse would be fine without such grooming at the moment, but he couldn't stop himself. It was as if he needed to take care of another the way he hadn't been taken care of himself.

"Christian?" Malinda had followed him into the barn.

"It's okay," he told her. It was far from okay. But it would be okay, he thought as he continued to brush the horse. It was no different than when Elizabeth died. In fact it wasn't even that bad. He and Hattie didn't have children together. They hadn't built a life over years.

It had just been a couple of weeks that he'd been hanging out with Hattie. It wouldn't take long for him to get over her. He just had to remember that the world kept turning even when a heart was broken. He had learned that lesson long ago. All you had to do was keep putting one foot in front of the other. Just keep waking up in the morning and going to bed at night and going through the motions during the day. Eventually the pain would dull until it didn't take your breath away. Because regardless of his broken heart, life went on.

Chapter 18

Hattie paused for a moment before opening the door to the popcorn shop. The door was glass and the front of the store all windows. It wasn't like they couldn't see her stop there and take a breath and try to gather herself. And they were watching. Most everyone in the shop was watching to see what happened between her and Christian. *Jah*, they were trying to be subtle about it. But she knew they had been watching. And they would watch her still.

She blinked back tears and opened the door. The bell rang its cheery warning. Everything in the shop was cheery. Red and white stripes with shiny chrome, bright lights, colorful popcorn flavors, even the red aprons that she and the other workers wore over their dresses and outfits. Everything about the place was cheery. And she gave a tremulous smile and hoped it matched.

"Is everything okay?" Elsie asked. She followed behind Hattie who smiled all the way to the back room. That's where she had been reorganizing their supplies before Christian had arrived.

"*Jah*. Of course. What could be wrong?"

"Well, he looked a little angry when he got here," Elsie said, still hovering at the door of the back room.

Hattie waved away her concern. "He always looks like a thundercloud." And that was the truth. But she hadn't seen him that way lately. She had started to not see his dark expression and see the thoughtfulness underneath.

"Okay. I'll bite. He looked a little more like a thundercloud than normal. Like a tornado cloud wall."

"Everything's fine," Hattie said. She picked up her clipboard, adjusted her glasses, and went back to her count.

She couldn't concentrate on anything, but she had to pretend. She had been stupid stupid stupid. And as a result her heart was broken. The bad part—the worst part of it all—was she couldn't blame anyone but herself. She didn't have to take Elsie's bet. She didn't have to join in the wager. She didn't have to invite Christian to the Sadie Hawkins whoopie pie benefit for Barbie Troyer. She didn't have to do any of those things. And yet she had to prove her point with Elsie. She just had to be right about it. About why Christian Beachy didn't smile. About bringing positivity to his life. She'd had to be right and now her heart was broken.

"If you guys didn't have a disagreement," Elsie started, "what happened?"

Hattie looked up from her clipboard, her smile firmly in place. Her cheeks felt as if they were molded plastic, and they were to be stuck in that position for a long time to come. Well, no matter. People would think that everything was fine with her if she just kept smiling. It was amazing how expressions could be so misread. It was amazing to her that everyone thought that Christian was unhappy and cantankerous and angry all the time when he was just thoughtful and his face had turned into a frown. She was smiling now even though her heart was broken. She was crying inside. She was unhappy and sad and remorseful and a dozen other negative emotions that just swirled around and pecked at her like mean birds. No, you really didn't know how a person was feeling. Not truly, deeply on the inside.

"Everything's fine," Hattie said, her voice as upbeat as she could make it. She would get through this. The best thing to do was to just keep believing. That everything was fine. That life was good. That God was good. Because all of that was true. It was her right now. Just her stupidity and her broken heart and her competitive nature. But she would get through.

"If you're certain." Elsie didn't sound like she wanted to leave. Her voice held a note that made Hattie think she wanted to keep prying and digging until she got to the truth. But Hattie's smile remained firm. "It's nothing."

"Okay," Elsie said, and finally retreated. But Hattie left that smile in place. She was afraid that if she let it drop, even for a moment, she would never be able to get it back.

That wasn't true. Life would go on; she knew that. It would go on without Christian. It would go on with Christian. It would go on despite her broken heart. And maybe soon her heart might find a way to put itself back together. In the meantime, she just had to keep smiling.

A week passed and Elsie started to get worried. Hattie was normally a positive and upbeat person. She smiled incessantly. She never worried about a thing. She just turned it over to God and kept on going. It was something that Elsie admired about her cousin even though she wasn't able to mimic that behavior. Hattie said give it to God and she did. Elsie prayed and prayed, confessing that she was giving it over to God and yet worrying about whatever it was relentlessly. Now she was worried about Hattie.

It wasn't that she hadn't stopped smiling, it wasn't that

she had changed her previous behavior except for perhaps now she seemed even more positive and even more hopeful if that was even possible. But as the days had gone by, the smile that had once been easy and quick to the lips had become stuck. It was as if Hattie smiled without giving her lips a break. That was unnatural. Not knowing what else to do, she walked to the B&B to talk to her friends.

"That's why I came down here today," Elsie said, looking from Millie to Sylvie and hoping for some sort of answer.

"And she didn't say anything happened between her and Christian?" Millie asked.

"You saw her last week at the meeting."

Sylvie nodded. "*Jah*. She was smiling and seemed happy enough."

"I'm sure it's an act. It has to be. It's the same smile all the time. It doesn't change. It doesn't grow in intensity. It's just the same. Always the same. As if it's the only smile she has now."

"You don't believe that," Millie said. She turned her attention away from Elsie just long enough to redirect Linda Beth. The sweet child was crawling all over the place and trying to get into everything she could reach. For having such a rocky start in life she was surely making up for it now.

"Just wait," Elsie told them. "Just wait and see how she is tomorrow night at the widows' meeting. See if I'm not right about what I'm saying. She flashes the same smile; sometimes she even leaves it on her face without relaxing, as if she let it go it would just drift off and never come back."

"That is troublesome," Sylvie said.

"'Troublesome' doesn't even cover it," Elsie said. She was thankful that they had let the bet go and continued to do the chores like they always had. It was a stupid bet anyway. They knew better than to behave like that. It just went to show how bad behavior could lead to bad other things. "You watch tomorrow and see. And you come by Wednesday and let me know what you think."

Sylvie nodded. "I have an idea." She turned to Millie excitedly. "I told Hattie that I would make some of my own award-winning beignet whoopie pies for the meeting, but I didn't have time last week. What with the hot water tank breaking and everything. But I can do it this week. If that doesn't bring a genuine smile to her face, I don't know what might."

"True enough," Elsie said. She didn't really know if that was the right answer or not. Whoopie pies surely couldn't cure what was wrong with her cousin. But it didn't hurt to have a great snack on hand either.

No, what she thought was wrong with Hattie . . . Well, Elsie had teased her about falling in love with Christian Beachy. Now Elsie believed that might just be what her cousin had gone and done.

He really should skip these things. Christian looked around the group of men as they discussed the upcoming ice cream social the next weekend. Maybe that was why he was there. *Jah*, ice cream was important. But mostly he was there to keep face.

"I'm just saying it might be fun if we made our own waffle cones or bowls." Vern looked around the group. "Especially since Christian here has an award-winning pancake recipe."

"What do pancakes have to do with waffle cones?" another asked.

"It's the same basic recipe just put in a waffle iron. Right?" Vern looked around for affirmation.

"I'm not sure how it would be for a waffle iron," Christian said. And he really didn't want to start experimenting with it now.

"We already have the cones on order," Thomas Kurtz said, bringing them all back to the original topic. "Let's use those for this year and then maybe next year we can start working on this a little earlier."

They all voted and the measure was tabled for a time. He supposed it would be rather tasty to have a bowl made out of fresh waffle mix to hold your ice cream rather than just a plain paper bowl or a commercially made cone. But he would have to look into it. They needed to look good as well as be functional and delicious.

"Are the cousins still going to supply us with toppings?"

Hattie and Elsie usually gave them all the toppings they needed from their own stock. What they didn't have, they grabbed at Buster's along with the fresh fruit and syrups that they would need. It made for a fun afternoon. Basically just a time to sit around and eat ice cream and get ready for Memorial Day. The unofficial start of summer.

"I think that about does it," Thomas said. He turned to Christian. "Can you go by and verify that with them?"

Christian coughed. He cleared his throat and shifted uncomfortably in his seat. "I'm sorry it's the beginning of the growing season, and I really don't have time to do that. Perhaps someone else can go by?"

"I can," Jason Stoll said. "I'm in town anyway." He turned toward Christian. "That way you won't have to make a special trip."

Christian breathed in an audible sigh of relief. He knew he would have to face Hattie eventually. He had avoided her at church yesterday, said he had work to attend to, and left almost directly after the meal. In fact he was fairly certain he'd left before Benjamin Lambright, resident dairy farmer. If anyone thought ill of it, no one said. And talk today hadn't been about him leaving church; most people were talking about Barbie Troyer finally getting out of the hospital.

"Good. *Jah. Danki*," Christian said. He knew that eventually his path would cross with Hattie's in a way that he wouldn't be able to avoid. And he would have to man up and talk to her, but in the meantime, he was just licking his wounds as they say. Patching up his broken heart and learning to get along without her.

"Is there any more business?" Thomas asked.

"Just next week's meeting," Uriah said. "Sammie Franklin came to me and told me that we can't have the community theater building next week. Seems they are starting a play and they need the building on Monday night. So, anyone willing to host?"

"I can," Christian said.

Truthfully he was surprised to hear his own voice. Why was he volunteering? Because he was doing his best to make everything look like it was normal. As if he wasn't heartbroken. As if he and Hattie had just had a minor encounter, a short-term friendship. A limited partnership in creating the second best whoopie pie in all of Paradise Valley. Hosting the meeting was just one more way to prove that to be the truth.

"All in favor?" Thomas asked.

There was the raising of hands, and it was voted in that Christian would host the next men's meeting at his house.

"I'd love a trip out to the country," Jason said. As if his whole life wasn't already pastoral.

But that was all right, Christian thought. Just as long as everybody believed that he was doing just fine.

Something strange was happening in Paradise Springs and everyone knew it. Elsie was certain of it as she bustled down Main Street toward the B&B.

Yesterday afternoon Malinda Beachy had called to tell Elsie that something was going on. Elsie didn't actually need Malinda to tell her that something was amiss. But she heard the woman out. And agreed with her wholeheartedly. It was as if Christian and Hattie had swapped places. No, not really places. They had swapped their roles in the community. Hattie had always been upbeat happy-go-lucky, even. She always had a smile on her lips and a light in her eyes that made everyone else smile. But lately she had done nothing but mope around. Only smiling when absolutely necessary.

Sunday at church she had done all but hide until it was time to go home. Elsie knew she was trying to avoid accidentally running into Christian. Not that she could blame her.

And after that, everything had changed. Hattie had cried and called herself an idiot for falling in love. Actually she didn't say those specific words, but she called herself an idiot and Elsie knew what she meant. She had fallen in love with Christian Beachy. And now she was not a better person for it.

The smile that had been plastered to her face disappeared and her normally happy and energetic cousin was neither of those things. And she was no longer pretending to be.

Then Malinda's phone call let her know that Christian had been going around smiling. Actually smiling. According to Malinda it was somewhat terrifying, this curve of his lips that didn't seem to suit him at all. It was forced and shaky and just a bit . . . well, terrifying. Something had to be done. So Elsie agreed to meet Malinda at the B&B this afternoon to try to work something out.

Elsie hustled up the stairs and into the B&B. Without hesitation she made her way into the common room where Malinda, Millie, and Sylvie were already seated.

"I'm sorry if I'm late," Elsie said. "I was trying to get out of there without Hattie getting suspicious."

"What did you tell her?" Sylvie asked.

"I told her I was going to the dentist." Heaven help her when she really did have to go to the dentist. But hopefully by then Hattie and Christian would be back together and life would be sweet. Then Hattie wouldn't even remember that today Elsie had lied to her about going to the dentist. See, it was perfect. At least she hoped it was.

Millie stood. "Would you like a cup of coffee?" she asked.

There were several snacks laid out on the coffee table between the women—brownies, cookies, and of course whoopie pies.

Elsie shook her head. The last thing she needed was caffeine to make her even more jittery. "How about some water?" she asked instead.

Millie went to the kitchen to get Elsie a drink as the other three filled their plates.

She was back in a flash and Elsie gratefully took the glass from her. She drank deeply, then set it on the coaster on the coffee table. She picked up a saucer and started stacking it with dessert.

She was absolutely too nervous for this. She had loaded up with a brownie, three cookies, and a whoopie pie and had been reaching for a second before she realized what she was doing and snatched her hand back. She had never been a nervous eater before, but this deal with Hattie was making her crazy.

If anybody thought it strange, no one said. There were no judgments in this group. Not even from Malinda who appeared to be just about as upset as Elsie herself.

"Too bad you don't have a cell phone," Sylvie mused, focusing her attention on Malinda. "I would've loved to have seen a smile on Christian Beachy's face."

Elsie figured they picked up the conversation where they had been before she interrupted.

Malinda shuddered. "You really don't want to see that at all."

"Was it that bad?" Millie asked.

Elsie swallowed the bite of brownie she'd been wallowing around in her mouth. It tasted delicious, but she was having to slow down so she didn't just shove the desserts into her face one after the other. "I suppose that it's about like looking at Hattie frown."

Hattie had frowned before, Elsie was sure. But now she walked around frowning. She didn't stop. It was a constant expression, as if her inner turmoil was displayed across her face. And inner turmoil was not what everyone was used to seeing from Hattie Schrock. She was positive, upbeat, uplifting. This was something else entirely.

"The issue is," Millie said, no doubt trying to direct the conversation back to productive footing, "what are we going to do about it?"

"What can we do?" Sylvie asked. "That's what we have to focus on. What can we do in order to get these two back to themselves?"

Malinda and Elsie both shook their heads. "It's never going to go back. He's in love with her."

"They'll never be the same," Elsie said. "Hattie's in love with him."

The two women spoke at the same time.

Then they turned to look at the other.

"You think they're in love with each other?" Sylvie asked.

"Absolutely," Elsie said, all the while, Malinda nodded.

"I mean to say," Malinda started, "Christian's never been the kind of smiling brother. I'm okay with that. But this smiling has got to stop."

"You're sure he's not just . . . happy?"

Malinda shook her head emphatically. "This is not happy. This is frightening."

"I just want Hattie to be back to Hattie, you know?" It was all Elsie could ask for. "This is all my fault anyway," she continued. "If I hadn't made the bet with her, then this would've never happened. She would've never started hanging out with him and she would've never fallen in love with him."

Malinda was shaking her head the entire time Elsie spoke. "I didn't mean to say it. The words came out and then I had to follow that with something else and before I knew what was happening, he was storming out. I couldn't convince him to listen to any more. It's my fault that he's acting so un-Christian like." She made a face. "That didn't sound like I meant for it to."

"The fact is we got to get the two of them together." Sylvie looked around at each of them to see if they were all in agreement.

"That's easier said than done," Millie put in.

"I agree," Elsie said. "Did you see how they avoided each other at church on Sunday?"

"It was almost comical," Malinda added. "I think Christian left before anyone else. And usually he's staying until the very end to help clean up."

"At least he wasn't smiling and scaring the children." Sylvie gave a tiny smile at her own joke.

"That was a blessing," Malinda said.

"So what do we do now?" Elsie asked. She took another bite of brownie. It really was delicious. She just couldn't believe she had taken it plus the cookies and the whoopie pies. Her dinner would be ruined for certain.

"Well, if they're not going to be able to get together in a natural occurrence, like church, maybe we have to just make them get together some other way," Sylvie said.

"That's not a bad idea," Elsie admitted. "But that's what I did with the whole Sadie Hawkins thing—" She broke off, shaking her head. "I'm not sure that's something I should be meddling in again."

"You've meddled this far," Millie said.

"Agreed," Sylvie reinforced. "We've already set the ball into motion. Now we just have to make sure it goes into the right glove."

Malinda shook her head. "I don't understand basketball metaphors."

Sylvie reached across the table to pat Malinda's hand reassuringly. "That was baseball, dear, but it's okay. We're going to get them there somehow."

They chatted for the rest of the afternoon over different desserts and finally they came to an idea. Elsie hadn't conceived the plan herself, but she thought it was a pretty good one. No, Malinda came up with the strategy and everything seemed to be falling right into their hands. As far as Elsie was concerned, you couldn't ask for more.

It had to be the dumbest thing she had ever heard of. Hattie loaded up the rest of the boxes into the back of her buggy and started out of town. Whoever heard of a popcorn shop catering a men's meeting? Who came up with such a plan? Probably Vern King. He loved to eat.

Hattie had thought Malinda was putting her on when she came into the shop and told her of the plan. They, the men, said they wanted to do some kind of game, something about taste testing the popcorn to see . . . What was it they wanted to see? Hattie tapped her chin. She couldn't remember. But who was she to turn down the opportunity for business?

It just seemed a little pushy that Malinda needed Hattie to bring everything out to their house. The men's meeting was to be at the house that Christian shared with his sister. Hattie thought perhaps Malinda could have gathered everything up herself while she was in town, but again . . . who was Hattie to question that? And that didn't even take into account why it was *Malinda* who was going around gathering up things for the *men's* meeting. Unless someone came up with the popcorn idea and Christian didn't want to see her. At all. Any. Like, ever again.

Most likely that was the case.

How could she blame him?

She had tried to call off the bet a couple of times and been goaded back into keeping the wager. She had even told Elsie that she didn't want out of their bet. But truthfully she should have never agreed to wager on anything that had to do with another person's feelings. Their life. People were too fragile. Sometimes even the strong ones.

It was a horrible mistake and she would regret it until her dying day. She wasn't trying to be dramatic. That's truly how she felt. If only she could make it up to Christian. She knew he would never forgive her enough to trust her again. He would forgive her, then hold her at arm's length. He was a smart man, after all, and she couldn't blame him for that.

That day in front of the popcorn shop, she had tried to apologize and she had meant every word. But only time would allow him to truly forgive her. Still, maybe she would have an opportunity tonight to apologize to him once more. She wasn't sure that she had to stay at the house. Malinda had just asked for the popcorn to be delivered. Maybe Hattie wouldn't see him at all. And maybe that was better. Maybe he needed more time before he could forgive her.

She was trembling by the time she got to Christian's house. There were several buggies already parked in the driveway, and she changed her mind about trying to see him. *Jah*, she would apologize to him once more. Some time or another. Maybe she could get him alone, even if for just a moment, to tell him again how sorry she was. She wanted to do that more than anything, but she didn't want to do it with an audience of men.

Her legs quaked as she climbed down from the buggy and fetched the two large boxes from the back seat. She wanted to walk sure and true, practically march to the front door and confidently knock to tell them she was here with whatever experiment they were going to conduct.

Yet she found herself walking slower and slower across the yard . . . up the stairs . . . across the porch . . . until she had no choice but to knock on the door.

The first time her knuckles rapped the wood, it was so faint she barely heard it herself.

"Chin up, buttercup," Hattie told herself. "You can do this."

She knocked once more. And then a thought occurred to her. There was a meeting here tonight at Christian's house and the chances of someone other than him actually answering the door were practically none. She was fixing to come face-to-face with him. And she wondered if she'd been set up. She wanted to knock loudly, then drop the boxes on the stoop, and run back to her buggy. But before she could execute such a move, the door swung open. Yet it wasn't Christian standing there. It was Malinda.

"What are you doing here?" Hattie looked at the woman, shaking her head. "You weren't supposed to be here. That's why I had to bring this all the way out here, *jah*?"

Malinda gave a small shrug as if it were truly of no consequence. And that Hattie hadn't wasted an hour of time running popcorn out when Malinda could've brought it home herself. After all, she just ordered it in the shop that afternoon. They hadn't had to make anything new. Everything came straight from the shelves.

"Hand me one of those boxes," Malinda said.

"You can have both of them," Hattie returned. She could hear the men's voices talking nearby though she couldn't hear what they were saying. It was just a low drone of deeper sounds. No words or thoughts detectable.

"I need your help," Malinda said.

Hattie shook her head. "I didn't sign up for this."

"Elsie promised me you would help."

"I'm going home." She thrust the box of popcorn toward Malinda, but the other woman refused to take it from her.

"Elsie promised." Malinda's tone brooked no argument.

Of course she did, Hattie thought snidely. It was always

Elsie promising this or that, then Hattie had to come behind and actually do the work. And where was Elsie? Training a new girl at the popcorn shop. Their roles could've just as easily been reversed. Elsie could've come out with the popcorn, and Hattie could have trained the new recruit. But no, somehow Elsie always laid it on her.

"I'm paying for this," Malinda said. "Now get in here."

Money isn't everything, Hattie wanted to yell.

But she could handle this. It was nothing. She would have to learn to be around Christian at some point. Tonight was just more like trial by fire instead of slowly getting accustomed to it. She was an adult. He was an adult. And somehow they would find a way.

She hoped anyway.

"In the kitchen," Malinda said.

Hattie carried the popcorn in its box through the house, past the room where she could hear the men gathered, and on into the dining area with a small wooden table. There were several bowls already sitting on the table though all were empty. They were of different sets. Different colors. Different materials.

Hattie set the box down in one of the chairs just as Malinda had.

"Okay," Malinda said propping her hands on her hips. "This is how it's going to work. We're dumping the popcorn into each of these bowls, then we'll take it around to the men and give them a little taste. They are going to guess what flavor it is. Then we're going to write down the flavor for them."

"Why are we going to write it down for them?"

"Because they're going to be blindfolded, naturally." Malinda looked at her as if she had lost her mind. Maybe, but she wasn't the one blindfolded for a popcorn test. Whoever heard of such a thing?

"Naturally," Hattie repeated.

"The one who gets the most flavors right is going to win a gift card to the popcorn shop."

She'd almost forgotten about that fifty-dollar gift card Malinda had come in and purchased that morning. At the time she couldn't for the life of her figure out why. They didn't give out prizes at the Whoopie Pie Widows' Club. But then again Malinda had never been to one of their meetings. Honestly, as far as Hattie knew, she had never been to one of the men's meetings either since they held them in the community theater and she was . . . well, a woman. But it seemed that Malinda had her own ideas about how the meeting should be conducted.

"I see what you're doing," Hattie started, "but why do you need my help?" She should just leave. Get out of there. Not worry about any more of this stuff and Malinda and Christian and the men and just drive home and forget tonight happened.

"I need your help marking down the answers. I will go by and give them the popcorn, then they can whisper their answer to you, what flavor the popcorn is. They'll have a clipboard and you can mark on it which popcorn they say is what flavor."

"Heaven help us," Hattie said. "Are you sure they're not in school, like this is the third grade class or something?"

Malinda laughed "Well, they are men."

"That's the truth," Hattie said. But one thing was certain, when she got back to town, Elsie owed her a big one.

"Follow me," Malinda said, and led the way back into the living room.

The men were all sitting, dotted around the furniture, bandannas tied over their faces to hide their eyes. Like hiding their eyes was going to change what flavor they chose. But Hattie supposed it would be harder to guess without seeing the food. She knew quite well that there was more to taste than just taste. Texture, smell, and sight were so important as well.

"I forgot the tongs," Malinda said. "Christian, can you run to the kitchen and get the tongs?"

Christian pulled his blindfold up just a bit and stared at his sister. "Are you kidding me?"

"No, I'm not. I need you to go get them now please and thank you. We need to get this started or we won't have time to finish."

"That would be a shame," Christian grumbled.

Some of the men laughed. But just only a little. Malinda was standing right there after all.

She went to give the first man his popcorn. "I'm just pouring a little into your hand," she said.

She started to do just that and turned to Hattie. "I forgot the Dixie cups. I was going to use them so the men could have their own serving. But I left them on the dining room table. Can you get them?"

Hattie went back into the dining room, noticing not for the first time that's where Christian had put the trophy the two of them had won for baking the pancake whoopie pie. They had split the prize money and she had tucked her half away to purchase a bicycle. Someday anyway. But the trophy . . . She had said he could bring it to his house since he had more room, and now it seemed like she would never get her turn. But it wasn't the trophy she wanted. It was the man she shared it with.

He looked so good tonight sitting there even with a blindfold covering his beautiful eyes. And she wished she could call back that stupid wager, do something to reverse the damage she had done. Her stomach clenched just thinking about it. It had been a stupid, dumb, ignorant thing to do. She was all three and more.

She turned her focus back to the task at hand. The little Dixie cups she was supposed to take back to Malinda. But they weren't in the dining room. In fact, she hadn't seen them when she had been in there earlier. She wondered if they might be in the kitchen. She pushed her way inside the kitchen only to find Christian standing by the sink holding up the bright blue plastic tongs in one hand. "Is this what you wanted—" He stopped when he saw it wasn't his sister but her. Hattie.

He turned back and grabbed the dish towel off the counter. He begin to wipe the tongs. Hattie didn't know if they were dirty or not. Perhaps they were and they needed to be wiped off. Or perhaps he just didn't want to look at her and it was the only thing he had on hand to do. Whatever it was, he did it meticulously. Wiping them with such deep attention to detail that she thought perhaps the mayor was coming to supper.

Here's your chance.

The voice whispered in her head. She wanted to shut it up. This was no chance. Yes, they were alone. But it was too soon. He could barely look at her, much less accept her apology. She wanted to. She needed to apologize to him so badly. She needed to know that she had his forgiveness.

They would never be more than friends. After tonight possibly no more than just church acquaintances. And she would keep that and hold it close if that's all he could give her. But first she needed his forgiveness. More than anything she needed to know that he forgave her.

"I'm sorry," she said.

He stopped drying the tongs and set them on the counter. Then he braced the heels of his hands on the edge of the sink but he didn't turn around.

"I said it so many times I don't want to say it again, but I have to say it again and again until you know exactly how sorry I am. It was a dumb thing to do." Tears sprang into her eyes as she tried to blink them back, but they only fell down her cheeks rolling in twin streaks to drop off her chin.

"You don't have to tell me you forgive me. But please one day think about it. I—" She almost said "I love you and I need you to forgive me" but she couldn't say that to him. It was entirely too forward. Some things were best kept to yourself. Or at least that's what her *mamm* had always said. "I care about you," she amended. "And I want you to know that I'm so very sorry. I'm sorry. I'm sorry. I'm sorry."

It was time to go home. They could have their popcorn tasting and do whatever, but she needed to leave. She had apologized to Christian. Once more she had explained as best she could, but explaining didn't help. It was a mistake, a terrible mistake that she had made and that she would never make again. Although they couldn't be more than friends at best, she needed his forgiveness.

She had to get out of the house. Out of the kitchen, away from Christian. Just out. She spun on her heel and raced back into the dining room out into the hallway and over to the front door.

"Hattie?" Malinda called after her.

But Hattie didn't stop. Twice as fast as she had come in, she flew down the steps and over to her buggy. She was just about to hop inside when a hand grabbed her arm. She gasped and whirled around to find Christian standing behind her.

Even in the dark she could tell he wasn't frowning. He wasn't smiling because that wasn't Christian. But he wasn't frowning at her. He was simply looking at her, openly and honestly, as he studied her features.

"Say it again," he commanded.

"Say what?" she whispered in return. The moment was soft and the darkness was between them.

"Tell me you're sorry."

"I'm sorry," she said. "I shouldn't have messed in someone else's life."

"I forgive you," he replied.

"You forgive me?"

He chuckled; the sound was rusty, as if he hadn't used it in a long time. And she supposed he hadn't. He just wasn't that kind. Not that she minded at all. "Of course I've forgiven you. I'm Amish."

"And that's the only reason." She couldn't have believed anything else.

His expression grew serious, his tone soft. "No."

She waited for him to continue.

"Promise me something," Christian said.

"What is that?" she asked. She should have said *anything*, but somehow she couldn't. She wouldn't be able to never speak to him again. She wouldn't be able to promise that she would never care for him or love him or want to be with him. Some promises she wouldn't be able to keep. Anything was definitely out.

"Promise me that you will never wager with your cousin again."

"I promise." That one was easy. She never wanted to make another wager with Elsie as long as she lived. Some things just weren't worth it. "In my defense," she continued, "I just wanted to make sure you were happy."

"What about now?"

"What?" She wasn't following him.

"Are you worried about my happiness now?"

"*Jah*. Always. You're a wonderful man, Christian Beachy." Okay, so that was a little forward, but it was the truth and she felt all the better for having said it.

That was when she realized he was standing a little too close to her. Not that she minded. She liked when he was close. She could feel his warmth and his strength and it made her feel cared for, protected.

Her heart was thumping in her chest. She could feel the blood rushing through her veins. It was like something out of a romance novel as she waited for him to continue.

"What about love?" he asked.

"Love?" She couldn't confess her love. She wasn't that forward.

"What if I love you?" he asked, though she couldn't believe her ears.

"What?" Her voice was barely a whisper in return.

"I love you," Christian said. "I don't know how or when it happened, just one day I realized that I wanted to spend all my moments with you. But then—"

She nodded. "The bet." That cursed bet was going to be the end of them. Some things just couldn't be forgotten, and its looming presence took away all the joy his words brought to her.

"I don't care about the bet," he said. "It took me a little while to come to terms with everything but I did. I have."

She nodded. And that was why he had decided to forgive her.

"Marry me."

Hattie drew back unable to trust her ears. "Are you serious?"

He nodded. "I'm so serious."

"Where will we live?" she asked. Like that was the most important aspect holding them back.

He shrugged. "We'll figure it out."

They would figure it out. Sure. He loved her and she loved him and they would figure it out.

"You're serious," she said.

"I'm serious," he confirmed.

"He's serious," Vern called from the porch. "Now quit talking about it and call the bishop."

Hattie turned to look. Everyone from the men's meeting, as well as Malinda, was standing on the porch trying to see what was going on over by her buggy.

"If you say yes, we can call the bishop," Christian said.

"Yes," she said. Loving the sound of the word on her lips.

Hattie laughed and Christian joined in with his sweet rusty sound. One that she hoped to hear again and again as they spent the rest of their lives together. Being happy, being thoughtful, frowning, smiling, laughing, loving, living.

Epilogue

Weddings were the best, Hattie decided. Well, she had decided that long ago, but standing next to Christian and promising her life to his was definitely the best. So maybe she would amend her conclusion to second weddings were the best and weddings in general a close . . . second.

She took a deep satisfied breath and looked out at the backyard belonging to Christian Beachy. Correction: the backyard that now belonged to the both of them.

"What are you doing out here?" Elsie came up beside her, nearly scaring Hattie out of her skin.

"I don't know," she said. "Just looking at everything."

"It's a pretty place he's got here."

Hattie nodded. It was pretty a place. Plenty of land with lots of room, large greenhouses and fields on either side filled with all sorts of crops. Well, in the spring they would be. For now everything was waiting expectantly for that time to come.

Tonight it was supposed to snow. But Hattie would be warm inside with her new husband.

"Are you sure you've got everything okay for tomorrow?" she asked worriedly.

Elsie gave her a look, one Hattie knew well. It said

Pu-lease, kind of like Stephanie, the *Englisch* girl they had just hired to work in Poppin' Paradise. "I think I can handle the shop for a couple of weeks without you."

A couple of weeks. How was Hattie going to survive that? What would she fill fourteen days with before returning to work? There were only so many clothes to move in and so much to rearrange. And truthfully only so much honeymooning at their age.

She had only wanted to take a week, but Christian insisted that she take longer. She had agreed because he had asked so sweetly and she did love him so. But now she was starting to regret that decision. Not that she didn't want to spend time with him, just she wasn't used to not staying busy.

"*Jah,* but—"

"No buts," Elsie said, shaking her head. "You're going to take two weeks off and you are not coming into work and you are not calling or driving by in the buggy or with a hired driver or in a golf cart. Did I leave anything out?"

Hattie frowned. "No."

"Good," Elsie continued. "You are going to spend that time with your husband."

And she could only hope that they wouldn't start getting on each other's nerves before the honeymoon was even halfway through.

Listen to her! Where had all her positivity gone? She supposed her doubts were a natural conclusion to the fact that she didn't understand how someone as kind and caring and frowny as Christian had fallen in love with her.

"It's too late now," Elsie said.

"What's too late?" Hattie dragged herself out of her churning thoughts.

"You two are married." She didn't have to say more.

Amish couples married for life. And though Hattie and Christian seemed about as opposite as two people could be, she couldn't imagine her life without him.

What she could imagine was the not-so-healthy relationship that could happen as a result of too much time together too soon. Or maybe it was two people who were too competitive living together.

Maybe if it were the springtime and Christian was out working in the fields, she wouldn't be so nervous. At least they would have Malinda there as a buffer. In a bit anyway.

The house was big enough for them to share and Hattie couldn't imagine making Christian's sister live anywhere other than the farm. Malinda had never lived anyplace other than her childhood home. Though she had agreed to get a room at the B&B for a couple of days so the newlyweds could have a little measure of privacy.

"There's nothing to be nervous about," Elsie said, low and close to her ear.

Hattie sucked in another breath and waved her cousin away. "I'm not." But that wasn't the truth and they both knew it.

"Don't stay out here too long without a wrap," Elsie said, then moved away.

Hattie didn't watch her leave. She just stood and looked out over the large backyard. The place where Christian had taught her to ride a bike. The place where their respective grandchildren would play together. Happy times were on their way. She shouldn't have a care in the world and yet—

"What are you doing out here?"

This time Hattie didn't start at the sound of the voice

behind her. She had heard his familiar step a moment before he spoke.

"Just looking," she said.

She smiled as he wrapped her shawl around her shoulders and pulled her in close to him. They were alone on the back porch while friends and neighbors, cousins and other family continued to celebrate inside.

Hattie sighed and leaned into him, soaking up his warmth and comforting scent. It soothed her nerves. She had nothing to be anxious about. She loved him and he loved her.

They would play cards. Or maybe . . . work a crossword puzzle. Or color in one of those crazy adult coloring books that she had seen while waiting in line at Buster's. *Jah*, coloring. There was nothing competitive about that.

"I have something for you."

She was so close to him she could feel the rumble of the words, deep inside his chest before he actually spoke.

She raised her head from his shoulder. "I thought we said we weren't getting each other gifts." She had wanted to buy him a new chess set that she had seen at the antique store in town. It looked to be made entirely of wood, gently carved into the correct pieces, then carefully polished to a delicate shine. She didn't know how to play chess herself, but she was willing to learn. But since they had agreed not to buy gifts, she had walked away from the beautiful set.

"This isn't that kind of gift," he told her.

"There's only one kind of gift," she said. "And that's something you give to another person."

He held one finger over her lips, then handed her an envelope. "Here," he said. "Happy wedding day."

Hattie frowned at him to show her disapproval of his

gesture, even though she was a tad excited by what she might find. Then she opened the envelope. Two bus tickets to . . .

"Branson?" she asked, looking up at him.

"I hear it's really something to see when it gets close to Christmas."

"It's getting close to Christmas now."

"I guess we had better go see it then." He smiled, and she felt warm all the way to her toes.

"When do we leave?" she asked.

"Tomorrow about lunchtime. And we'll come back in ten days."

Ten days. Ten glorious days with him. "I love you, Christian."

"I know. And I love you too."

She could tell by looking into his eyes that he felt the same about her. He didn't need to say it. But she was thankful that he did all the same.

She also knew that he felt the same as she had about finding love in the first place. She hadn't been looking. She had never even dreamed that she would get married again. Much less to him. And yet here they were.

"As soon as everybody leaves, we'll pack," he said. "The driver will take us into Warrensburg to the bus station and come and get us when we come back home."

It was the perfect plan. And the perfect gift. She couldn't have asked for anything better. She sighed, the relief of the promise that everything was going to turn out just fine washing over her.

Tonight they would pack and tomorrow morning she would head into town to pick up the chess set and a book on how to play. And maybe she would drive by the popcorn shop and make sure everything was okay there too.

Or maybe not . . .

"Hattie," Christian said, pulling away to look at her face. "Were you worried?"

She shook her head, scoffed. "Of course not."

"*Jah.*" He said the word slowly and nodded in a way that said he didn't believe her for a moment. But he wasn't going to call her out on it. "You know what you have to do whenever you get worried."

She nodded and stepped in close to him once more.

"Give it to God," they said together. Then they laughed, shared a brief but sweet kiss, and made their way back into the party.

Visit our website at
KensingtonBooks.com
to sign up for our newsletters, read
more from your favorite authors, see
books by series, view reading group
guides, and more!

BETWEEN THE CHAPTERS

Become a Part of Our
Between the Chapters Book Club
Community and Join the Conversation

Betweenthechapters.net

Books by Amy Lillard

The Wells Landing Series
CAROLINE'S SECRET
COURTING EMILY
LORIE'S HEART
JUST PLAIN SADIE
TITUS RETURNS
MARRYING JONAH
THE QUILTING CIRCLE
A WELLS LANDING CHRISTMAS
LOVING JENNA
ROMANCING NADINE
A NEW LOVE FOR CHARLOTTE

The Amish of Pontotoc Series
A HOME FOR HANNAH
A LOVE FOR LEAH
A FAMILY FOR GRACIE
AN AMISH HUSBAND FOR TILLIE

The Paradise Valley Series
MARRY ME, MILLIE
THE AMISH MATCHMAKER
ONE MORE TIME FOR JOY
WHEN HATTIE FINDS LOVE

Amish Mysteries
KAPPY KING AND THE PUPPY KAPER
KAPPY KING AND THE PICKLE KAPER
KAPPY KING AND THE PIE KAPER

Sunflower Café Mysteries
DAIRY, DAIRY, QUITE CONTRARY
A MURDER OF ASPIC PROPORTIONS

Published by Kensington Publishing Corp.

WHEN HATTIE FINDS LOVE

Christian nodded toward the step where she sat. "Do you mind?"

Hattie scooched over closer to the wall and patted the wood next to her.

He came closer, eased down on the step, brushing against her leg as he did so.

Really, the staircase was too narrow for two large adults to sit there. Unlike her, Christian wasn't chubby; he was just solid, thick, and broad.

"You're upset with me," he said. He was sitting a hair's breadth away, and she could feel the rumble of his words as his shoulder touched hers.

They had sat this close together in the buggy. Maybe not quite *this* close, but near enough. Yet there was something a little more intimate about sitting on this step while a party raged in a nearby room. And they weren't in a buggy.

She started to tell him that it wasn't true. That she wasn't upset with him, but she couldn't bring herself to lie. "You're a very special man, Christian Beachy," she started slowly. "But if you go around frowning at everyone and scowling all the time, well, no one will know that you're as wonderful as you are."

He seemed at a loss for words. So Hattie continued. "I know you're just thoughtful. But the world doesn't know that. They would have to spend a great deal of time with you to really understand." That was what she had done. She had spent a great deal of time with him these last couple of weeks, and in truth it only made her want to spend more time with him . . .